The Hope of Rage

Book Six of Rage MC

Elizabeth N. Harris

ISBN: 9798707118654

This is a work of fiction. Names, characters, businesses, places, events, and incidents are either the product of the author's imagination or used in a fictitious manner. Any resemblance to actual persons, living or dead, or actual events is purely coincidental. This book was written, produced and edited in England, the United Kingdom, where some spelling, grammar and word usage will vary from US English.

Elizabeth N. Harris
The Hope of Rage.
Book 6 of Rage MC.

© 2021 Elizabeth N. Harris
ElizabethnHarris74@outlook.com

ALL RIGHTS RESERVED. This book contains material protected under International and Federal Copyright Laws and Treaties. Any unauthorised reprint or use of this material is prohibited. No part of this book may be reproduced or transmitted in any form or by any means, electronic or mechanical, including photocopying, recording, or by any informational storage and retrieval system without express written permission from the author/publisher.

Cover by Filipe Almeida, courtesy of Unsplash.com.

The Hope of Rage

For years she loved a man who was incapable of loving her back. Pain and constant yearning became her life until she said enough. She refused so suffer any further, now she wanted a life, and now she was going to get one. Her whole life, she'd never run until now, and now she was making the rules.

He'd loved her ever since he set eyes on her, but she was out of his reach. His past was bleak, and he couldn't drag her into his mess. So he did the honourable thing and stayed away. Shame no one else thought it was honourable. His club was splintering, sides were being taken, and he knew it was his fault.

When she returns, she's different, more distant, and he realises he's lost her forever. Even worse, a man has followed her home. Two sides of him warring, one to claim and one to protect. But it's not going to be easy, not when she becomes a victim and his urge to cherish is stirred. He failed her twice; he won't fail her again. The question is, can she forgive him?

Books by Elizabeth N. Harris

Rage MC series.

Rage of the Phoenix.
The Hunters Rage.
The Rage of Reading.
The Crafting of Rage.
Rage's Terror.
The Protection of Rage.
Love's Rage.
The Hope of Rage.

Love Beyond Death series.

Oakwood Manor.
Courtenay House.
Waverley Hall.
Corelle Abbey.

Hellfire MC Series.

Chance's Hell.

Chapters.

DEDICATION..6

PROLOGUE..7

CHAPTER ONE...17

CHAPTER TWO...40

CHAPTER THREE...63

CHAPTER FOUR. 89

CHAPTER FIVE. 114

CHAPTER SIX..135

CHAPTER SEVEN. 157

CHAPTER EIGHT..182

CHAPTER NINE..203

CHAPTER TEN. 227

EPILOGUE. 245

CHARACTERS. 251

Dedication.

To Joy and Leia, gone but never forgotten.

Love

Mum.

Elizabethnharris74@outlook.com
Elizabethnharris.net

Prologue.

3rd January 2016

"We sure it's Crow they found?" Texas asked.

"Yeah, asshole's been identified, it's a waiting game," Drake replied, gazing around the table at those present. Ramirez's phone call a few weeks ago hadn't been fuckin' welcome. Detective's Ramirez and Benjamin had both been removed from the case, deemed too close to Rage MC for the Chief to be sure of a clean investigation.

From intel, Ramirez had spat the dummy out big time and was on 'vacation'. Everyone in Rapid City understood Ramirez was clean, by the book, and loyal to his department. To insinuate otherwise was asking for a fist in the face. Ben wasn't holding up much better. Rumours were in the wind that Ben had approached Hawthorne's for a position. For two top detectives to take umbrage at rumours meant the RCPD was in serious shit.

"Ramirez and Ben gonna quit?" Axel boomed,

looking worried. Rage encouraged a beneficial relationship with the RCPD because of the two detectives. The others were okay in the department, apart from Hernando Hawthorne, who was like Ramirez and Ben, but Rage wouldn't trust them as far as they could throw them.

"Dunno, backed off Ramirez for a while, sent him our support, told him we were backing away and giving him space. His career is important, ain't gonna let him crash for us," Drake said firmly. Nods met him from every side. No one disagreed with that. Ramirez's job was sacrosanct.

"We've no information on who informed the police where to find Crow's remains?" Gunner asked. Lex leaned forward.

"The only ones with the knowledge are sitting here," Lex stated. "After what happened with Artemis, I'm not prepared to believe those here are involved in this shit-storm."

"No, Artemis cleared out the shit we had left. Could be Jacked or Gid told someone in case of their deaths," Slick replied.

"That may be true, but why wait so long?" Ace asked.

"Don't have answers, gotta wait on the cops to make their move. Our information line at RCPD is dead, and I don't think we should ask Hawthorne to ask his brother for an inside line," Axel boomed.

"No shit, we lose Hernando Hawthorne; we not got an in with the cops. I wonder how close the Chief is to losing his two best detectives?" Lex murmured.

"Ramirez has never pulled his punches before; despite our relationship with him, he still wouldn't have done so," Drake said.

"So we sit here waiting for the hammer to fall? Bullshit!" Ezra spat. Lowrider nodded.

"Heard they brought in two New York cops to investigate this. The Chief wants it done above board," Slick said.

"Bullshit, Chief's fuckin' frightened of the power Phoe and Artemis wield. He can point the finger at the New York cops if this goes tits up," Apache growled.

"Too fuckin' right," Manny agreed. Mac nodded as well.

"We need to shift the other bodies?" Rock asked as several of his brothers turned to him, stunned.

"Fuck!" Texas spat.

"No! If the cops are aware of them, they could be sitting on them, waiting for Rage to turn up and trap us. We don't go anywhere near," Drake said, shaking his head violently.

"So we sit and twiddle our thumbs," Lowrider said, and that sat badly with each of them. Rage didn't sit quietly and knit in a corner.

"We cover each other's backs and watch for shit," Axel said, pointing a finger at them.

"That goes without saying," Ace replied.

"Anyone gets a knock, you shut the fuck up and call our lawyers. They've been instructed to contact Ace and me if someone gets swept up, you keep your fuckin' mouths closed. That includes you too, brother," Drake said, eyeing Ace. Ace grinned in reply, and Drake shook his head.

"Not a word outside this chamber, the newer brothers, prospect and candidates, don't need to know shit," Ace warned.

"If you think one will turn, get rid of them now," Texas said belligerently.

"Brothers and prospect no, candidates, ain't sure. Keep your mouths shut," Drake said, rising to his feet.

"Check with Blaze, he still feels eyes on him," Fish said, and Drake nodded.

"Check him now, see you at the bar tonight," Drake said and left the sanctum. Apache turned off the jammer they'd got from Artemis and passed it to Texas. Shit was coming; Apache felt it deep in his bones. Crow was the beginning; someone was making Rage fight a war on multiple fronts. Rage wouldn't break. Someone was about to get that bad news.

I looked around, and my heart froze in my chest as I saw the woman plastered across Apache's chest. She was beautiful and well built, with curves to die for, tall and slim. Apache was smiling at her with his hand on her hip, and I hated it. Phoe followed my gaze, and her face hardened.

"Silvie," she said, and I shook my head.

"No. No more Phoe, I can't take anymore," I whispered. I don't know how Phoe heard me over the band playing, but she did. She put her hand out, and I shrugged it off. Autumn twisted to face me, dislike etched on her face. Skank, she mutely told me, and I nodded. Gunner came across and dropped a kiss on Autumn. Autumn whispered something, and Gunner glanced at Apache, and then his eyes found me. Pity shone in them for a second, and then it was gone; Gunner wasn't aware of the second kiss between Apache and me. They'd traded blows twice over me, no more.

My heart breaking, I gathered my purse and phone together and knocked back the last of my drink and then banged the glass on the table. I felt the old ladies' eyes on me, each of them worried.

"I'm out, catch you Monday. Honey, I'm taking tomorrow off, if that's okay?" I asked Lindsey as I rose to my feet.

"Take it as vacation, Carly can operate the desk," she said, sympathy in her voice.

"Actually," I paused, "can I take the week off?" Worried eyes met mine, and Lindsey nodded.

"We'll manage. Do what you got to do," Lindsey replied, her hand reached out to touch my arm. I let her give me love for a few seconds, and picking up my purse, I walked away from the women who were my sisters. Gunner appeared at my side.

"Silvie," he said. I looked up and smiled sadly.

"I can't do this anymore, Gunner. Shit, I'm thirty-five in a few months, and I need to start living," Gunner's eyes flashed, worry in them. I stood on tiptoe and kissed his cheek.

"Silvie," he hissed.

"Take care, Gunner, of you and Autumn, I'm going to get a life," I told him and deftly dodged as a woman staggered towards him. She tangled him up, allowing me to escape. I ran out to my car and jumped in just as Gunner got to the door. I gave him a fake jaunty wave and sped out of the bars car park and drove home to the nasty apartment I lived in. The desire to escape was an overwhelming sensation.

When I got home, the apartment was in darkness as Carly was at the bar. I grabbed an old duffel bag and crammed clothes into it. Frantically, I grabbed my wallet and slid it into my jean pocket and then looked at my phone. I guessed the MC might phone me, and if they didn't, the old ladies would. Despite this, I needed time alone to figure out what I was going to do.

I'd loved Apache over half my life, ever since I'd walked into Rage with an old girlfriend and set eyes on him. At first, I thought Apache wasn't interested because I was so young. Then I realised over time Apache just wasn't interested. Since that day, I hoped he'd wake up and realise what was in front of him, but Apache never did. Now the brothers were getting old ladies, and I was the odd one out.

Drake had given me old lady status even though I didn't have an old man. I hoped he'd done that out of respect and not pity. Who knew with Drake? Drake did as he wanted and was a law unto himself. I put my phone on the table where Carly wouldn't miss it and then wrote a note. Looking around at the shithole I'd lived my adult life in, I walked out and closed the door behind me.

Lindsey looked up as Lowrider walked into Made by Rage with Apache on his heels. He looked to the desk and frowned. Apache turned his head and looked around the workshop, and his frown deepened.

"Where's Silvie and Carly?" he asked.

"Silvie is taking the week off, and I don't know

where Carly is; she's late."

"Silvie's taking the week off work?" Apache asked, sounding surprised, Lindsey glared at him, and he looked shocked.

"Yes," Lindsey said curtly. "Silvie asked I give her a weeks' vacation." Apache studied her.

"Where she gone?" Lowrider asked. "She's okay? Not ill?" he asked, making Apache's head snap towards Lindsey. She loved Apache like all the brothers but was too angry at him.

"Silvie's gone away for her health," Lindsey replied, Apache's eyes narrowed on her.

"What's going on?" Apache growled. Lindsey opened her mouth to answer when the door flew open, and Carly sped into the shop. She flew past the two men and barrelled into Lindsey, who wrapped her arms around Carly automatically.

"Oh my God, Carly, what's wrong?" she cried, alarmed.

"I don't understand if she's coming back," Carly wailed, and Lindsey's heart sunk like a stone.

"What?" Lindsey hissed. Carly pulled away and handed Lindsey a crumpled note. Tears streaked down her face.

"Read it. I don't know if that's goodbye goodbye, or goodbye for now," Carly sobbed. She collapsed into an armchair, and Lindsey unfolded the screwed-up note. Reading it, her skin chilled, and fear ran through her. Lowrider gazed at his beloved wife and put his hand out for the letter. Lindsey handed it silently to him.

"Dear Carly,

Hey sweetie, I'm going away for a week, maybe

longer, I don't know. The rent is paid for the next three months, so you don't need to worry about that if I don't come home straight away. I've a lot of thinking to do and need to get my head straight. I can't keep doing what I've been doing, and I need to work out what I want.

You've been the best roommate a girl can ask for. Don't make the mistakes I made, sweet girl, don't get to my age and be full of regrets. I hope to exercise some of these regrets this week. Maybe they'll need longer. I don't know, I'm afraid I understand nothing anymore.

Honey, I'm lost, confused and hurting and need to heal or at least begin to heal before I come back. I've left my phone, I don't want anyone interfering, even with good intentions, I want to be alone, please make my sisters understand that. God, I need to be alone. Can you ask them to please give me that? All my love, sweet girl, Silvie." Lowrider looked stunned as he read the note out loud. Carly burst into sobs again.

"What the fuck?" Apache asked, looking like he'd been beamed with a four by four.

"Silvie's gone," Carly sobbed. "I want her to come back." Lindsey gathered the teenager up in her arms.

"She'll be back. Silvie loves us, she won't stay away too long," Lindsey soothed, but her was heart breaking. She understood Silvie needed time alone, but there was no way of contacting her. Lindsey feared the worse.

"I'll get Hawthorne's on it," Apache said, turning towards the door.

"You leave her the fuck alone," Lindsey hissed. Apache stared at her, shocked. Lowrider took a step towards Lindsey, and she held a hand up to his face.

"What the hell, woman?" Apache asked, anger creeping into his voice.

"You and I Apache both know why Silvie's gone. Fuck, the entire club will guess why she's gone. You leave her alone. Silvie needs time, we're gonna give her time," Lindsey told him. Apache's eyes narrowed on her, and Lindsey squared up for battle. It was a testament to how far Lindsey had come that she'd square up to a brother. A far cry from the abused creature she'd once been.

"If I want to find Silvie, I will," he growled.

"No, you won't, you've played with Silvie's emotions long enough. You let her fucking heal," Lindsey shouted, hate in her voice and Apache rocked back on his heels. "Silvie saw you last night with that tart, she's waited twenty years for you to notice her, and you play her like a fiddle. You fucking leave her alone!"

"Control your woman," Apache snapped at Lowrider. Lowrider glared at Lindsey, who glared straight back.

"Don't you dare say a word," Lindsey yelled, pointing at the man she loved. "You fucking leave her alone. Silvie's dedicated her life to this club; now she's asking for time. You're going to give her time," Lindsey shouted at them both. A noise came from the adjoining door to the shop, and everyone jumped. Drake, Ace, and Lex stood there, Gunner to one side, his face impassive.

"No one tracks Silvie down, you leave the woman alone," Drake said his piece, and no one could go against it. "Don't you ever speak to a brother like that again, woman," Drake said, pointing at Lindsey. She sniffed at him and turned her back on them. But Lindsey didn't know that her face reflected in the mirror, and they could see the silent tear that ran down her face.

Chapter One.

15th January 2016

Content, I sank my feet into the golden sand and relaxed onto my back. Heat tickled and warmed my skin. This was my second week here, and I loved the ocean views and the golden sands. I'd not visited the beach and the ocean before, and I was grateful to experience it. After the first week, I'd contacted Lindsey and told her I needed more time. We'd agreed on three more weeks, Lindsey insisted on paying me and bullied Gunner and Manny into it as well. I don't think there was much bullying to be had, considering Gunner's relationship with me. And I'd worked for them for well nearly two years and never taken one day off. Lindsey must have thought she owed me a good vacation.

I'd requested an update on Harley, and Lindsey sadly explained that there was no change. Phoe refused to give up hope, but it was fading. Harley remained in the coma, breaking hearts. When asked how Phoe was holding up, Lindsey sighed. Phoe's pregnancy was hard, and Drake didn't stop hovering. Sin and Marsha both looked ready to explode. I missed them but had no intention of returning, not until I'd licked every wound and done some healing at least.

A shadow fell over me, and I opened an eye to see Brady standing there. Brady was smiling and holding two chilled drinks. Cheekily Brady blatantly eyed me up in my bikini and then dropped in the sand next to me.

"Hello again, Miss Silvie," he teased, I laughed and sat up, reaching for a drink. Teasingly, Brady moved it out of my reach and kissed me on the cheek when I grabbed for it. As we broke apart, I grabbed the drink and took a sip.

"Hello, Mr Brady," I said finally. Brady winked and leaned back on his elbows, enjoying the sun.

"So," Brady said and stopped; I arched an eyebrow.

"So?" I asked.

"Silvie, I leave in two days, I want to stay in contact." I flipped on my side and faced him. Brady and I met two days after arriving here. At first, I'd thought Brady was hitting on me at the bar and told him firmly I was recovering from a broken heart. And I'd no intention of a vacation fling. Brady had laughed and informed me he'd just been dumped at the altar for his best friend, so he wasn't looking either.

Brady was gorgeous. His ex must have been one dumb idiot, he was kind, friendly and educated.

Surprisingly, we'd clicked as friends that night, and both of us spent the night cursing those who'd broken our hearts and damning them to hell. We'd ended up back at my room, where I'd fallen into bed, and Brady slept on the sofa. Brady didn't once try to take advantage of me.

We'd ended up spending most of our time together, going on excursions and sight-seeing. Brady was funny and charming; I thought his ex was off her head to have dumped him. And his best friend was a jerk. Laughingly, I offered to buy a voodoo doll and stab pins in it, and Brady chuckled.

After a few days, we both got rip-roaring drunk and opened up more about our heartaches. Not only did I discover Brady's ex dumped him at the altar, but the bitch was knocked up by his ex-best friend. And I thought I had issues! We comforted each other by extolling each other's virtues and making many digs at those nasty heartbreakers.

The truth was we'd become good friends, and it was nice, no pressure or demands, no pining after Apache. Brady distracted me and was what he appeared to be, a decent, well-mannered man, a good man. Sometimes, I wished I'd met Brady before Apache. Maybe I'd have had a chance.

"Brady, I don't like that you're leaving," I said honestly.

"Can we stay in touch?" Brady asked.

"Yeah, but you're aware I don't have my phone, but if I give you my email?" I offered, and Brady nodded.

"Email is fine. Just check-in, let me know you're okay and alive," Brady laughed.

"Okay, I promise to send emails when I arrive," I

agreed. Brady was worried over the next trip I'd planned. I'd booked several hotels with long drives in between destinations, and Brady concerned I was on my own.

"Promise?"

"Yes, Dad," I teased, Brady slung an arm around me, and we both laughed. Caught up in Brady, I missed seeing a man take a picture of us. If I'd seen him, I'd have reamed him a new one. Davies got back in his car and headed towards the hotel to mail the picture to Hawthorne and Drake.

Two days later, I said goodbye to Brady and headed out myself. I'd spent two weeks in California and was now heading to New Orleans for a week, then back up to Colorado and finally home. Truth was, it was a hell of a lot of driving for one person, but I could manage. I'd driven to California after all.

New Orleans was a blast, and I'd gone mad there with the unique sights and sounds. Brady and I emailed each other daily, and I sent loads of pictures on a burner phone I'd ended up buying. He laughed when I told him I allowed a woman to drag me into her shop and cut and style my hair. I was amazed at the difference it made. Brady said it made me look even more beautiful, and I sent a vomit sign to which he replied with a bucket emoji.

Brady loved the cheeky braids the hairdresser had woven in, and I felt better than I had for years. I ended up extending my week into two weeks, after requesting extra time from Lindsey. Lindsey emailed back saying my job was safe and to take as long as I needed. So I did. Happily, I discovered another way of doing my makeup and bought myself lots of rocking clothes and jewellery. Falling in with the atmosphere, I went batshit crazy in New Orleans and decided I was allowed to treat myself. This was the new me.

Each night, I dined at a different restaurant, took ghost tours, and toured the bayou. I danced in various clubs, from jazz to rock. New Orleans brought out an entirely new side of me, one I never guessed existed. The truth was, I laughed and flirted more than I'd ever had before, allowing nothing to develop beyond a flirt. Life was fast and furious, but if I wanted it, there was slow and magical. Every night a different man courted me, and while I took none back, my confidence grew. They made me feel attractive and special. With great sadness, I said goodbye to New Orleans and considered extending my stay longer, but Colorado called and off I drove.

Colorado was fantastic and cheap because I stayed in a vacation home of Phoe's. Phoe was so relieved to know where I was, she'd offered it on the spot. I wandered on long hikes, did some horse riding, and chilled out. With a sad heart, I said goodbye to my vacation time, but I drove home on Friday so I could get ready for work on Monday.

The six-week vacation had done what I'd intended. My head was clear around Apache, and I decided to be friendly but distant. Yes, I still loved the man, but I couldn't let that rule my life anymore. If a guy asked me on a date, I was going to give him a fair chance. He would never know about Apache and my feelings for him. It was time for me to live and stop wallowing in what my future could have been. With a far lighter heart, I began the drive home.

I wasn't expecting a welcoming committee on Sunday morning, but there was one. Carly had obviously been keeping an eye out, and as soon as I pulled up, she was out of the door and hurtling towards me. Happily, I opened my arms, and Carly flew into them crying. I swallowed my own tears at the warm welcome from the girl I'd taken under my wing and hugged Carly tightly.

Carly helped me carry my cases up to the apartment and then fetched the rest of my bags. We chatted about my trip and what I'd done, and Carly kept exclaiming at my new look. Hours passed with us eating pizza and staring at the photo's I'd taken. Carly teased me about Brady, especially when I told her we were still in touch, and she made me text him from my phone. That night we went to bed late, and when I woke the following day, I knew I'd be able to cope.

I walked up behind Lindsey and hissed a boo in her ear, she shrieked and spun around, grabbing me in a bear hug. Lindsey pushed me away to check me critically, and her eyes grew wide and soft, and her mouth formed an 'O'.

"What's up, Lindsey?" I asked, smiling.

"Silvie, you look amazing. Oh my God, you're glowing, it's a new Silvie. And I love your hair and the braids, your makeup really highlights your eyes, and those clothes are to die for!" Lindsey exclaimed. I squeezed her to stop her frantic babbling and grinned as Lindsey opened Made by Rage. As usual, I dumped my bag next to my desk and hit the coffee maker. The next hour I grumbled that the temp Lindsey had hired had messed up my mojo. Halfway through telling Lindsey about my trip in New Orleans, the door opened, and the atmosphere turned electric.

Confused, I glanced at Lindsey and saw she was glaring at whoever had walked into the shop. I was stunned when I looked up and saw it was Apache. He looked me over and then turned his head to Lindsey and met her stare for stare. What on earth was going on? What had I missed?

"Hey, Apache," I said easily. Apache turned back to me but didn't smile, his eyes raked me in, and I smiled. Gleefully, I saw the surprise in Apache's eyes at my appearance, and I took intense joy in that. No more drab, colourless Silvie.

"Hey Silvie," he rumbled, and while I still felt the pull, I knew I had it under control now. Those six weeks away and Brady's help had got me to the point I would no longer mourn what could have been. No, I hadn't fallen out of love with Apache, as I had hoped, but I could now handle my feelings. I wasn't going to allow them to push me into despair again.

"Anything I can do?" I asked, wondering at the strange atmosphere. Lindsey's back was up, and so was Apache's.

"You look different," Apache stated baldly, I nodded.

"Yup. Amazing what a six-week vacation can

achieve and male attention." As I said my last words, the atmosphere turned flat and then heat flared. I looked puzzled at Apache and saw something in his eyes I couldn't explain.

"Met someone, did you?" Apache asked with a bite in his tone.

"Yeah, he's called Brady, they're texting and emailing each other, it's sweet," Lindsey said with venom in her voice. Surprised, I glanced over, but Lindsey wore a sickly-sweet expression on her face. What the fuck? Apache's mood darkened and then sank even further when Gunner appeared at the joint entrance, vaulted it, and dragged me into his arms for a tight hug.

I hugged Gunner back tightly and murmured that I'd missed him, subtext, I hadn't missed Apache. Gunner's arms clenched, he dropped a kiss on the top of my head, took a step back and checked me over.

"Wow, looking good," Gunner said shortly and dragged me in for another squeeze and gave Lindsey and Apache a chin lift and walked out. Apache stared for a few seconds more and stormed out of the shop.

"What on earth is going on?" I said, spinning around to face Lindsey. She looked shamefaced, but her shoulders shot back.

"Things have been strained since you left," she murmured. I blinked startled.

"What?" I asked.

"Okay, I told Apache off the day after you left. Apache was going to find you, and I shouted at him. Once the other girls realised what was happening, it's as if we've split into two sides. The brothers and the old ladies, shit's strained at the club. We've been hanging out at the Reading Nook more often. It doesn't help that Harley hasn't woken up. Gunner and Apache are barely tolerating each other too."

"Because of me?" I said, stunned.

"Yes," Lindsey replied shortly. "Apache thinks Gunner drove you away when he chose Autumn over you. Gunner thinks Apache drove you away because he's an asshole, and the old ladies took Gunner's side. Drake's ready to kill half of us, and his tempers been foul. The only light is the pregnancies. Shit's been hitting the fan, and it's got to the point I've banned Lowrider from mentioning Rage at home."

"Holy shit!" I exclaimed. Lindsey worshipped the ground Lowrider stood on. Damn, how had my actions led to this? "Oh honey, put this aside, I'm okay, everything is cool. You know I didn't leave because of Autumn, I released Gunner, and I'm ecstatic that he's with Autumn. Gunner needed to be loved the way Autumn and those kids can love him, and I'm overjoyed for them both."

"No, it's not cool how Apache's treated you and chased you away. Drake put his foot down with the old ladies and told us we had no right getting in a brother's business. After that shit got worse, we didn't want to be around Drake when he disrespected our feelings like that. That's when we moved to the Reading Nook. Shit's got rougher the last two weeks." My mouth dropped open and remained open when Phoe and Marsha rushed through the doors. Artemis was on her way with Sin, Penny and Autumn planned to come later, they told me.

Phoe explained more about what had been going on, and despite my intentions, my leaving harmed no one, it seemed I'd caused a rift. Phoe wanted to meet up that night, but I declined, and her eyes narrowed. This was the hard part. I planned to slowly unravel my ties to the women and the club and distance myself from them. My plans even included finding a new job, I'd someone in mind who might hire me; it was time to move on from Apache. During the last two weeks, I'd realised that being around the old ladies meant seeing Apache, which meant torturing myself unnecessarily.

After a chat, Phoe quizzed me about a night out Saturday, which I declined again. A hurt look crossed Phoe's face, and I informed her I had plans. Which was not a lie, I'd contacted the Hawthorne women for a night out, and they'd readily agreed. Dylan Hawthorne's sister and cousins never needed an excuse to party. Offering Phoe a balm, I asked her if we could meet Wednesday night and go for a meal or a drink. Phoe agreed, but she was wary. I could sense it. Guilt hit hard because I realised they'd taken my back, yet I was planning to distance myself from them.

Lindsey kept her own knowing gaze on me when the old ladies left, and I guessed she was beginning to suspect things weren't back to normal. Distracted, I filled the air and time with chatter about Brady and my vacation. Carly also sensed something was wrong, but I headed both girls off before they could pry deeper. When I returned home, I knew something had shifted between us, and that was what I'd intended. Sadly, I'd treated Lindsey more like a boss today than a friend.

Wednesday night came around, and while it was

fun and laughter, it was stilted, and I could tell the old ladies had guessed I was planning something. I didn't stay late, as I usually did, and when a guy gave me his phone number, they were shocked when I texted him mine. Further shocked when I agreed to a date on Friday night. Phoe pulled me to one side and asked if I was sure, I told her, of course, I was.

I got ready Saturday night and put on a short black dress that hinted at cleavage and dropped to mid-thigh. The dress was a lacy number I'd picked up in New Orleans, and it was far different from what I was used to wearing. A quick glance in the mirror told me I was ready, and I walked into the living room, where Carly met me with wide eyes.

"Wow," Carly gasped as I spun on the spot.

"Okay?" I asked, and Carly nodded. I was meeting the Hawthorne women at the Rage bar, although I'd not wanted to. We planned to move on after a few drinks to warm us up before hitting a club. A knock at the door surprised me, and Carly walked over and frowned before opening it.

"Brady!" I exclaimed in surprise and dashed across the small living room to hug him. Carly stepped back with her mouth open as Brady swung me up and hugged me back.

"Hey, drop dead and gorgeous," Brady chuckled.

"What are you doing here?" I asked happily.

"Thought I'd take a drive and surprise you; I can stay in touch with the company through my laptop and phone. I missed you," Brady chuckled again. My mouth made an O shape, and Brady pulled me closer.

"Missed you too, my friend," I whispered, and Brady dropped a kiss on my head. "I was going out with friends, let phone and me cancel…"

"Nope, how about I accompany you? Unless it's ladies' night, and then I don't have the right equipment," Brady teased. I aimed a mock punch, taking in his suit pants and shirt and tie. Brady looked amazing, totally edible, and I'd be beating the Hawthorne women off him.

"Yeah, you'll pass for tonight," I winked, happiness colouring my tone.

"Not ladies' night?" Brady asked, and I shook my head.

"No honestly, just a night out, but my friends are man-eaters, Brady, be warned. Keep by my side," I insisted.

"Man eaters, damn, I'm handcuffing us together, you'll protect me, right? Hey there, you have to be Carly," he charmed. Brady turned to Carly and extended a hand. Carly smiled and held his hand briefly and then kept a distance.

"Yeah," Carly said, her gaze swapping between us.

"You're not coming out?" Brady asked.

"Not old enough, I got a movie night planned," Carly replied, and Brady nodded.

"Pleased to meet you, Carly, I've heard so many good things about you, I feel I know you already," Brady smiled, keeping up the effortless charm.

"Heard lots about you too," Carly muttered. Worried, I shot Carly a look to check she was okay and realised Carly was uncomfortable there was a man in our apartment.

"Okay, we're off honey, don't wait up," I said, stepping forward and hugging Carly. She nodded and kept a wary eye on Brady, who escorted me from the apartment.

"Is Carly okay?" Brady asked as he walked down the stairs.

"Carly's shy and definitely doesn't like strangers, especially men. Give her time to know you," I replied. "Oh my God, I can't believe you're here! What about work?" I asked excitedly and hopped on a stair to Brady's laugh.

"As I said, the company is fine, I've left my second in command in charge, and he's doing fine. We've worked hard this last month to cover the changes I've made in staff, sacking the asshole was the first. Can you believe he'd no intention of quitting? Luckily, I had him on various issues, and we had a solid basis for firing him.

Then I had to replace him, and I promoted internally, and I've replaced several other staff who were loyal to him. Think they forgot it's my company and not his. They were shocked when they thought to give me an earful, and I sacked them." I laughed at Brady and squeezed his arm.

Brady had been straight with me from the start, I understood he owned a well-known crockery company. It had been started by his grandmother on his mother's side, and his mother had taken over before Brady did. He didn't think it emasculating that he ran a company that specialised in vases, plates, etcetera. The company was famous for its high-end goods, and Brady hadn't made a big issue of his wealth.

"Did they go quietly?" I asked, seeing strain around Brady's eyes.

"Nope, but the guy who's in charge now, I've had my eye on for a while. He's got the balls and determination to help run the company. He's on a three-month trial basis, and then we've agreed for the first five years, he'll get a yearly contract judging on his performance. Don't mind saying, I've added significant benefits to his package, I've a good feeling about him." We got into Brady's rental, and I punched the Rage forecourt into the sat nav. We chatted about various things as Brady made the drive, and I showed him where to park on the forecourt.

Calamity came from the clubhouse as I got out, and I lifted my hand in a wave. Calamity waved back, and his hand froze mid-air as Brady walked around the rental to my side. Calamity's eyes narrowed in on Brady's arm around my waist, and then he offered a stilted chin left and disappeared back inside the clubhouse.

"One of the Rage members?" Brady asked curiously as I led the way out of the forecourt.

"Prospect, he's the one who saved me," I replied. There was no need to explain further. Brady knew about Frenzy and the attack. Ever since I'd mentioned it to Brady, he'd kept a sharp eye out for media articles that might upset me. As I said, Brady was a good man. I led the way to the bar and entered first.

As per usual, it was crowded, and we had to push our way through the crowds. Klutz and Mac were behind the bar serving alongside Banshee, known as Shee and Bear from Hellfire. Bear and Mac's eyes narrowed straight in on Brady as we approached the bar.

"A diet coke and a Southern Comfort with coke, please," Brady said to Mac, whose eyes narrowed as he studied the 'suit' with me.

"Mac, this is Brady, we became friends in California. He's driven down to visit this weekend," I said, giving Mac a warning glance. Mac responded with a sharp nod and got our drinks. I felt eyes glaring and spied Bear standing like the mountain he resembled, with his arms folded across his chest and a dark look on his face. Mac slid the drinks towards us, and Brady paid. Brady winked, and I smiled; he felt the tension as I did but was going to be a gentleman instead of reacting.

"Holy moly! Who is this hunk of gorgeousness?" Maria Hawthorne spluttered, approaching, eyes wide at Brady. Brady unruffled, smiled and took the hand she offered.

"This is Brady Whittaker, a friend of mine," I introduced them. Maria blatantly checked Brady out and grinned.

"Wanna be my friend too, Brady Whittaker?" Maria purred, and Brady took on a deer in the headlights look. I chuckled and laid my hand on his arm. A simple claiming gesture, but one Maria would understand.

"Friends sure, any friend of Silvie's is one of mine," Brady said warily, and Maria tossed her head back and laughed.

"Don't worry, friend, we don't poach, got the lady code, you know?" Maria said and began dragging us to a table where the Hawthorne women were. On the drive, I'd explained about the Hawthorne women.

Still, I got the impression Brady thought I was exaggerating. One glance at the rowdy bunch at the table changed Brady's mind, and his arm crept around my waist. I patted his hand reassuringly as Marissa Hawthorne checked him over and whistled.

"Damn Silvie, that's one hunk of a man," she grinned and shook Brady's hand happily.

"Thanks?" Brady ventured as Imelda was next to introduce herself. Within minutes Brady's head was whirling from the women and their names, and I kept whispering reminders of who was who in his ear. Despite being the only man present, Brady was a good sort as he bought a few rounds of drinks and kept a careful distance between wandering hands and leading comments.

"Silvie, we're off to Washington's," Marissa squealed, and I stepped back in surprise.

"Honey, didn't James ban you last time?" I asked quietly. James nearly had a heart attack the last time Hawthorne women attended his club.

"Yup, but I know James didn't mean it!" Sophia smiled. Shit, she was the quiet one compared to her sisters and cousins, and yet she was leading Ramirez around by his balls. Sophia was known as Sweet Sophia, but Ramirez had found himself with a wildcat on his hands, from the tales I'd heard, the moment he'd shown an interest. Luisa Hawthorne smiled, and Brady bristled. That smile had trouble all over it.

"The Hawthorne's get wild, they've been banned from five clubs and two strip joints," I explained, and Brady's eyes widened.

"They've what?" Brady spluttered as the Hawthorne's began gathering up their purses and whatnots.

"Yeah, they're widely known as the Hawthorne Females," I sighed, "they're wild women. Their fathers are three brothers who married wild women. Dylan Hawthorne runs Hawthorne Investigations; you may have heard of him?" Brady nodded, so I continued. "These women are his sister and cousins. Dylan's male cousins are law enforcement, private eyes, fire rescue or similar. They often get called to come to restrain their female cousins."

"Shit," Brady muttered, "and I'm the token male tonight?" I nodded, and Brady paled.

"They're good people Brady, honestly, wouldn't harm anyone unless crossed," I reassured as Luisa passed with a squeeze on Brady's butt cheeks. Brady jumped, and Luisa blew him a kiss.

"Washington's is a club?" Brady asked, and I shook my head. "Washington's is the premier strip joint in Rapid City. Dead classy, and you have to be a member to enter. James has revoked their membership so many times I'd be rich if I'd a dollar for each. But the women ignore James, and his front door men are terrified of the girls, so they let them in," I giggled. Brady downed the rest of his drink in one and put his arm out.

"Lead on, Silvie," he said grimly, and I laughed, delighted at the humour in Brady's eyes. I was secretly wondering which of the Hawthorne women I could set him up with. They'd keep Brady on his toes, and everyone knew the Hawthorne's male or female, came with a bucket load of loyalty and respect. One of them would be great for my friend.

As we made our way to the exit, I felt eyes on me,

and a pang of guilt stabbed me straight in the heart. Phoe and the old ladies sat at a table, eyes on us. With them sat their husbands or partners and Axel, Ezra, Apache and Slick. Drake's face was blank, as were most of the brothers, but Apache's eyes burned with fury. Jauntily, I waved at them and led Brady from the bar.

Brady offered to take three of the Hawthorne women in his rental, while the others got taxis. They booked them for the forecourt so Brady could follow the others to Washingtons. As we approached the rental to wait for the taxis, the clubhouse doors slammed open, and Gunner shot out. Long muscled legs strode in my direction, and Gunner's vibes hit hard. Worry, fear and anger sparked off Gunner as he stopped a few steps from us.

"Uh oh," Marissa muttered.

"I'm Gunner. Who the fuck are you?" Gunner growled, eyeing Brady up and finding him lacking.

"Brady Whittaker, a friend of Silvie's," Brady said, putting his hand out. The expression on Brady's face said he wouldn't back down. Gunner stared at Brady's hand and finally took it.

"How d'you know our girl?" Gunner growled, arms folded across his chest and legs splayed.

"That your concern, bud? Silvie told me everything about you and her. Great you found happiness but looking out for Silvie is no longer your concern," Brady said, throwing down. I gulped.

"Gunner!" I hissed angrily.

"Silvie, you're my one, and you know it. No bullshit, I'm gonna keep you safe," Gunner growled, and Brady grinned.

"Well, Silvie's not your one, Autumn is, but man to man, I admire a man who's looking out for his friend. You've got nothing to fear here, man," Brady said, but Gunner's eyes narrowed.

"Think I'm gonna take your word for it?"

"Nope, but take Silvie's, think you know what an excellent judge of character she is," Brady challenged, and I winced. I'd had bad feelings about Frenzy and not spoken up, which led to me being attacked.

"Sayin' you know Silvie better than me?" Gunner asked, astounded.

"Not a chance in hell," Brady demurred. "No one could understand Silvie better than the man who's stood at her back most of her life. I'm not here to tread on toes. Silvie helped me through some stuff that happened, kept me sane these last few weeks. I'm here as a friend," Brady stressed the last word, and Gunner searched his face.

"My girl's got a good heart," Gunner grunted, and Brady nodded. "Harm her…"

"Stop right there, bud, I'm not interested in hurting Silvie, got my own past, it's not for your ears, but Silvie's aware. We're friends, and that's where it ends," Brady said firmly. Gunner turned to me and caught the rage on my face, and winced. Angrily, I lifted an eyebrow, and Gunner winced a second time.

"Done comparing dick sizes?" I asked caustically.

"No, you left me, woman, don't wanna go through that again," Gunner muttered. I raised up on tiptoes and kissed Gunner's cheek.

"Reel your dick back in, Brady's cool," I said as taxis arrived on the forecourt. Brady and Gunner exchanged one more glance, and then Brady helped us into the vehicles. Gunner watched us pull away, and I squeezed Brady's leg in apology.

"Don't, it's nice to see Gunner still cares for you," Brady murmured as Luisa, Marissa, and McKenna whispered in the back of the rental.

"Gunner cares for me but loves Autumn, I worried about the dynamic at first. Would Autumn cause trouble, would she see me as a threat?" I replied.

"And?"

"Autumn's wonderful, everything Gunner needs and as she has Calamity, she understands better than I thought she ever would."

"Each Rage brother isn't satisfied by one woman?" Brady asked curiously.

"Oh no, they'd never be unfaithful once they claim a woman!" I exclaimed. "It's more a case of the women seeks an alternative. Sometimes we can't speak to those we love, so we have someone we can. It's as if we have a second husband but without the bond or sex."

"We?" Brady asked, and I realised what I'd said.

"That came out wrong," I whispered, "I'm trying to pull back. Protect my heart, you understand." And Brady understood; he'd suffered and been betrayed as I had. Out of everyone, Brady understood what it was like to love someone and not have it returned.

"Silvie, just do what's best for you!" Brady said with heat. He hugged me tightly and the rest of the journey passed in silence. Brady looked surprised when we pulled up outside Washingtons, it was a classy joint, not a scummy one. The doorman looked terrified as the Hawthorne women piled out. I began giggling, and Brady glanced at me curiously.

"The doormen and bouncers are terrified of the women," I whispered as Luisa strode over and placed her hands on her hips.

"Luisa, you're barred," the doorman muttered, and Luisa cocked an eyebrow. That single action did it, and the poor man stepped aside, and Brady chuckled.

"They really are wild, and the men won't tackle them one on one. He'll call for backup before any of them get close. Hey Tony!" I said, grinning at the doorman speaking on a radio.

"Silvie, you with them?" Tony asked.

"Yeah," I grinned. Brady and Tony exchanged looks, and we followed the Hawthorne females inside. Tony's was full of sympathy, and Brady's full of trepidation. The girls hadn't got far, and as Brady and I pushed through, Adam, James's second in command, stood in front of them, arms folded.

"Oh no, you don't!" Adam said firmly as Marissa pushed forward. "Don't start, Marissa, follow me," Adam said, and we exchanged glances. Luisa stepped up and followed Adam, and we trailed behind them. I grinned when I saw where Adam was leading us too. There was a curved seating area to the left of the stage that was cordoned off from the public. A round booth held a large table and an excellent shot of the stage. It could hold at least twenty people easily and if we pulled up chairs even more.

"James said you stay here, no ripping up the club, no mayhem, and you get a server. This is the Hawthorne VIP area, and there's one downstairs too in the male strip club. You don't leave this booth unless you're tipping a dancer and only in twos for the ladies' room, which is right behind you," Adam said, frowning at the girls.

"James got us a private booth?" Marissa asked, lighting up in joy.

"Fuck woman, you set a club on fire? Got you a private booth with fucking sprinklers above your head. You lot don't behave, then you are permanently banned. And don't even fucking think of terrifying Luka who's watching over you," Adam pointed at Sophia, who looked insulted.

"I've never terrified Luka," Sophia argued back.

"One of ya's handcuffed Detective Benjamin and offered a lap dance. My bouncers are fucking terrified of the lot of you because of who ya brothers are. Now enjoy your night and fucking behave!" Adam warned, and I grinned. I glanced behind me at the blackout glass panels above the bar where James's office was. They were a two-way glass, and I guessed James was watching. I lifted a hand and hoped James had seen.

"They set a club on fire?" Brady asked, and I nodded. "They handcuffed a cop?"

"Told you, they're wild, and they're behaving. This is the women dancer's floor, the males are below, but the girls thought you'd be uncomfortable," I replied.

"They ain't?" Brady asked. I started to answer, and Justine screamed instead.

"Shake that ass, baby!" Brady turned with wild eyes as the girls began screaming and shouting at the dancers, encouraging them. Catalina jumped to her feet and threw some dollars at the stage.

"Fuck me, why don't I have tits like that?" Carla moaned, looking at her own boobs. Brady wide-eyed stared at me and sank back on the seat. I bit my lip to stop from laughing, and Brady's eyes lit up with unholy mischief.

"This is going to be an experience to remember," Brady laughed as a round of shots appeared.

"You can bet on it," I agreed, slamming one down. Brady put an arm out, and I tucked myself under it as we watched the floor show offered by the dancers and the Hawthorne women.

"Who is he?" James asked, his eyes narrowed on the man who had an arm around Silvie.

"Don't know, as soon as he offers a card to pay, we'll run him," Adam said from behind him.

"Yes, run him, I want to know everything, if he's with Silvie… just run him, Adam," James said, observing. Silvie appeared happy enough and was animatedly talking to the stranger. But until James knew he was kosher, he wasn't taking chances. James owed Silvie big time. If not for her, he'd be dead, and so would his brother. Yeah, no punk was latching onto Silvie because of her connections.

Chapter Two.

I yawned as I walked into Made by Rage the next day and found myself facing the firing squad. Every single old lady was present, even Penny, and several didn't appear happy. With a sigh, I dropped my bag on my desk and turned to face them.

"What's going on?" I asked, yawning again. It had been a late-night yesterday, and I'd fallen straight into bed.

"That's what we want to know, you've stopped hanging around the clubhouse, and you don't spend as much time with us. What are you doing, Silvie?" Phoe asked.

"I'm living Phoe, is that wrong?" I asked, sitting my ass on the desk, and facing them. Autumn pointed a finger at me.

"We're worried," she said.

"Why?"

"You're different," Lindsey said, folding her arms across her chest. Oh, I recognised that look, although it was usually aimed at Lowrider. It wasn't comfortable being at the end of one myself. This was the showdown I wanted to avoid and wasn't going to be allowed to, judging by their faces.

"It's not you guys, it's Apache. The vacation I took was to get my head together, and I did, and I made decisions that you may disagree with. I love Apache, I always will, it's something rooted so deep inside me, I can't cut it out," I said, taking a deep breath.

"Silvie," Marsha said, and I waved a hand.

"No, let me finish. This is harder for me than you. You have your men, I don't, so give me the respect I've earned over the years and listen." The old ladies nodded. "I spent weeks coming to terms with my feelings, and I have. But in doing so, I realised the cycle I was on wasn't healthy, it was killing me slowly. So I've changed the cycle, and no one's going to stop me. I will still see you once a week, I'll visit Rage once a week. I've Calamity and Gunner there and Drake.

But I'm no longer going to be the old lady without a fucking brother. I won't watch Apache whore himself out to every woman he wants while I stand there with my heart breaking. So it means I make other friends, I date other men, and maybe one day soon I can find a man who's going to give me everything I deserve. Fuck, it may be too late, but I want a family, a husband, the dream home, I deserve it, and I want it."

"Oh, Silvie," Marsha said, heartbroken.

"Yeah, I love you guys, but I can't hang around you, swallowing bitterness that your men can give you what you need. Apache treats me like shit, and I'm swallowing that every day. No more, I'm getting me a life, and you need to understand, I'm searching for another job. Even working here isn't healthy, because I'll see him every day and I'll fall into my old cycle. It's destructive, and I'm not paying for a man who's too bitter, stubborn and too much of an asshole to see I deserve love," I said and folded my arms.

"Apache…"

"No, Phoe, I understand what Apache is and what he isn't. He's not got the damn balls to man up and take the love offered him. That's his mistake, not mine, he's a pussy, and I deserve a real man. I can't stop loving him, but I sure as hell can find someone else to love and who'll love me. Apache is cold, manipulating, and selfish; he's an out-and-out bastard. And I'm done loving that. Yeah, I get you're hurt, so am I. Never wanted to lose Rage, but for me to be healthy, that's what I got to do," I said. My head dropped and lifted; determination written on my face.

"You can either support me or go against me, it's your choice. But you don't get to make me suffer guilt for being the idiot who loved a brother incapable of love. You don't get to make me feel shit for removing myself from a poisonous situation."

"Silvie, you have my support," Autumn said instantly, she knew about guilt too.

"I can't imagine not working with you," Lindsey said, stunned. Her entire body was closed in and her arms folded across her as if protecting herself.

"I love you, you're my sister, but Lindsey, surely you don't want me to suffer?" I asked, and she shook her head instantly.

"Of course not!" she exclaimed.

"Good, because I'm done letting Apache make me suffer. He can go to hell and fuck who he wants. But he's done fucking with my life," I said heatedly. A noise near the joint doors between Made by Rage and the Rage shop made us turn around. Standing there was Drake, Ace, Apache, and Gunner. Drake's face was set in stone, same as Ace. Apache's was deadened, no emotion, nothing. Gunner was furious, anger bled from his body, and I recognised the signs of Gunner ready to explode. No need to ask what they'd heard; judging by their expressions, they'd heard everything.

Gunner slammed away from the other three, and I saw him storm past Made by Rage's windows, and moments later, his bike hit the street. Taking a deep breath, I turned back to the other three and held their gazes. They gave nothing away, and neither did I.

"Phoe you need to get to HQ, Sin and Penny off with you, Reid will burn the Reading Nook down to its foundations. Autumn office now, Marsha clubhouse and rest, Artemis go feed those babes.

Lindsey, we need to go over the orders," I bossed the old ladies to their businesses. Without a second look at the three men, I walked around my desk and sat.

For several long moments, everyone stood rooted in place, and then Phoe nodded and tilted her head towards the door. One by one, the old ladies left, leaving Lindsey, Carly, and myself alone. I opened my drawer and pulled out the order book.

"Are you ready?" I asked, looking at them. Lindsey nodded, and I opened the folder. Boots stomped away, but I refused to glance up. Rage was no longer part of my life. Not now, never again.

Carly sat next to me after I ordered take out for dinner. Brady was staying in town for a few weeks, but he was attending a meeting online, so had begged off for tonight. It was just Carly and me tonight, and we needed this.

"Are you okay, honey?" I asked as Carly curled into herself. Carly studied at me for ages.

"Yes, unlike the others, I understand. I believe you're doing the right thing for you, but is Brady the one for you?" Carly asked.

"Brady? No, we need each other. Brady had his heart broken the same as mine. Together we're helping each other heal. There's nothing sexual in it. Just two friends supporting each other," I explained.

"I liked Brady, he seemed nice last night, and he survived the Hawthorne's," she giggled.

"Yeah, something few can do. Brady was a good sport about last night, they tried to behave, but you know them," I giggled. Brady had been horrified when Justine had got up on stage with one dancer and stripped to her underwear. As she wasn't hurting anyone, Luka, our bouncer, had left her there strutting her stuff. But I'd bet good money her two older brothers, Arturo and Hernando, as well as her male cousins, were furious this morning. For once, they hadn't ripped up the club, the Hawthorne's happy in their VIP Hawthorne area.

"Did Gunner come back?" Carly asked.

"No, I didn't see him return," I said, upset. Gunner will take me pulling back and leaving hard, but I was comforted by knowing he had Autumn and the children. Gunner would make it through, he'd begun repairing his relationship with James, his older brother, and he'd a family. Yet again, Gunner had everything I wanted, but there was no way I'd ever hold it against him.

"I'll miss you; I can't imagine working without you. Lindsey is the skill and talent behind Made by Rage, but you're a vital part and have been with her since day one. Designs by Lindsey is as much yours as hers," Carly said, and my stomach churned. Carly was correct, I had been with Lindsey before Design's by Lindsey even had a building. And I'd put a huge part of myself into helping her get it off the ground. Would the next office manager take it as diligently as me?

"Carly, I can't stay around Apache and stay sane. That won't work for me anymore. These few weeks away have shown me I'm attractive and people like me. They don't take me for granted. Oh, honey, there's something I didn't tell you," I said and jumped as someone knocked on the door. Desperate to escape Carly's sad eyes, I scurried over and accepted our takeout, paying the kid before busying myself serving our meal.

"Tell me," Carly said as I sat.

"Apache kissed me twice and got handsy. The first time, Gunner punched him over, the second, Gunner has no idea happened. After Gunner and I broke up, Apache thought Gunner had taken my virginity, and that made it okay to fuck with me. When I told him Gunner hadn't, Apache backed away like I was diseased," I muttered, ashamed.

"You're still a virgin?" Carly gasped. Trust Carly to latch onto that!

"Yeah, I've waited for him all this time. And now…"

"Fuck me!" Carly exclaimed, and her hand shot to her mouth. Carly was fire and ice, calm and collected on the outside, but I sensed a maelstrom of emotion beneath her facade. She was cautious with who she let in and rarely cussed or lost control of her emotions.

"Yeah, shameful at my age," I agreed as Carly's enormous eyes studied me.

"I'm shocked," she admitted.

"So am I!" I laughed and stuffed food into my mouth.

"Wow, so you and Gunner?" Carly asked after a few moments.

"We fooled around, but it never went the full circle. Gunner was very much aware I was a virgin and held back. Now he has Autumn, I'm glad he did. But in a way, I'm disappointed he didn't. That man certainly has moves, Autumn's one lucky lady," I laughed, and Carly's eyes grew even larger.

"Wow," she said again.

"While we on the subject of hot and sexy bikers," I said, and Carly's face became expressionless.

"Yeah," Carly replied warily.

"Rock," I said succinctly, and Carly turned red and then white.

"Rock?" she asked, and I raised an eyebrow. Really, was she going to pretend there wasn't serious chemistry between them?

"Carly," I said and let it hang.

"Oh, okay," Carly exclaimed and flung herself backwards on our shitty couch. She raised an arm and covered her face. Huffing a breath, Carly flopped onto the cushions behind her.

"I like Rock, seriously like Rock. I mean, honestly, what's not to like? He's dark and handsome, a tall, delicious drink of yumminess. But he is twelve years older than me and doesn't want to settle with one woman. He's always with a skank from the club, and he's not interested in me. And there're things you can't outrun," Carly denied. I studied her and caught something in Carly's expression.

"Carly, we've never talked about how you landed at Rage," I said, and Carly stiffened.

"Nothing to discuss," Carly denied.

"Are you sure? If there's something dark in your past, we can help. The brothers can help if you're running from trouble," I pushed.

"Drop it, Silvie, I love and respect you, but there're things that not even Rage can solve. I'm happy and content, and that's all you need to know. Excuse me, I wanted an early bath today," Carly said, springing to her feet and running from our tiny room. My mouth dropped open in surprise as I watched her disappear.

What on earth had just happened? Carly had never discussed her past, we knew nothing about her, but this excessive reaction was beyond Carly. She never mentioned family or friends or even where she'd previously lived. When she arrived, she'd not even had a bank account, I couldn't even hazard a guess if Carly had a birth certificate and identification. My girl was definitely running from something, and something had terrified her in her past.

It was not for me to bring this to Rage's or Rock's attention, but I could drop a whisper in Lindsey's ear. But on the other hand, although I'd caught Rock watching Carly, he'd not made a move, nor had he stopped his man-whoring ways! Decisions, decisions, everything was so complicated lately!

Three weeks later, Drake picked up his phone as it rang, he glanced around the clubhouse, spied several skanks, and walked to his room. Ramirez cut off and rang back straight away, and Drake hit answer.

"Ramirez," Drake said.

"Evidence was found on the body Drake; I don't know whose, but they're coming for one of you. Get a lawyer," Ramirez said and disconnected.

"Fuck!" Drake roared and punched the wall. He knew who'd taken care of Crow, who'd beaten the man to a pulp and then killed him. Drake called his lawyer and put him on standby; his brother would need him soon. As Drake walked back into the clubhouse, he caught Ace's eyes just as there was a loud rap on the doors, and they were pushed open. No less than eight cops walked into the clubhouse, and the sound died, and the music cut off with a shriek.

"What do you want?" Drake asked, stopping in the middle of the room, his legs splayed and arms folded. Menace drifted off him in waves.

"We'd like to speak to Ace Blackelk concerning an ongoing murder investigation," one cop said, stepping forward. He was dressed in a shabby suit and looked worn and tired.

"Yeah? Got a warrant?" Drake asked as Ace came to stand at his side. In the blink of an eye, Artemis stood at Ace's side, her face expressionless.

"It's just a friendly chat," the cop said.

"Friendly chats don't include bringing eight cops

onto Rage," Drake said.

"Ain't no fool, no one walks on Rage without back-up," the cop sneered.

"Why's that? Ain't been no trouble from Rage with the law for years. So why is Rage a threat now?" Drake bellowed, and the cops hand went to his belt.

"You draw that, you can kiss your job goodbye. My husband's right, Rage has worked with the cops for years, so what the fuck do you think you're doing?" Phoe spat. She stormed across the room, stopping at Drake's side.

"Lady, this ain't got shit to do with you. So why don't you go return to where you came from and keep your fucking nose to yourself?" the cop sneered. Phoe began laughing.

"You have no idea who you're talking to," she said when she stopped giggling.

"We're aware of who you are, it just has no bearing on this. Now you can come quietly, Ace, or we'll get a warrant," another plain-clothed cop said, elbowing his partner.

"Get a fuckin' warrant," Drake spat. Apache laughed.

"Get the fuck off our land," Apache growled.

"Don't bother, I'll go with them for a chat," Ace said with his own sneer. "Call our lawyer and inform him how the cops turned up in force for a so-called chat and get a complaint put in. Make it fuckin' air-tight against the assholes."

"That ain't necessary," the first cop said.

"Oh, there's a huge fuckin' need for that. Look around, asshole," Drake sneered as the cops did. "You came onto my land, my clubhouse, with eight armed cops. Cops and Rage worked together for years; you just blew that relationship right out of the water. We got fuckin' kids and babies here," Drake roared, and the second cop looked worried.

"All we want to do is have a chat with Mr Blackelk," he said, putting his hands up in peace.

"Asshole," Nova said, "that's my Dad, and you thought it's a good idea when my baby brother and sister are here?" Nova rose to her feet and glared.

"Calm down," Axel boomed. His large hand slammed on Ace's shoulder. "Artemis, take care of Nova now. If my man's coming to the station, you're taking me with him, until his lawyer gets there. And you don't talk to Ace in the car or interview room until his lawyer gets there. If this is a fuckin' friendly chat, you don't walk Ace to the interview room until Rage's lawyer is present. You don't fuckin' agree, get a fuckin' warrant, and we'll see you in court." The two New York detective's swapped glances, and the second one nodded.

"Deal," he said.

"Lucas, tell the chief whatever agreement Rage had with the RCPD just expired. Ain't got a problem with cops wanting to talk to my brothers, we ain't got shit to hide. Do have a problem with eight armed cops charging into my clubhouse when we got our babies and kids here. One of you assholes got trigger happy.

Our kids could have been shot. So tell the fuckin' chief, by authorising this shit, he blew our deal," Drake hissed. Officer Lucas paled and put a calming hand up.

"Drake, you got to understand we wouldn't have come in firing…"

"Fuck that Lucas, Rage had good relations with RCPD. We work fuckin' closely with your department keeping crime down in our town. Chief authorised this shit, we're done. Solve your own fuckin' crimes. And tell the chief, good luck bringing in Romeo Santos on his own. Now get the fuck out of my clubhouse and off my land!" Drake roared. Ace smirked and then walked out the door, Axel on his heels. The two New York cops offered their own sneers and then left.

"Drake, the chief isn't aware, he's at a conference. This move wasn't his. Make the complaint formal, all the way to the top," Lucas said. Drake picked up the undertone. The cops present hadn't wanted to be there. They'd been forced there by the two New York detectives. But it didn't remove the fact they'd come armed, and Drake wouldn't forgive or forget that fact.

Ace sat in the interview room, arms locked behind his head, and impassively watched the two detectives as they organised their paperwork.

"I'm going to repeat you're not under arrest," the first said, and Ace said nothing.

"Your names would help," Mr Etherington said, the club's lawyer.

"Detectives Williams and Johnson," the second replied. Ace gave a slight chin tilt.

"So Ace, do you understand why you're here?" Williams asked. Ace shrugged.

"Nope," he replied.

"We found the body of a member of your club, Kyle Reeves, known as Crow," Williams said, an intent expression on his face.

"And?" Ace said. Williams frowned.

"You're not surprised or upset we've found a body," Williams said.

"Nope," Ace said, determined to be unhelpful. These fuckers had invaded Rage with weapons. If they'd been the old Rage, there'd have been a firefight. Luckily, they were led by Drake now.

"So, you're not upset or surprised we found a body. Can you elaborate why?" Williams pushed, and Ace glanced at Etherington.

"Crow was thrown out of the club when we split. He was dirty, so no, I'm not surprised he's dead. No, I'm not upset a known drug dealer is dead," Ace said. Williams made a note and shuffled his paperwork.

"So you disagreed with Crow?" Jackson asked.

"Nope, I don't like what he did or what he became. But once he was kicked from Rage, he wasn't my concern," Ace replied. Williams lit up with an unholy gleam in his eye.

"Kicked from Rage?"

"The club split, Crow left, didn't like what Rage wanted to become. That's clean, those who were dirty, fucked off from our club."

"Did you have a hand in helping them leave?" Williams asked, and Etherington shook his head at Ace.

"Yup," Ace drawled, and Etherington shot him a sharp glance.

"Would you care to elaborate?" Williams asked with a hint of frustration.

"Nope," Ace replied with a grin.

"No? You just claimed you had a hand in forcing them out. Did you beat and torture them? Shoot them?" Williams pushed.

"Nope," Ace drawled, knowing his one-word answers was driving the cop mad.

"Well, we need an explanation, Mr Blackelk," Jackson said.

"I voted against them staying," Ace said and shut his mouth. He slowly relaxed his arms and leant on the table.

"You voted against them staying?" Williams said with pure disbelief. "So you didn't hurt them or kill them?"

"My client already answered that," Etherington said. "Move on, Detective."

"You're an enforcer," Jackson said, and Ace bared his teeth at them.

"Nope." Williams frowned and checked his notes. Ace tapped his patch that said VP, and they flushed.

"So you're second in command of Rage, gives you a lot of power," Williams said.

"Is there a question in that?" Etherington asked with a sigh. Both detectives shot him a frustrated glance.

"Well, your client is hardly forthcoming," Jackson said.

"Why should he? You invaded the Rage clubhouse with eight armed officers supporting you. Mr Blackelk's wife, teenage children and two babies were present. Alongside other women and children. So ask questions and stop wasting our time," Etherington said.

"Crow was tortured before someone put a bullet in his brain. Would you know anything about that?" Williams asked.

"Nope," Ace said, holding up a hand to forestall Etherington.

"Yet you own a reputation for being ruthless and violent," Jackson chipped into the conversation. Ace turned a blank face to him.

"And you have reputations of coming to RC and being assholes. Fuckin' throwing your weight around as if you're special because you're from New York. You made a real impression in the few weeks you've been here," Ace drawled and smirked. Williams bristled.

"Mr Blackelk, are you saying your reputation is unfounded?" Williams asked in disbelief.

"Got witnesses? Proof?" Ace asked and knew they hadn't. No witness had been left breathing.

"Your wife is a well-known mercenary," Jackson asked.

"Yeah, and legal. So what?"

"Could she have been the one to torture Crow?" Williams asked. Ace laughed, startling everyone in the room.

"Fuck me, how thick are you bastards? When did he disappear?"

"The bones are estimated to be approximately nine years old. Crow died in two thousand and seven. When Rage got themselves clean."

"Artemis disappeared in two thousand and two, she wasn't in this country. Next stupid question," Ace said and leant back. He exchanged a look with Etherington.

"So you deny harming, killing or shooting Crow, or having knowledge of who did," Williams said.

"My clients already answered that," Etherington said.

"Crow disappeared during the time Rage fought to get the club clean, co-incidence?" Williams asked. Ace grinned.

"Must be, lots of co-incidences around."

"So can you tell me why a long black hair was found on Crow's cut?" Williams said, grinning as he laid his trump card. Ace stared at Williams for several long moments and threw back his head, and roared with laughter. Williams and Jackson swapped confused glances.

"One long black hair, that's what you got? Fuck me,

you dragged me in here, raided Rage with weapons because of one long black hair? Jesus, someone put a real cop in charge," Ace laughed.

"No need for insults. Insults are often used by guilty people," Williams said, but his smugness was rocked.

"Ain't insultin' when it's the fuckin' truth. Shit man, you dragged me in here for one long black hair?" Ace sneered.

"We've got evidence," Williams said irately.

"You got shit. Wanna know how you got shit? Take a forensics team to Rage, check every single brother, I bet you find my hair on their cuts too. Fuckin' pricks, causing this shit, destroying a relationship between cops and Rage that lasted ten years. You got fuckin' nothing," Ace spat.

"You're claiming that your hair ended up on his cut accidentally?" Williams asked.

"Ain't claiming shit, telling you, check any cut at Rage, I bet you find my hair on at least four of them. Jesus Christ, what a waste of time," Ace said. He clapped Etherington on the shoulder. "See fucker, I just slapped him on the back, my fingerprints now on his clothing, nice leather jacket Etherington. So he walks out of here and ends up dead you're gonna arrest me because of my fingerprints on his jacket? Get fuckin' real."

"So you can't explain why your hairs on Crow's cut?" Williams said, trying to regain control of the interview.

"Think I just gave you a reason, ain't my place to do

your job. If that all you got to say, I'm done. Fuckin' waste of time, and you gonna answer for this," Ace said, getting to his feet. Etherington reached out and touched Ace's arm.

"You have anything else?" Etherington asked. Williams sourly shook his head.

"Was that a threat?" Jackson asked.

"Huh?" Ace grunted.

"That we're gonna regret this," Jackson repeated. Ace grinned nastily.

"That was a fuckin' promise. See, my Prez's woman is already over this shit. Lawyers are drawing up complaints, and you just wrecked a relationship between Rage and the local cops, that brought down many criminals. Rage has helped RCPD bring in plenty of scum, and you assholes walked into my club and destroyed that in minutes. Chief will have your fuckin' balls, and you'll be back in New York with lawyers right up your ass," Ace said. Etherington rose to his feet and led the way out of the interview room, shaking his head.

"They've got nothing, Ace," he whispered as Ace grunted. He knew that, but he was furious.

"Keep you updated, man. Thanks for coming," Ace growled as they left the building. Calamity sat outside in a pickup with Axel. Ace shook Etherington's hand and climbed in.

"Talk," Axel boomed.

"Call church," Ace ordered, and Axel texted Drake.

"Is Ace okay?" I asked Lindsey as she brought Carly and me up to date on last night's happenings.

"Yes, furious, and there's a war meeting with lawyers and whatnot today. Heads are going to roll," Lindsey said, sitting back in her armchair.

"God, the kids were there?" Carly asked.

"Those detectives are disgusting," I agreed. How dare they act like that? Rage had been legal and clean for years.

"Well, Ace is back; he said they've shit on him," Lindsey whispered, chewing a sausage roll from the Reading Nook. Sin sat with us, having her lunch.

"Don't care, those cops came armed for trouble, unnecessarily. Rage hasn't exploded in years," I said, frowning.

"They used to?" Sin asked, leaning forward, eager to learn more about the club.

"Clubs been clean years now, when Bulldog ran the club? Yeah, armed cops would have been needed. Bulldog would have been the first asshole to pull a weapon. I'm disgusted with this," I said, shaking my head.

"I don't like what I've heard about Bulldog," Lindsey said, shaking her head.

"Bulldog was a murderous, greedy asshole, he'd no moral compass and grasped the reins of Rage tightly. Drake and Ace had a real fight regaining Rage, but they won. That's all we need to know," I said.

"I don't care. Lowrider's a good man," Lindsey said

with stubbornness in her voice.

"Not just Lowrider, all of them are, they're each special. Even Apache," I smiled, and for once, bitterness didn't tinge my smile. I was letting go, moving on, and it felt bloody fantastic.

"You think Ace did it?" Lindsey asked, and Sin peered at me curiously.

"Does it matter? Ace is good and honest, protective, and loving. Nothing means more to Ace than Rage, his brothers, and their old ladies. I honestly don't care if Ace did it, or if they've got blood on their hands, I couldn't give a fuck. Don't start doubting Rage Lindsey, because none of them deserves it. I may pull back, but I'll hang before I ever judge Rage and to be honest, you should feel the same," I said firmly.

"No, Silvie, you've mistaken what I meant. I wasn't judging Ace. Do we need to circle the wagons?" Lindsey said, laying her hand on mine.

"No, because Drake, the brothers and Artemis, will have circled the wagons. Your role is to support Lowrider and make sure he's healthy, loved and happy at home. You get that right, then he can handle what's being flung at him from outside home and Rage. This is part of being Lowrider and Jett's old lady. This is your role. Don't falter now," I said. Lindsey and Sin nodded.

"I won't!" Lindsey swore fervently.

"Good," I said. Engrossed in our conversation, none of us saw Apache and Texas standing watching us. Apache's eyes blazed with a fierce light as I came to the defence of his son while Texas nodded approvingly.

"Silvie's always been a wonderful woman, never strayed from Rage's path. Shame to lose her like we're going to," Texas rumbled. Apache grunted; Texas could take that however he wanted. For now, Apache wished to gaze at the precious woman he longed to claim but couldn't. He wouldn't get many more chances, Drake had informed him; he'd received two reference requests from people interested in offering Silvie a job.

Silvie's friend Brady (and Apache wanted to punch his lights out) had offered Silvie a serious job as his personal assistant. Lindsey had told Lowrider, who told Apache, Silvie was considering it, but she didn't want to ruin their friendship. Apache hated the man but admired him for firmly sticking to his words. All Brady truly wanted was friendship. Brady had returned home; Apache didn't care where it was as long as the man stayed there. Apache swallowed his bile and closed his eyes briefly. It was March. How much longer did he have her?

I gazed across the forecourt with the sensation of something being wrong. Turning, I checked the bays seeing brothers and mechanics milling about and then turned my gaze to the clubhouse. Nothing there either. So what was bugging me, Blaze was crossing the forecourt heading to the office when he stopped, and his gaze began searching around him. Not just me, Blaze sensed something wrong too. His eyes met mine and took in my puzzled, cautious look.

"You sense it?" Blaze rumbled, and I nodded.

"We're being watched," I said, and Blaze grunted an agreement.

"Walk you to the shop. Drake's there. Let him know what you sensed," Blaze said. Slate joined us, his own head twisting as he sensed the same as us. A minute later, I was inside Made by Rage and talking to Drake, whose frown would have been terrifying if I didn't understand his expressions.

"And you saw no one?" Drake mused.

"Nope, but we were definitely being watched."

"You got shit on you? Mace, alarm?" Drake said, and I shot him a worried glance.

"Always," I replied.

"Make sure the others are fully kitted out, Silvie, do that now. I'll call our supplier, let him know you'll be dropping by," Drake said.

"Okay, I'll tell Lindsey."

"Do that, and Silvie…" Drake stopped and stared at me.

"Yeah?" I asked.

"Don't want you to leave woman, you're a vital part of the old ladies," Drake said and held up a hand as I started to interrupt. "But I get it, just wanted you to know, I get it. And you'll always have my love." Drake walked away, leaving me in a puddle of swallowed tears and guilt. Damn Drake Michaelson to hell!

Chapter Three.

I ran down the road as fast as I could. I'd lost my shoes a long way back, kicking them off to run faster. A pang of regret struck at losing my Manolo Blahniks, but I had to get to our territory and let the brothers know. I didn't have a choice; they needed the information on what I'd just overheard and seen. The club depended on me, even though they weren't aware of the need.

Rudely, I'd left Luisa, Justine, Marissa and Lina at the bar we'd been at, when I'd come across what I was now running from, frightened beyond belief. They were safer there than with me, and I needed to reach Rage. Despite my withdrawal from them for the last couple of weeks, I was still Rage, and I'd information they needed.

Headlights turned the corner, their beam piercing the darkness. The clubhouse was ten minutes away, but I was tired and hurt. Pinhead had caught me and began beating me when he realised who I was, the bastard. He hadn't expected me to scratch his eyes as I'd been told to and tear myself away.

Silently, I ducked behind a car as headlights again came my way. These were worrying as I could tell they weren't a car, they were bikes. Fear made me shake, not the fear of being killed, I was resigned to that. Pinhead made that fact plain. No, it was the terror of my knowledge dying with me. The pipes grew louder, and I crouched as small as I could, my ribs hurting from the punches I'd taken.

Pinhead had broken at least two, judging the sharp pain, and I cursed the asshole to hell and back. Small comfort knowing Ace would beat the fuck out of the guy and make him suffer. I'd suffer first. Yanking a tissue from my purse, I took the time to wipe the blood from my nose and prayed it wasn't broken. The bikes passed, I waited a few minutes and then rose cautiously to stand. After a quick glance around, I saw no one and began running again.

My feet were cut to shreds, and I was leaving a bloody path, but I just had to get to our territory. Once there, they wouldn't, couldn't touch me. Pinhead had stamped on my phone, and I couldn't call for help. So it was on me; I'd information the MC desperately needed informing of, before blood spilt on Rage land. Before there was another shooting like Gunner. There was no one else but me to get them this information.

Warily, I turned the next corner and sighed in relief. Two more streets, and I'd hit a patrol, I knew I would. As out of touch as I was with Rage, they still ran their patrols. One of them should find me.

Focused, I kept running and didn't see the figure that stepped out of the shadows. Pinhead caught me around the waist and covered my hand with his mouth. I tried biting him, and he released my mouth and punched me in the head. Stunned, I stopped struggling.

"Time to die, bitch. You're gonna send a message," Pinhead growled. I whimpered and began struggling again. Pinhead dragged me towards the road, and I saw a truck coming towards me. I tried digging my heels in but scraped my feet raw as the car neared. A sick feeling and regret swamped me, when Apache's face came to me. The brother I loved more than anything else in this entire world. It was too late, and he'd never understood how I honestly felt, we'd never get a chance to fix what Apache had broken between us. Yeah, I was stupid, I'd still hoped even though I'd pulled away from Rage. I still worked at Made by Rage, looking for a decent job that paid well. Now I'd a taste of a good job, I wasn't going back to bartending, or so I told myself. Too late now, Pinhead shoved me in the road, and for a second, everything froze.

The truck hit me at speed, and I tumbled up on its hood. Just before my head hit the windscreen, I glimpsed a face I'd not seen for a long time. He wasn't smiling at me, and it was wrong. Worry was in his eyes and regret. But my head hit hard, and I lost my train of thoughts as everything faded to black. The truck skidded to a stop, and I tumbled off into the road. Pinhead approached.

He made a motion with his hand, the truck reversed and came straight at me, I couldn't roll out of the way properly, and my legs screamed in agony. I couldn't do anything except embrace the darkness with Apache's stunning eyes gazing at me. It was my fault; I should have taken what he was willing to offer. And even as peace and darkness claimed me, I'd never felt in life swept over me, I'd done right. But fuck, who wants to die a virgin? Bollocks.

Drake looked up as Ramirez walked into the clubhouse, his face expressionless and blank. He came alert, and the vibes warned his brothers. Relations were tense between Rage and the RCPD, Rage pulling back and stopping their help. But Drake hadn't turned his back on Ramirez, Ben and Hernando Hawthorne. The chief tried contacting Drake several times, and each time Drake ignored the calls.

Phoe's complaint landed two days after Ace's chat, and a fire had been lit under the chief. The man claimed he honestly hadn't had any idea what the two New York detectives had done, and having a lawsuit brought by Rage and Phoenix infuriated the chief. The chief promptly kicked the two detectives out, Ramirez told Drake severe reprimands had been lodged on their file, but the lawsuit hadn't been dropped. Drake had a point to make, and he was making it.

Ramirez stood in the doorway, stared at his feet for a few seconds and then looked up, squaring his shoulders. His face impassive, Ramirez strode towards Drake, whose stomach dropped, and he glanced around checking his brothers. Not everyone was accounted for, and Drake's worry rose and then Ramirez blew Drake's world apart.

"Do you know Silvie Stanton?" Ramirez asked. Drake stiffened. Of course, they knew Silvie Stanton, but Ramirez had to ask. Procedure. Ramirez saw awareness in Drake's eyes and guessed the man he called brother, realised the reason he was there.

"What happened to her?" Drake asked hoarsely. No way, not Silvie, he'd expected Ramirez to say a brother, not Silvie. Drake tensed, and his fists clenched, not their women again.

"Please, Drake, you need to confirm you know Silvie Stanton," Ramirez repeated.

"Yeah, she's part of the old ladies here."

"She have an old man?" Ramirez asked. Again Ramirez knew the answer but fucking procedure. Drake shook his head.

"No."

"Tonight Miss Stanton was run down, there's a few witnesses, she'd been running towards Rage, and was injured. A man was seen walking out of nowhere, catching her and then throwing her under a car. Silvie hit the hood and then rolled back to the ground; the truck then ran her over a second time before pulling off with a biker behind it. Asshole wore a cut, but we've no description of the patch," Ramirez said, giving him it straight.

"Jesus fuck," Drake roared, his mouth tightening. Behind him, Calamity made a wordless noise of pain. Texas rose to his feet and grabbed Axel's arm as the big man rocked backwards, rapidly paling, and his legs weakened. Lindsey screamed as Lowrider made a noise of disbelief, and Phoe collapsed in a chair.

"You're named as her next of kin. Silvie was DOA," Ramirez muttered. A roar came from behind him. Drake caught sight of Apache moving towards him, pushing brothers out of the way. Ace dived on his father and brought him to his knees. Deftly Ace locked his father's arms behind him. Artemis flew across the room to wrap her arms around her father-in-law's neck. Apache kept roaring but stopped moving. Ramirez looked back to Drake.

"No, old man?" he murmured. Ramirez understood what had happened, Silvie giving up on Apache and pulling away. Even though he'd kept his distance since Crow's body had been found, he'd stayed in touch with Drake and Dylan Hawthorne.

"No, the asshole still didn't claim her." Drake suddenly looked tired and worn out. He lifted his hand and rubbed the back of his neck. The fuckin' drama over the last six weeks, Silvie pulling away, Apache's temper becoming uncontrollable, was wearing thin. Old ladies taking sides. Ace's chat with the cops. Drake hoped it'd blow over, not now. Christ, Silvie. Drake's heart broke as pain swept through Rage. Everyone underestimated Silvie's value. Drake wordlessly reached for Phoe.

"I'm so sorry, Drake, we're investigating this as murder," Ramirez whispered. He turned on his heel and walked away. He hated delivering news of a death to a person's family. This one was even worse. Ramirez had known Silvie and respected her. His phone rang as he got to the door and he answered it. Drake saw his body go tight, and Ramirez spun around and looked horrified.

"Get your ass to the hospital. Silvie's alive, they're working on her now," Ramirez snapped out. "Fuckin' hell, Silvie was in the morgue. Get there now!" Ramirez was moving when Apache threw Artemis off, and she fell into Lowrider's arms. Apache snapped his shoulders and dragged his arms forward, and Ace let go. He was moving past Drake before anyone could say a word.

James looked up as Adam strode into his office, his face impassive. Adam hadn't knocked, and James recognised that whatever Adam brought him was going to be a shitstorm. James reached for the whiskey as Adam paced.

"Someone attempted to murder Silvie Stanton tonight. A car hit her and then reversed over her to make sure she died. She's alive barely, she came to in the morgue. Got eyes and ears on the streets," Adam drawled, his mind flicking to when Silvie had been in Washingtons, dancing happily.

"Say that again," James said, shocked. Adam repeated his message.

"And there'd been no chatter on a hit on Rage?" James asked, and Adam shook his head.

"Truthfully, the hit appears opportunistic. Think she overheard or saw something. Rumours are she was fleeing towards Rage," Adam said.

"Get my car," James said, and Adam nodded and placed a file in front of James. James glanced down and saw it was the file on Brady Whittaker. Too late now. If that fuck had something to do with the hit on Silvie, Brady Whittaker was a dead man walking,

James promised.

Yet again, the waiting room in RC Regional Hospital was full of bikers and old ladies. Dana, Hawthorne's office girl, was standing to one side and looking worried. With her were Dylan Hawthorne and several of the Hawthorne women. Marissa was pale, and her friends Lina and Mackenna were crying. Drake hadn't realised that Dana was familiar with Silvie and guessed Silvie had found another wounded chick to take under her wing.

Silently standing, anxiously, in the waiting room was Ramirez, Ben, and Nando Hawthorne. Dylan Hawthorne moved to his men and began giving orders as they left in twos and threes. Hawthorne's women had been out with Silvie and had been questioned. All they could say was one moment, Silvie was dancing and then the next she disappeared. When Silvie came back, she looked shell-shocked and told them she had to leave.

They'd offered to go with her, but Silvie brushed them off cheerfully, they'd thought nothing was wrong. She said she'd received a phone call from Rage, and someone was sending a brother for her. A blatant lie, Silvie had been protecting them from whatever she'd witnessed. The Hawthorne's let her go, trusting in what Silvie told them. The women arrived at the hospital and been questioned before Hawthorne sent most home in tears. When Drake looked up, it looked like the entire Hawthorne agency had arrived, along with several of the man's male cousins. Drake didn't care; he was grateful the man was there.

"Any idea why you're her next of kin?" Mac asked, walking towards him. Drake shook his head, and Phoe shifted uncomfortably. Drake pulled her in close and wrapped his arms around her.

"What do you know, Phoe?" Drake asked her gently. His wife punched him in the shoulder.

"Silvie's been Rage, how long? *And you don't know.* What the fuck, Drake?" Phoe snapped. Phoe had tears in her eyes, and Drake understood she was lashing out because one of her girls was hurt.

"Baby. We don't do that shit," Drake reminded her gently. And they didn't, Rage looked after their old ladies, and they cared a great deal for them. But fuck, they didn't pry into an old lady's life, not unless there was danger threatening them. There'd been no need to investigate Silvie, she'd been with them too long. But Drake hated the sensation in his gut. He knew little about Silvie, and he doubted anyone, but Gunner, did.

"What? Show interest in a woman that's covered for your club and old ladies for twenty years? None of you knows shit about her," Phoe spat. Drake looked lost as Lindsey came over and wrapped her arms around Phoe. Lindsey laid her head on Phoenix's shoulder and whispered something in her ear.

"Silvie's got no one," Phoe whispered, but everyone in the room heard it, felt it. "Silvie had the club and us. She's a wonderful woman but alone in this world. As club president Silvie put you as next of kin, there was no one else who needed to be informed. You'd inform everyone who needed to know." Phoe let out a sob, and Lindsey followed suit. Lowrider strode across the room and dragged his woman into his arms.

"What do you mean, Silvie has no one?" Apache asked from his chair where he hadn't moved.

"Silvie's got no one, fuck me, Apache, didn't you pay Silvie any attention? When did she go home, when did Silvie meet with family? Jeez, are you so fuckin' self-absorbed?" Marsha hissed from Fish's arms. "Silvie named Drake as next of kin because if she died, there'd only be us to care. We're it. All of it. Her family."

"That's enough," Apache bristled, Marsha's words stung. It hurt that Marsha thought poorly of him, as she'd been Rage's single old lady for years. Fish rubbed her protruding stomach, and Marsha sent Apache a glare.

"Silvie's an orphan?" Ace asked, his hand on his father's shoulder. Phoe grew silent, as did Lindsey, Autumn, Penny, Artemis, Sin and Marsha. The women stared at their respective men and zipped it.

"Woman," Drake warned, growling.

"You brothers have your secrets. Us old ladies have ours," Phoe said. "You twats close your circle barking brotherhood at us, well this is sisterhood." Drake dropped his head. He recognised he wouldn't get shit out of Phoe. Not now she'd dug her heels in, Drake sighed.

"Babe?" Ace asked Artemis. Artemis turned on her heel and faced him, hands on hips. Ace took one look at her face and wished he had said nothing.

"As Phoe said, you have your shit, we have our shit. Silvie had no one, and yeah, it sucked that her next of kin would be the president of an MC where she's tolerated. None of you bothered to get to know her, other than trying to her in her pants." Artemis pointed at the brothers, who she noted looked shamefaced. "When you couldn't get in her pants, you ignored her. Silvie wasn't worth dick to you."

"That's bullshit Artemis," Drake snapped, eyeing Gunner as Artemis's words aimed and fired, hitting her targets. Gunner's eyes registered the hurt her words caused.

"Where she live, Drake?" Artemis sneered; she knew Drake didn't know. "Ace? Mac? Lex? Where does Silvie live? Gunner, you're close to her. Where does she live? None of you know. What's Silvie enjoy eating? What's her favourite movie or song? Anyone? Come on, one of you give me a single personal detail about her. No one? What a surprise."

"Artemis," Ace growled, his wife looked at him.

"Ace," Artemis growled back. "None of you learnt your lessons when we said enough bullshit. When we took her back, you thought it'd blow over, that everything will be forgiven. That because you got cocks, and we let you be protective and shit, you'd the right to deride Silvie. If one of us treated a brother the way Apache treated Silvie, you'd have banned her from Rage. You'd have taken up arms to protect your brother, but it's okay for you to treat a woman like that? Fuckin' bullshit. Silvie's been around twenty years, and all you understand is she's kind and gentle and loyal. Because Silvie shows that every single fucking day and you, each of you, take that from her and give her nothing back." Artemis pointed her finger at each of them.

"Silvie takes a month away because she can't cope

anymore. Shut it," she snapped at Ace. "It's time someone brought this bullshit into the open. I love you, Apache; you're my father-in-law, I respect and love you, but you're a dick. Silvie loves you. Truly loves you, she's been in love with you from day one, but you brushed her off as she was nothing. Silvie never once forced that love on you.

You brushed it off as that Silvie had the hots for you. How fucking dumb are you? Silvie wasn't good enough for you, your actions told her you'd fuck anyone but her. Silvie's held that pain inside her for years. Woman takes a fucking vacation to mend her heart and start living, and you sent your dogs after her," Artemis spat, pointing at Drake. Drake didn't say a word.

"You did what?" Phoe asked, horrified.

"Drake sent Hawthorne's to monitor Silvie. Aware you did it because you care, Drake, but Silvie never asked Rage for anything. The one time she did, you couldn't respect her feelings. Silvie pulled away from us, and we realised she was doing it. Silvie didn't choose that by choice, it was the only way she could hope to have a happy life. We were losing her, bit by bit and day by day, and none of you gave a shit." Artemis took a deep breath and carried on.

"I love you, all of you, I'd take a bullet for any of you, any day and time. Yeah, you're good guys. But I'm aware that you're freaking Neanderthals and that the MC is sacred, a brotherhood and women don't get a say. But shame on you, for not seeing that for twenty years, you've been that woman's life and family.

Silvie never mentions a man, never mentions

dating, never mentions anything private. Brady was the first guy you ever saw hanging around, and he's her friend. You're way too happy not to look beneath the surface of a woman because if it does, you may find beauty, a life, a fuck load of magic. The only value a woman that hangs around the club to you guys is pussy. Unless she is an old lady."

"That's enough," Drake ordered. He sounded harsh and meant to be brutal. Fuck Artemis's words stung as they'd more than a grain of truth in them, and he saw his brothers feeling that truth too. Gunner was beyond fury. Autumn eyed him with trepidation.

"Yeah, I'm done," Artemis said and walked towards the door.

"Where you going?" Ace asked, standing.

"Where you think? Hunting," Artemis replied. "I'm more than a pussy for you to dip your cock in when you need a fuck. A sister was lying in the morgue presumed dead. Silvie woke *in a body bag*," Artemis hissed. Ace flinched. Artemis watched him with frigid eyes. "Yeah, I'm going hunting." Akemi materialised from the walls and walked out at her side.

"Fuck," Ace muttered. He met Fish's eyes and acknowledged further blood would be spilt tonight. Last time someone hurt a sister Artemis had taken forty-eight hours to put twenty bodies in the ground and five more days to disappear anyone affiliated with them.

"If I get bodies tonight…" Ramirez warned. The cop sighed and rubbed the back of his neck. "Fuckin' Rage, fucking Artemis."

Phoe pulled away from Drake, and he saw the

reproach in her eyes. Drake guessed Phoe was pissed, but she was biting her tongue. They didn't need trouble between them, not with Harley still in his coma and her pregnancy. Drake rubbed the back of his neck as he considered Artemis's words. Did the women honestly believe Rage thought of them like that? Surely the women understood that to their husbands, they were the most precious thing in the world. Phoe walked to Lindsey and Sin and dragged them towards Dana. Marsha, Penny and Autumn joined them. The women formed their own clutch, and the men clearly weren't welcome.

"Silvie's private," Apache muttered, looking like his daughter-in-law had punched the hell out of him.

"Didn't try, Dad," Ace disagreed. His wife's words had hit hard and deeply hurt him. Artemis was right. None of them knew anything about Silvie, she'd had shitty jobs, and they'd looked out for her. Offering back-up when Silvie needed it, but she'd never asked Rage or the brothers for help. Marsha would tell Fish, and Fish brought the problem to the brothers. Silvie had been so grateful when they gave her the job working for Made by Rage, and none of them had asked why. Artemis was right, they took Silvie for granted.

The new Silvie of the last few weeks rocked them but again, as his wife said, none of them pried. Only Ace knew Drake had confronted Silvie a week ago, but the man hadn't stuck to his guns. Drake let her brush him off and close him out. Ace guessed Drake was hurting the same as the rest of them. Silvie was much like Phoe, but remained in the background, happy to help and not push her own needs on anyone.

They looked up as Doc Paul walked in, and Drake, Lowrider, Ezra, and Jett looked sick, they'd been on the end of this before. Drake walked forward with Ramirez at his side.

"News," Drake snapped out.

"Sick of seeing your women in here, Drake," Doc Paul said sadly.

"You're not alone, bud, in that," Drake replied.

"Silvie flatlined in the ambulance, they tried everything to get her back and failed. They didn't know that the monitoring equipment was faulty. They'd brought her back, but the machine still showed a flat line. Silvie was declared DOA and taken to the morgue after a colleague of mine declared TOD."

"Silvie woke in a body bag, Doc," Drake said harshly.

"Yes and no, Silvie began moving in a body bag, and the assistant noticed and hit the alarm. The assistant unzipped the bag and had it undone when Silvie opened her eyes. Silvie gave her a message and lapsed into a coma. Silvie didn't know she was in a body bag, which is a great kindness. She's critical. No lie, Drake, this is the worse I have seen. Silvie chances are low; I'd offer generously, twenty percent."

"Shit," Drake whispered.

"What was the message?" Ramirez said.

"The assistant said that Silvie said, 'Tell Drake we've a Mexican ghost.' Silvie attempted to elaborate but couldn't. Does it mean anything?" Doc asked before Ramirez could. Drake bent his head and looked at his boots. A Mexican ghost? Could Silvie mean Santos? Had she seen something?

"Nothing," Drake finally said. "Ask the brothers and old ladies." But they'd nothing. No one understood what Silvie meant.

The brothers took familiar turns guarding Silvie. Drake put a full watch on her. What with keeping Harley company and now protecting Silvie, Rage was stretched. They also had their day jobs to do. Apache spent the first three days and nights at the hospital, but Silvie remained in her coma. Apache found it hard to gaze upon her apparent wounds. Her body was covered in bandages and stitches, and two heavy casts.

Finally, Apache left but returned the next night, although he went back to the clubhouse during the day for sleep. Gunner took the days. For three weeks, they kept this up as they waited for the woman who none of them had bothered to get to know, to wake. The old ladies took turns spending time at the hospital during visiting hours and glaring at whoever tried to get them to leave.

Apache felt the division keenly between the old ladies and the brothers. Guilt hit Apache and Drake hard when baleful glares were aimed at them. The women had made their point, and it was a point the brothers were having trouble swallowing. The old ladies were solidly keeping Silvie's secrets to themselves. Apache had empathy for how they must have felt when the brothers did stuff and didn't discuss it.

What made it worse was Artemis was hunting. Artemis had gone home while Ace was at the hospital and packed a bag, and no one had seen her or Akemi since she left. Ace was pissed the fuck off, and his temper wasn't helping anyone. Everyone helped with the twins. Nokomis and Nashoba were being looked after by Ace, the old ladies and everyone else linked to Rage.

Life wasn't good for Rage. Crow's body still hung over them. Despite the fact the New York detectives were sent back in disgrace, the murder was still open. Ramirez point blank refused to take charge when he'd been offered it, as had Ben. Nando copied their actions, and the chief had a mutiny on his hands. The case was quickly passed to the two newest detectives on the squad. Not ideal, but the chief had no choice.

The old ladies continued to spend half their evenings at the Reading Nook, and Drake felt the MC was fracturing. Apache and Ace agreed, and they were trying to heal the wound that kept growing bigger. No way could they allow the old ladies to lead them by the balls, but surely a balance could be found. Drake suffered the slow realisation that the old ladies were the backbone of Rage, not the brothers.

Without the old ladies' support, shit hit the fan. Drake noticed an influx of new women hanging around the clubhouse, tempers were frayed, and fights occurred. For once, it wasn't Apache and Gunner swapping blows, but the others. The inner circle came to the reluctant conclusion that the women soothed most of their tempers, and without that buffer… shit hit the fan. Dragging Hunter and Blaze apart two nights ago caused bloodshed when Hunter promptly belted Fish, who now sported a black eye. They needed the women back to keep a lid on the tempers.

It was a harsh reality that the brothers confided in the women, even if they weren't one of the old ladies' alternatives. Rock had made the point at their last church, and most offered a brisk nod, agreeing. So Drake needed to discover a way to heal their wounds, one way or another. The question was, how?

The first body hit the street two days after Silvie had been hit. No information flowed from the streets. Ramirez, Hawthorne and Rage discovered nothing. A well-known snitch suddenly disappeared and couldn't be found. Drake had been at the hospital when Ramirez called saying that the snitch had turned up dead, one bullet to the brain execution-style. Artemis, Drake guessed correctly. Next to the snitch was a confession that he'd been working for a rival biker gang. What a rival biker gang had to do with Silvie, no one understood. Silvie must witnessed or overheard something that caused her to run.

The next body turned up two days later, another snitch, but again no information. Rage hadn't heard from Artemis for days, and Ace was worried, even though he wore a constant scowl. The word filtered through Ramirez that the witness hadn't been able to pick out a patch, and everything stagnated. Silvie remained unconscious, and her attackers remained free. Artemis remained missing until three more bodies turned up, and she sauntered back into the clubhouse.

"Where the fuck have you been?" Drake spat at the diminutive assassin. Artemis arched an eyebrow.

"Out hunting," she spat back.

"Tell me you found something," Ace said, striding forward and snagging her around the waist.

"Sanctum," Artemis said, nodding towards the room. Drake led the way, and Ace and Artemis followed him.

"I got whispers and nothing else. The whispers are Silvie saw someone she recognised, and that's as far as we got. Someone reported seeing her staring at a man looking like she'd seen a ghost. No idea who. There's nothing but silence on the streets. Adding facts together, a biker was seen, but no club is claiming the attack, there's not even rumours amongst local clubs, who was behind it. The only fuckin' discussions on the streets, is who offed Silvie and Rage have a bounty for information. But none of the clubs I infiltrated has anything to offer.

The other whisper is an MC has jumped into bed with Santos, but again no one knows anything. It's rumours and little else, I had the clubs watched and discovered nothing. The silence on this is deafening, which leads me to believe that maybe the Santos and MC rumour could be true. Only Santos has the power to keep this silent. Washington hasn't heard anything either; he's torn apart the same people as me and found nothing. His contacts have nothing but the same whispers I had.

It's got me thinking that Santos has raised his head, and Silvie either saw something or heard something she knew we required. I can't find anything on a dead Mexican ghost either, so that's baffling. I'm thinking we got trouble heading our way. The silence on the streets is eerie. The fact nothing is doing the rounds, Drake, well, we know what that means," Artemis said, sitting back with a sigh.

Yeah, Drake did, something big was going down, and it involved a rival club. He rubbed his chin and let his mind make connections. Artemis had got nothing more than mere wisps of information.

"Why is Washington taking this to heart?" Drake asked.

"Because he owes Silvie his life," Gunner said, entering. Drake frowned.

"Huh?"

"Silvie overheard the plan to kill Autumn, me, James and Frank. She went to James with the information. James owes her," Gunner explained. Fuck! Drake roared in his head. What else didn't he know about Silvie? Woman had fingers in more pies than he'd been aware of, and she stayed beneath the radar.

"Get Texas to dig into our relationships with other clubs. Any little slight they may think they have against us; I want noted. Check Hellfire's prospects, do a deep dive on them, deep dive on our allies' members and prospects. Could be one of them had ties to ex Rage members," Drake drawled, and Ace sat forward.

"You think Silvie's hit and run has something to do with Crow's body being discovered?" Ace asked.

"Could be; it's one explanation. Silvie might mean a ghost from the past, someone we dealt with but has come back to haunt us," Drake said.

"That's a leap, but I can see where you got it from,"

Artemis said, tapping at her phone. "You get Texas on it; I'll get Nigel to dig. Maybe one of us can find something the other doesn't."

"We need to find out who this biker is, we find him, and we find why Silvie was attacked and left for dead," Ace agreed.

"When we find him…" Drake hissed, and the other two nodded.

"He'll talk before he dies," Ace promised as fury bled into Artemis's eyes.

"I can promise," she spat, "my girl will have revenge."

"I've four bodies, Drake and two missing snitches. Artemis has gone too far." Ramirez snarled.

"Got proof?" Drake asked. Ramirez looked at him, frustrated.

"For fuck's sake, Drake, Artemis told everyone in front of me she was going hunting. We both know what hunting means with her. I got to bring Artemis in for questioning. I stand by you, but can't condone this," Ramirez said tiredly. He'd not be able to protect the woman from her actions this time. If they found a shred of evidence she was involved, she was going down. Drake turned stiff.

"For what?" Artemis asked from the doorway.

"You need to come with me, got questions for you," Ramirez said, turning to face her. He placed his hand on his cuffs as Artemis wrinkled her brow.

"For going hunting? I have a permit," Artemis said innocently, and Drake caught the hint of smug in her voice, and his eyes narrowed.

"You don't have a permit for hunting men, Artemis, and putting bullets in their head."

"No, but I have a permit for hunting deer, and I brought in two bucks, twelve rabbits and other shit. I was at my cabin in Colorado. Check flight times and shit, check the rangers who I spent a couple of cosy nights with over a campfire. I'm sure they can prove I was there.

Also spent time with Akemi and Master Hoshi, making smores and hunting a stag for several days. Again, I'm sure they will be happy to provide an alibi if I need one. And spent time with other hunters, they're people I've hunted with before, so again, I'm sure they'll provide an alibi," Artemis said calmly. Drake just stopped himself from rolling his eyes.

No question, Master Hoshi and Akemi would back Artemis up, but other hunters and rangers? Fuck, Drake realised that she'd pull in Revenge members to alibi her that no one had seen before. Yeah, she'd an alibi, alright, one that couldn't be questioned, but they knew it was fake. Drake wondered what Ramirez would do.

"I give up," Ramirez said. "One day, you'll slip Artemis, and someone who is not me will be there. I'm handing this over to Ben; I'm too close to the MC for this shit. While you may not respect my job, I fucking do," he snarled at her. Well, shit just kept hitting the fan, didn't it? Drake thought ruefully. Artemis wouldn't let Ramirez get away with that though, she tilted her head and wet her lips.

"Ramirez, you're the best cop in RC, you are the most dedicated, loyal, diligent cop I've ever met, and

I've met a load. You can't be turned, bought or threatened. Everyone in Rapid City knows that. You've a brother bond with an MC president, but it doesn't affect your job. Tonio, you're whiter than white. And you got my respect, you want me to come in and talk to Ben, I will. But don't you ever, ever think I disrespect you. As much as I'd lay my life down for the MC, I'd do the same for you, because you, honey, are a good guy. I'll go and meet Ben," Artemis said, placing her hand on his arm. Ramirez glanced at it, and Drake saw the visible struggle.

"Talk to Ben Artemis," Ramirez growled, and she nodded and skipped away. Ramirez rubbed the back of his neck and paced back and forth; Drake let him regain control.

"One day, Drake Artemis is going to slip," Ramirez warned. Drake gave a chin tilt, but that was all the acknowledgement he'd give that the man was right. As much as Artemis had returned to Ace, the girl she once was, died long ago.

Artemis had no qualms about killing if it protected the MC. Something had long ago twisted in her. Although Artemis openly loved Ace and Rage, they accepted she'd a dark, twisted side. And it'd never heal. Artemis would never stop in her pursuit to first protect the old ladies and second the MC. The fact she only went after the guilty gave them some relief. Artemis would never, ever harm an innocent.

Drake bent and laid a kiss on Silvie's head. Her bruises finally healed a week ago, the machines still monitored her and never showed a blip. The stitches had been removed, and the cuts were red against her pale skin. Her arm and leg remained in a cast, and while she looked better, Silvie wasn't better. Drake realised that, like his son, Silvie may never wake up, and he sucked up the pain. Doctors had induced the coma because of the swelling of her brain, and they'd even cracked her skull to let the swelling out.

Drake hadn't even been able to be shocked as he'd been through this with Harley. Her skull was healing up and her brain back to normal, but Silvie remained sleeping. The good news was there was brain activity, but Silvie was taking her sweet time. Drake needed them both to wake up, Silvie to heal the rift, Harley to heal his wife and himself. This should be an era of beauty and peace for Rage. They'd found old ladies, they'd began having legacy children, shit with Santos was under control for now, it should be a time of beauty. What the fuck had gone wrong that this shit kept seeking Rage out and making them pay? Was this karma, with each brother's bounty, came pain and hurt to overcome? Drake prayed not.

Drake sat on the bed and grasped Silvie's hand, giving it a gentle squeeze. He waited minutes for a response, but as usual, nothing. Drake stroked her face and prayed for Silvie to open her eyes and give him that sweet smile. The one Drake now realised held trust and affection for him and his club. Silvie didn't react, and Drake's heart broke a little more.

"Wake up, sweet girl," he whispered. Drake watched for a few minutes and left when Gunner stamped into her room.

Apache rested in a chair, he hadn't been sleeping

well, worried about his family and Rage. He accepted what his own actions had wrought and blamed himself bitterly. He'd allowed the fuckin' past to control his future, and now he and Rage were paying the price. Apache tried speaking to the old ladies, but the freeze-out on him was in full motion. Lindsey glared, and Sin avoided, Penny tried to be balanced, but it was apparent she was firmly with the women. Marsha was too busy with the babes, and Phoe and Artemis were leading by example.

And what an example, both strong-willed and leaders to the boot, the old ladies were punishing him for his arrogance. He longed to tell them the reasons behind his actions but opening those wounds would irrevocably harm Ace. And his son came before his own feelings and needs. If Elu… no, Apache wouldn't consider it. Fuck Elu and fuck everything else, he was bone tired. Wearily closing his eyes for a few seconds, Apache tried to wipe the inner voices from his head.

"Tell Drake we have a mole, tell Drake we have a Mexican ghost," a hoarse unused voice whispered to him. Apache's eyes flew open, and he sat up straight in his chair and looked at the bed. Silvie's eyes were open, and she repeated her whisper. Apache met the bed in one stride and hit the call button. Silvie stared at him, but there was no recognition in her eyes, she repeated her words for a second time.

"It's okay, baby, I got it. I'll tell him." Silvie looked at him, and Apache felt fear hit his gut. Was Silvie even aware he was there? Was she aware of what she was saying?

"Tell Drake we have a mole, tell Drake we have a

Mexican ghost," she whispered over and over. Apache tried soothing her as the nurse came running and followed by the doctor. And even while they examined her and tried to question her, Silvie kept repeating those words.

Finally, the extent of what the club meant to Silvie hit him hard, and Apache puked in a bin. With the back of his hand, he wiped his mouth, aware of Silvie's eyes still on him, focussed on his patch, and she still repeated her words. So desperate to warn the club she loved. Apache tried to soothe her again as Silvie got agitated, it was as if her brain couldn't understand her message was getting through. His heart for the first time in years fuckin' hurt beyond belief, if he'd offered Silvie what she needed and desired, she'd be safe. Not this fuckin' automaton repeating the same words.

Apache stroked the hair away from her face as the doctor gave her a sedative, and she finally slept. Even fading, Silvie kept muttering, her brain stuck on the last words she'd thought before passing out. Silvie remained trying to get her message to Rage. The last name she said before the sedative kicked in was,

"Drake…"

Chapter Four.

    Quietly, I yanked on jeans and did them up, keeping an eye out for someone coming. Outside my room, noise abounded as nurses hurried around and patients groaned in pain. A week had passed since I'd woken properly. Apparently, I'd started coming out of the coma seven days before but took a whole week to wake up properly. Whatever, the fact remained, I'd had enough. Rage was like a rash, an uncomfortable rash, I didn't mind the old ladies, but the brothers? Diligently paying attention for a week? Nuh huh, something was off with the lot of them.
    The weirdness started with Apache refusing to leave my side now I was awake. The blasted man even took showers in my bathroom! Sweetly cooing nurses kept a gleeful eye on the comings and goings. And Apache had been a constant presence for the last five weeks, spending each night in my room. My days

were taken by Gunner, who kept a continuous watch over me. Irately, I fielded questions asking who I was, what made me so special. The answer was no one special. The nurses couldn't understand how I'd an entire MC jumping. Who knew that answer? Damn sure it wasn't me! Drake, too, had been a constant irritant by the nurse's accounts. No question, Rage had lost their tiny minds.

The nurses claimed they'd been told by Doc Paul four days after my admittance, that it was best to let Rage come and go as they pleased. Which, according to nosey nurses, meant there was a constant presence of Rage guarding the door and someone in the room. Apache was the most persistent culprit, but Gunner ran a close second and Drake third.

Life had become a merry-go-round of Rage brothers. No sooner had one left, another popped in less than a minute later. Exasperatingly, they brought books and shit, and I was deadly suspicious of them. The MC did not act like this! The old ladies, yeah, not the MC! Doc Paul was amused whenever he visited, and the nurses were curious, now they were used to the constant presence. To be honest, the brothers were driving me insane.

Whatever I'd been attempting before the incident, my intent to keep Rage at arm's length hadn't worked. The men completely over-ruled any objections raised, and the women were just as obnoxious. Efforts to push them away hadn't worked, and now the old ladies were clinging even more tightly. Apache was one of the worse, and every time he caused a stab of pain in my heart. The distance I'd gained inch by painful inch was gone, and Rage was in my face again. And they were killing me; it hurt to see their caring and understand I'd have to distance myself again.

I'd been told when I first awakened, I'd kept nagging Apache to get Drake and then fallen back to sleep. Anyone would have thought I'd slept enough! When I came to a few hours later, Apache, Drake, Gunner, Ace, and the old ladies were present. At the time, I noticed the four guys looked rough, but Phoe crying and Lindsey grabbing my hand in a death grip distracted me.

Drake asked what I needed to tell him so urgently. What was so important that someone had tried to kill me? Blankly, I stared at Drake and realised there were gaps in my memory. Was there a message I'd been racing to tell Drake? Gunner gently explained my last words before lapsing into a coma, and Apache repeated what I'd said when I first woke. But I was a blank canvas, I remembered running, being in the club, but nothing else. There was an infuriating niggle, but when I tried to recall it, the memory fled. Surprisingly, Drake ordered me to let it go. Shit didn't matter. The only thing that mattered was I was alive and going to be okay.

But I couldn't let it go. I could sense whatever it was at the back of my mind, and it kept teasing and fading away. The sensation made me frustrated and angry. Someone had tried to kill me for something I knew, but I couldn't damn well remember what that was. An underlying feeling bothered the hell out of me, that what I knew was important. Very important, but the more I tried to grasp the elusive thought, the more it ran. Artemis explained the streets were silent.

Even the usual snitches offered nothing.

Ramirez had interviewed me, and while I could remember snatches of being in the club, I couldn't offer any answers. Tonio said I'd left the club and tried hailing a taxi but had started running instead. RCPD found my shoes just off a street and knew the route I'd taken. When Tonio said a biker had been seen throwing me into the street, I was gobsmacked. Why on earth did another MC want to hurt me? Shit just didn't make sense. What had I seen someone do that forced me to run miles to get to Rage? I cried tears of anger while Artemis soothed me, and I curled in a ball, annoyed at my fragility.

Still pushing at my weak memory, I stood on my feet and swayed. Angrily, I stretched out, picked up the top from the bed and slipped it over my head. There was nothing worse than weakness. But I was getting stronger as each day passed. I'd managed to get my bra on, and now I was escaping. Desperately, I wanted to escape the hospital and the way too friendly bikers! I'd been kissed, hand held, hugged, studied, read to more than enough! Rage was out of character, and I didn't enjoy it one bit.

Those thoughts making me growl, I slipped my feet into the new sneakers that Lindsey had brought and eyed the door. Sneakily, I'd grabbed a nurse earlier when Apache went to get coffee and made it very plain, I was discharging myself. Doc Paul had disagreed and threatened to call Drake or Apache, and I told him if he did, I'd cut him out of my life for good. Yup, that was a significant threat as Doc Paul backed down and got the discharge papers. Yeah, I liked Doc Paul, but there were limits to being smothered.

Quietly I wrote my address to send the bill to and ignored the sharp look Doc Paul gave me when he recognised the slum where I lived. Luckily, I'd insurance, but no doubt there'd be a bill somewhere. Firmly asking a nurse to book a taxi to arrive in the next ten minutes, I gathered my belongings together. It was easy to get rid of Apache by telling him I wanted buns and coffee from a coffeehouse fifteen minutes away from the hospital. Apache had grumbled but reluctantly gone. This was my time to escape, and I was making a break for it.

Outside, a nurse waited with a wheelchair, sternly frowning, but I wasn't staying here. In my opinion, I was fine to leave, and no one had ever looked after me. No need for someone to start now. The nurse glared disapprovingly, but I squared up and sat in the wheelchair, and she pushed me to the exit. The taxi sat outside, and I clambered unsteadily out of the chair and into the taxi.

Phoe had brought my purse, and I checked there was enough cash to get home. Unfortunately, twenty bucks wouldn't get me far. Politely, I asked the driver to stop on the way home to get some money from an ATM. Twenty-five minutes later, I was struggling up the two flights of stairs to my shitty apartment. Wearily I opened the door and nearly fell backwards at the musty smell that greeted me. Violently coughing, I choked, kicked the door shut and hurried to get the windows open to let fresh air inside the shithole. I hated this apartment, but it was what I had. For years now, I'd saved hard for a deposit on a house which meant, for now, I stayed in this three-room shithole.

Carly usually bunked here, but Phoe had bullied Carly into living with her and Drake. Phoe had literally stolen Carly away the night I was attacked. Carly was now residing at Reading Hall in a cottage Phoe had provided. Carly said the tiny cottage was way nicer than the apartment. And I couldn't blame the kid. Carly being safe was an enormous weight off my shoulders. Carly shouldn't be going into this shithole alone.

The apartment wasn't fantastic. Not even the furniture was great, bought from thrift stores. Or (my coffee tables and drawers) discovered on the side of the road. Since I was born, I'd never had good stuff and still didn't. Past jobs had barely covered rent, utilities and food, my wages never had much left out of them. Not until I began working for Made by Rage and working for Lindsey.

Now I was earning four times what I had two years ago. Lindsey, Gunner and Manny paid generous wages, and yeah, I worked hard to earn them, but I knew Rage had been looking out for me. That had allowed me to save up nearly twenty thousand dollars, which was a damn fortune. Even the vacation hadn't affected my savings much as I'd still been paid. Roughly, I figured in another year and a half, I'd have saved enough for a deposit on a house and not just the deposit but new furniture as well. Life was to be endured until then. Miserably sighing, I dropped my bag on the bedroom floor and crashed on the sofa, the windows open and air freshener sprayed.

Hungrily, my stomach grumbled, and I grabbed the landline and dialled for takeout and then waited the hour it took to deliver. In the meantime, I dozed lightly on the ratty old sofa with its saggy springs and near flattened stuffing. A knock at the door heralded food, and after paying for it, I kicked shut the door, sliding the deadbolts and the chain into place. Someone somewhere out there was after me, and I wouldn't be an easy target for no one.

Two days later, I was relaxing after ending a call from Lindsey when there was a loud hammering at the front door. Clumsily, I pushed up from my sofa and hobbled to the door and peered through the peephole. Oh, hell no! Apache's extremely pissed off face glared back, and I saw two brothers behind him. Uh oh.
"Go away," I shouted.
"Silvie, open up now!" Apache hollered back.
"Go away!" I yelled back, leaning my head on the door. Jesus, I didn't need this, I needed to rest and regain my strength. My pride was too great, and I didn't want Rage to see the dump I lived in.
"Baby girl, you better not be leaning your head on the door," Apache shouted. Huh, baby girl? I glanced up in surprise, and a thud echoed. Horrified, I gasped, as I realised Apache had put a shoulder to the door. My hands flew and opened the deadbolts as the door shuddered, and one came away completely in my fast-moving hands. Growling curses, I opened the door and glared as Apache prepared to kick the door at the bottom. Slowly Apache lowered his foot and glared.

"What the fuck?" Apache bellowed and carried me inside the apartment. My mouth opened in shock at Apache's highhandedness, and I shut and opened it again like a stunned goldfish!

"What the fuck, what the fuck?" I snapped back. Apache placed me gently on my feet. Glowering, Apache put a hand to my chest and pushed me gently onto the sofa. Apache stared around the shithole and put his fists on his hips.

"Blaze, Rock, get Hunter and Calamity to pack Silvie's shit up," Apache ordered, and my mouth fell open.

"What the fuck!" I yelled.

"You!" Apache said, pointing a finger. I slapped at the finger in anger, and Apache snatched it back. "Maybe this, 'Oh, Apache, I want coffee and those sticky buns from Heaven's Delight'. Oh, I got the fuckin' coffee and sticky buns, and you ran out on me!" To my amazement, Apache looked thoroughly insulted. He was making my head spin. Twenty years of ignoring my existence, and now Apache was in my face constantly!

"Apache, you were smothering me," I hissed, sitting up and crossing my arms. Apache leant forward and got into my face.

"Uh-huh, smothering you? Maybe I should've handcuffed you to the fuckin' bed, woman."

"How dare you!" I shrieked.

"I'll fuckin' dare anything where you're concerned. You got hit, got run down because of Rage! That shit happens, the brothers take your back, you know the score, Silvie! You take Rage's backs, we fuckin' take yours, woman."

"Well, forgive me for getting fed up being smothered. Fuck Apache, I couldn't even pee alone. One of you stood outside while I went!"

"Wanted to make sure you didn't fall," Apache muttered. Out of the corner of my eye, Rock and Blaze swapped grins.

"I was sat on a toilet. How on earth could I fall?" I said mulishly.

"Don't know, don't care," he replied.

"Oh my God, get out," I snapped as Blaze and Rock grinned.

"Yup, we'll get out, pack Silvie's shit," Apache growled.

"I'm not going anywhere; this is my home!" I squealed, thoroughly pissed off now.

"This is a shithole," Apache said, echoing my thoughts, I glared. "Fuck me, you're not staying here."

"Lived here for twenty years. Why on earth does it matter to you now?" I hissed, folding my arms over my boobs. Damn it, why couldn't Apache have acted like this sooner? I'd never seen him so het up over a woman.

"You lived here twenty fuckin' years?" Apache yelled, getting louder. Uh oh, what had got into him?

"What's got into you?" I asked. Rock grinned again as he directed Blaze into my bedroom.

"You! You ran out on me," Apache shouted.

"Well, I apologise, now get out," I snapped, pointing to the door. Apache wasn't paying attention. No, instead, Apache was wandering around picking shit up and putting it back. Apache opened cupboards and saw my two plates, two bowls and two cups and growled at the pathetic sight. Lips set, Apache peered into my pan cupboard and saw my one garage sale frying pan and two garage sale saucepans.

"Make that pack Silvie's clothes, make-up and women's crap and leave the rest of this shit." Apache changed directions and peered into the bathroom. He pulled his phone out and angrily pressed buttons, and put it to his ear.

"Shit's worse than we fuckin' thought," Apache snarled at someone, and I had a sinking feeling it was Drake. "Yeah, brother, not one decent thing in this shithole, it's second hand or garbage, Silvie's been making do for years. Don't know how she and Carly have managed. Yeah, you keep Carly there." I straightened my shoulders; yes, I'd had shit jobs, but I'd never scammed Rage for money. How dare he! I'd always managed on my own, and that was a matter of pride. I was going to kick Apache's bloody ass.

"Yeah, packing Silvie's shit, might wanna get the old ladies over to see what we leave behind and decide what's good, and then I'm taking her… Yeah, get them over. Rock will leave with Hunter and me, Blaze and Calamity will stay and pack Silvie's shit. Got ya, brother," Apache hit end and glared. Arms crossed, and in sheer disbelief, I glared back.

"Packing? Apache, I'm not going anywhere, and my stuff is shit because if anyone has something new here, it gets nicked. Puts a target on your back, ya know?" I stated firmly and calmly. Apache gazed at me, and something crossed his face that I wasn't sure I liked the look of. Seconds later, when Apache opened his mouth, I knew I hadn't appreciated that look.

"Silvie, you're coming home with me. Someone tried to fuckin' kill you. Do you get me? *Someone tried to kill you.*"

"Artemis is dealing with it," I said snottily. Apache's eyes narrowed.

"Twenty years I fucked around woman, guessed how you felt. Been a real asshole. Denied my feelings, couldn't let me feel for you." My body rocked in pain, and I drew in a sharp breath. "Ramirez came in and said you were dead, and my world fuckin' fell to pieces. There was nothing, no colour, no love, no noise. Nothing. The world ended for those few minutes, nothing ahead of me but darkness. Then I find out you're alive. Jesus Christ, baby, you woke in a body bag in the morgue." Apache's face contorted, and pain shot across it; I stepped back.

"That wasn't my fault," I whispered. That didn't bother me as I'd no memory of the body bag, but the fact haunted the old ladies and Rage.

"Yeah, I've got a second chance, but you're in a coma, not waking. I sit there, *fuckin'* pray you come back. You sleep for four weeks, four weeks, and I understand the world ain't ever gonna be the same again, shit's gone. Then you open your eyes, and all you do is tell me over and over to warn Drake we've a ghost and a mole. Silvie, I don't give a fuck about a mole or a ghost at that moment, I want you to see *me*.

And you're so fuckin' loyal, so much love for the club and the brothers, *you can't see me.* All you see is warning Drake. Yeah, I threw you away for twenty years and closed my eyes to you. Ain't closing them again, got a second chance, and I'm taking it." Apache leant into me and looked into my eyes to make sure I understood what he was saying. Nope, I beat my traitorous heart down; I couldn't consider the possibility, I shook my head in numb disbelief.

"No, I don't want you," I whispered, "I won't be your pussy. Fuck, I deserve better than that."

"You think I'm not aware of that, Silvie? *Twenty years!*" Apache seethed. "You've not had another have you?" The truth of the words hit hard, and I rocked back again. My eyes were fixed on Apache's face as it softened, and Apache raised a hand and cupped the back of my neck and dragged me forward.

"Apache," I whispered. No, I couldn't do this, couldn't be Apache's whore, his pussy, he'd break me. I opened my mouth to tell Apache, and he placed a finger over it.

"Givin' you me, baby girl. Silvie, I'm givin' in. You deserve so much fuckin' better, but you want me, and I'm gonna give you everything you want. Wanted you to have perfection, 'cause baby, I ain't perfect. Was hoping you'd get perfection. Instead, you're gettin' me, and I ain't letting you go. You waited nearly twenty years baby, you're never gonna wait for anything again." Tears gathered in my eyes, and I thought I got what Apache was trying to say.

"We're going to be together?" I whispered, swallowing tears. Apache stroked his thumb down my face and nodded.

"Yeah, baby, I'm gonna give you me, all of me. No holding back, no secrets, you ever try to walk, I won't let you go. But I'll break my fuckin' back to make it right for you. Put my ring on your finger 'cause no matter how hard I fought you, you've always been mine and in my heart." This time my sob escaped. Apache dragged me into his arms and wrapped them tight around me. This couldn't be happening! This was always my dream.

"'Bout fuckin' time." I heard Rock mutter.

"Pack Silvie's shit," Apache said, and picked me up and carried me down the stairs. Outside, Drake's truck sat.

"That's Drake's," I said stupidly.

"Yeah, Drake lent it to me so I could get you, back of a bike, not a good idea," Apache said as he placed me gently inside of it. He strode round to the other side, climbed in, and pulled out of the parking lot.

I stared at Apache for the entire twenty minutes as we drove to his home. I expected to be taken to the clubhouse, but no Apache was taking me to his house. In twenty years, I'd never visited his home and was excited at finally getting to see where he lived. Apache drove towards the Black Hills and then out into a wooded area. Despite Apache's declarations, a small part of me kept waiting for him to jump out and laugh. I expected Apache to say everything was a cruel joke, and this was Rage's way of keeping me safe. But on the other hand, Apache and Drake might pull that, but Gunner's temper would tear them apart. That single thought mollified me.

"Phoe and Drake are ten minutes that way," Apache said into the silence, pointing. "Ace and Artemis five minutes that way." He pointed in a different direction. "Lowrider and Lindsey, ten minutes that way and Jett and Sin over there." I twisted my head around to look, and he pulled into a secluded lane that led to an opening and a drive. A beautiful house came into view.

Damn, it was stunning. An A-frame house with a massive, decked space in front of it. Attached behind the house was an extension. It was built with wooden beams that held substantial glass panels that opened every room up to the nature surrounding it. I saw a couple of stone walls, and from where I stood, the glass looked tinted, but I could see the furniture inside, and I nearly leapt from the truck. Apache grunted and grabbed me to stop me from doing that.

"Apache, I want to see," I said excitedly, making Apache smile.

"Let me get you out safe, baby," he said and swung out of the truck. Apache jogged to my side and helped me clamber out carefully. I was nearly hopping from foot to foot in excitement, and Apache laughed, and I stopped and stared at him in amazement. Apache rarely laughed; he chuckled, he grinned and smiled, but laughter from him was rare. He scooped me back up in his arms and carried me up the steps to the decking and then through the double glass doors.

"Oh, my God!" I exclaimed. In front of me was a sunken living space with an immense stone fireplace in the middle. Haphazardly surrounding it were sofas and small occasional tables. To one side was a four-seater dining table and a bar opposite that. More sofas were placed into a semi-circle facing a massive flat screen tv on the other side. Large white fluffy rugs were scattered around, and pictures of bikes hung on the walls.

Behind this, I could see the extension which held a state-of-the-art kitchen. My mouth drooled. I walked down the three steps and wandered through the living area, determined to get to the kitchen that looked brand new. Stainless steel appliances, a vast Aga cooker with eight, yes eight hobs! A full wine fridge and a second fridge of beer, a substantial double fronted fridge, and a separate double-fronted freezer. I guess Apache liked his wine and beer.

At the far end, I spied a door and clumped through it, clapping my hands at the oversized utility room I discovered. It was terrific; I spied another door and discovered a downstairs wet room. Great for dogs! Turning back, I wandered back to the kitchen and began opening doors and peering in the cupboards, looking at the contents. Apache stood with a hip cocked on the island, and I caught sight of a discreet door and wandered through it.

I realised on opening, the door folded back, and the separate dining room, once the door was folded back, became part of the kitchen. I wandered past and found a study, which was a monumental disaster. Tongue in cheek, I frowned at Apache, who clearly disliked paperwork, he grinned, and I wandered to the open stairs.

Apache was behind me in an instant. He held my waist as I wandered upstairs and found a mezzanine level overlooking the living area with a huge leather sofa and bookshelves. A gleaming black glass coffee table stood inches away, and I spied a carved wooden guitar standing near the couch.

"You play?" I whispered. Apache lifted the hair from my neck and dropped a kiss on my neck.

"Yeah, at home, I do," Apache whispered back. I reached out and touched his arm, and wandered to the first closed door. It opened into a peaceful bedroom that was a guest room, the room opposite that was identical. The third door opened into a family bathroom and the fourth into a smaller, tastefully decorated guest room. I finally opened the door at the end and gasped as I walked into Apache's bedroom.

The walls were glass apart from the back wall, which was bare stone. On the wall were two huge prints, one of Ace straddling a bike and looking ten years younger and gazing at Apache standing by his side. Both men sported shit-eating grins, and it made my knee's weak. The second was of a bike's exhaust and the rider's foot and partial leg. It showed the bottom half of a bike, and it was freaking amazing.

The two glass walls overlooked the forest, and the view was beyond stunning. Gleefully, I saw an outside hot tub on a second decked area from the window on my right. The window on my left overlooked a third decking with a big grill. I looked at Apache's bed, and my mouth twitched as I saw it was a king-size bed with black covers.

"Not satin?" I asked, "or silk?"

"No, Silvie," Apache laughed.

"Well, you're a well-known man whore," I quipped as I continued gazing around. I missed seeing Apache's mouth tighten and guilt hit his eyes.

"No woman has ever visited here, you're the first," Apache said. I nodded as my eyes sought details I'd missed and filed away that information for later. There similar white fluffy rugs scattered around and two further doors. One led to a stunning ensuite bathroom, and the second led to a hell of a walk-in wardrobe.

"This is heaven," I gasped, looking around in happy shock.

"Women and closets," Apache grunted.

"Yeah, and you don't even use a tenth of it," I said, gazing around with enormous eyes making Apache chuckle.

"Fill it with your shit," he muttered, prowling towards me and wrapping a muscled arm around my waist. Fuck. Apache up in my space. Happily, I leaned my head back on his chest, testing out new boundaries, and Apache tucked his chin on the top of my head.

"My shit won't even take a tenth of that space," I whispered.

"Baby, get ready to be spoiled. Think I don't see you gazing at shit in the shop? You want it, you get it, and stick it on my tab," Apache whispered his mouth near my ear. I shuddered under the soft sensation.

"Hey, I earn money," I said, my pride stung. Didn't Apache realise I depended on no one to support me? I was unsure whether or not to be insulted.

"Know you do, but as my woman, you get to have what you want, when you want it. Silvie, you don't struggle for shit, you don't go shopping with the old ladies and watch them come back with ten bags to your one tiny bag. Christ, you don't bitch or whine, you just take pleasure in your simple purchase. No more, baby. Not gonna watch you struggle again."

"I'm saving for a house," I whispered, and Apache turned me in his arms and frowned.

"A house?"

"Yeah, my money from Made by Rage, I put into a savings account." I got excited at telling him. "I've twenty thousand saved so I can put a big deposit down and take a whack off a mortgage. Before Made by Rage, I couldn't save lots, but I've been saving hard since working there." Pride shone in Apache's face as he assimilated my words.

"Damn proud of you for working towards your dream. Babe, you had shit jobs and barely broke even but still worked towards your goal. Don't think I didn't notice you going without, and now I understand why. Fuck, I knew you were hard up, but I didn't help you out." Apache's eyes gazed into mine.

"Apache, I don't need a handout," I said mulishly.

"Ain't a handout when we're together. Silvie, you're gonna move in with me, woman," Apache said firmly, using his finger to lift my chin to meet his gaze.

"I am?" I asked. Damn, I was scrabbling for firm ground. I didn't understand what Apache wanted from me. Apache had literally flipped my world on its head today, and while I believed he meant what he said, I wasn't sure if I believed him. Apache had gone from a snail's pace to lightning-fast in the blink of an eye.

"What did you think I meant when I told you I was all in, that I was gonna give you me?" My cheeks blushed red, and shyness rose inside me.

"Thought you meant we were going to go steady or something." Apache laughed again, a soft, amused noise.

"No, I meant baby that you're mine. On the back of my bike, on my arm, in my bed, woman. Silvie, my bed is here, which means you're here. My cock is gonna be inside you, I'm fuckin' claimin' you,"

Apache said firmly, and my cheeks got even redder. "I'm the dumbass who fuckin' ignored you for years. Took your near-death for me to get my head out of my ass. You're mine, Silvie," Apache stressed and dropped his mouth to mine, and his lips grazed mine gently.

Happily, I murmured and leant into the kiss. Apache, the big strong biker I'd always known, surprised me by cupping my face and gently deepening the kiss. I pressed my body against his and touched his erection. Apache moaned as my hand slid to cup him, and he broke the kiss. This felt different from our earlier meetings. This wasn't about sex, and I felt Apache showing genuine emotion. He gathered me to him gently, handling me with care. There was heat between us, but Apache was well aware of how he'd treated me before. Apache was taking care to show this meant more.

"You get me as hard as a rock with a touch, baby. Your body isn't in good condition to take me. Not with what I wanna do to you, I've got fuckin' years of pent-up frustration for you."

"Apache, are you seriously saying that after our other encounters, you're going slow?" I asked in disbelief, scrabbling for my thoughts. Seriously, Apache decides we're getting together and then denies me sex? I wanted to bash his brains in.

"Yeah, gonna do this right, Silvie, fucked you about long enough. Now, I got something to prove. The darkness in me is so fuckin' deep, and you're so light, so bright, I can't risk dimming that light in you." Apache's eyes looked sadly into mine.

"Apache, you're one of the most beautiful men I

know. Inside and out," I said, cupping his face.

"And I hurt you," he gritted out.

"Yeah, you did, nearly destroyed me when you thought you'd fuck me because you thought Gunner had. That broke me, and that's why I left. That night kept eating at me, and maybe you're right, we need to go slow. Apache, the pain you caused can't be swept under the rug no matter how much I want to be with you or love you," I said.

"And I agree, Silvie, I've been a shit, and God knows I wouldn't blame ya for walking away," Apache muttered.

"If we're going to do this, you need to explain why you denied us twenty years, Apache. No more secrets," I said, and Apache blanched. What on earth was he hiding? Whatever it was had kept us apart for too many years. Yeah, no lie, I wanted to be with him, be Apache's life like he was offering, but with his secret between us, I had to wonder if we'd make it. Apache was on board now, but one wrong word and shit could blow up again. I couldn't bear it if Apache offered me everything and then snatched it away again.

"Honey, I won't," Apache said, and I realised he'd been watching my face. I smoothed my worries away and stared.

"This is hard, I want so desperately to grasp what you're offering. At the same time, I'm battling the part of me that is screaming not to trust you. I don't want to feel this, I want to fully trust and rely on you, but I am holding back, and I can sense it," I whispered. Apache moved swiftly and knelt by my feet. He reached up and took my hands.

"Fuck Silvie, I know, know what you're feelin', know I can't undo twenty years of pain in the blink of a fuckin' eye. But I swear, on everything I hold sacred, I'm yours. Gonna prove what you mean to me, what you've always meant to me. Believe me, I'm fuckin' aware of how much pain I caused you because I suffered myself. When Ramirez said you were dead, I couldn't breathe, ain't lyin', I couldn't get air into my lungs. Wanted to crawl in that body bag and die with you. Wanted to offer my worthless life for yours, but God didn't answer," Apache whispered, and pain rolled off him in waves. He meant it, Apache actually meant what he was saying, and the disbelief disappeared slightly.

"I understand, I've experienced that myself, usually when you disappeared with a skank. But Apache, I mean it, no more lies, only the truth between us now," I insisted, and he nodded.

"Silvie, you need to give me time. What I hold deep inside, it's gonna be hard to let out, I've held it for longer than I've known you. To give you this not only affects my life but several others, not sayin' I won't tell you, but I gotta have time, Silvie. Ain't as simple as spilling my guts," Apache said, holding my eyes.

"Okay, but soon Apache, you need to tell me soon."

"I can do that. Just give me time," Apache whispered, his hands cupping my face gently. "Fuck Silvie, you got no idea how much I loved you and still do. Fuckin' killed me to stay away, and then you with Gunner, slew me. But if Gunner made you happy, I could step away, and fuck me, I tried."

"Apache, you were a bastard," I said without rancour.

"Oh yeah, I know, baby, you got no idea how fuckin' hard it was me for, the first time I kissed you..." Apache broke off and offered a smug smile.

"It was heaven," I whispered.

"Yeah."

"Do you blame me for trying with Gunner?" I asked, wondering if he did. Apache had never once said a word, but I'd caught sly glances, and now I had to ask.

"No, I'd never blame you for seeking human comfort and happiness. Fuck knows I never gave ya it. Felt like a kick in the teeth when Brady followed you here. Wanted to rip his fuckin' head off," Apache growled.

"We're friends, that's all. Did you hate me for Gunner and Brady?"

"Never! I was jealous as shit, wanted to be the one holding you, whose lap ya sat on, who you curled in to at night. Instead, I was forced to watch as Gunner did everything I wanted to. Then I was forced to watch as Brady made you light up in happiness." Apache shook his head, pain flashing across his face.

"Gunner didn't do everything," I denied shaking my head.

"Not the stuff that mattered, Gunner held back from that. Deep down, Gunner understood I loved you. But he took a lot of your firsts I wanted to give ya," Apache grumbled, and I smiled.

"But not the ones that mattered," I repeated, and Apache glowered and then grinned, and I blinked as he dazzled me.

"No, your virginity is mine to claim, and I'm havin' it. Everything about you is mine to claim."

"Same goes for you," I chided, and Apache grinned.

"Whatever you want you get, ain't gonna deny you shit. We both waited too long for this," Apache replied. He gave a slight groan as he got up from the floor, sat on the bed and drew me into his lap.

"One thing, children? I want children, Apache," I said honestly. This would be the breaking point for us.

"Had Ace, he wasn't a problem. Ace turned out pretty damn good, I can go for another couple. Bit weird that they'll be younger than their aunts and uncles but fuck it. Told ya Silvie, whatever you want," Apache said after a minute. He shrugged, and I could tell he wasn't bothered by the thoughts of kids running around, causing mayhem.

"Hey, you're just thinking of your legacy!" I accused, and Apache grinned. Bloody minded man. The Rage brothers each had that singlemindedness, get an old lady, and knock her up fast. Since Drake took back his club, there was one ideal they never came away from, family. Each brother seemed to knock his old lady up within a year of meeting her. It was funny watching but a profound yearning, desiring family, guided the brothers.

Few of the brothers had family, certainly not close family, and they'd banded together to create their own. For many of them, the choice of the word brother, wasn't one just linked to an MC. Every member of an MC was a brother or sister. But these men meant the word brother, they may not have blood ties, but the bonds Rage had forged were set in stone. There were no lengths they wouldn't go to for one of their own. That was why Rage didn't recruit prospects straight off the bat, but candidates, Drake and the inner circle had to know if the candidate would fit in with their ideals.

Drake and his father had seen a club where like-minded men were brought together to form the club's basis. They wanted families to develop, the brothers to grow and nurture them, and finally have sons to run the club. Rage was meant to be handed from father to son. Instead, Arrow had died, and Bulldog had gained Rage, and everything precious went to shit. Now Drake was working his ass off to make Rage the ideal his father had dreamed of seeing.

"Yeah, I want a legacy; I was the only second-gen to have provided a son, I want more, although they won't be third gen like Ace," Apache teased. I rolled my eyes. Rage grouped gen's together, meaning generation. Axel was first gen, he was a founder of Rage, second generation was the next group of brothers to be recruited, only Texas and Apache remained. Third-gen was everyone in the club left apart from Blaze, Hunter, Jett, Slate and Calamity, who were fourth-gen.

"Well, we might have girls," I teased, and Apache's eyes softened.

"Yeah, I'd be happy with princesses," he mumbled. My ovaries clenched in anticipation. Down, I whispered to them.

"Are we going to fast?" I asked. This felt too fast, far too fast.

"Who the fuck cares, Silvie, we've loved each other for too fuckin' long to mess around now. We know each other well, although you manage to surprise me, we ain't just met, girl. I want everything with ya

Silvie, please try to trust me and look to our future."

"Apache, I'll be more relaxed when I understand what the deep, dark secret is," I replied.

"Yeah, you will, give my word. Just need to get the shit straight in my head before dumping it on you," Apache drawled. His cavalier attitude didn't fool me. Apache was deeply hurt by something, I'd always suspected so, but now I knew. He most definitely was, and I'd be there by his side and wouldn't judge. Apache needed love, not condemnation, and I had a gut feeling that what he'd tell me would change my life forever. And not in a good way.

Chapter Five.

Apache led me to the ground floor, where I perched on a kitchen stool as he prepared food. It was too late for lunch but too early for dinner, so Apache was making omelettes. Apache briskly chopped peppers and mushrooms before chucking them into a frying pan. Idly, Apache chatted about inane things I'd missed during my time away from Rage and what had happened while I was in a coma. I realised Apache was nervous and found this endearing. Apache was never one for idle chat, so this humoured me, Apache was making an effort, but I wondered how long that would last.

"Apache," I finally said when he broke for breath, "this is me. Stop with the nervous shit. What do you think I'm going to do?"

"Run," Apache muttered honestly. Quickly, I rose from the chair and walked around to him and wrapped my arms around his waist. Happily, I leant my head on Apache's chest and sighed.

"Honey, we're making a go of this, remember, no running for either of us."

"Can't stop worrying, Silvie, you ran on vacation, ran when you got back home. Honey, you've been running ever since I fucked up in my room," Apache murmured, dropping his chin to rest on my head.

"And now I'm here in your home," I said.

"No, our home," Apache snarled. That punched straight in my heart, I nodded against his chest, and Apache clasped me tightly and let go.

"Our home," I agreed. Apache relaxed and turned to the stove.

"If ya wanna change the décor, go ahead. Drake and Lowrider keep bleating on about cushions and knick-knacks," Apache offered, disgruntled. I giggled.

"Throw cushions and knick-knacks?" I asked, knowing full well what Apache meant.

"Drake says Phoe can't go to a shop without returning with something. Lowrider bitches Lindsey's the same and the other old ladies. Fish don't know what to do with Marsha. He thinks she's nesting," Apache said, sending me a baffled glance. Oh, this was too funny, I began laughing. The brothers wouldn't understand what it took to make a home. Even though Apache's house was gorgeous, it lacked the softer woman's touch.

"Anything?" I asked, and Apache offered a concerned look.

"Within reason. Anythin' with a plug I buy, anythin' else is yours," Apache said. Ah, the old, if it has a plug, men knew best idea!

"Okay, so pick me up a new blender, I don't see one here and a new air fryer? I hear they're healthier," I said mischievously. Apache looked horrified.

"Huh?" he asked.

"Honey, you said anything with a plug you have to buy, and I need a new hairdryer and curling iron," I grinned as Apache twisted to face me.

"Anythin' big with a plug I buy, little shit you get," Apache amended with a light in his eyes. Yeah, he knew what I'd been doing.

"Okay. Can we just get one thing straight? I'm moving in here?" I asked, needing to hear but not for the reasons Apache might have guessed. Damn, Apache's scowl descended rapidly.

"Nope, you ain't moving in, you've moved in, as of now," Apache said, pointing the spatula at me.

"Okay, then I need to know what is outstanding on your mortgage," I said, and Apache scowled once again.

"Why?"

"Well, if I'm living here with you, then I pay my way. Apache, I don't freeload, I've never freeloaded. And I don't plan to start now," I said as Apache served up an omelette and put it in front of me.

"Fuck off," Apache said, and I gasped.

"Seriously?"

"Baby, you ain't paying the mortgage."

"Apache, I don't freeload, you need to let me pay half," I insisted.

"Nope, I don't, I own this outright, no mortgage and even if there was, you wouldn't contribute," Apache said, putting his own omelette on a plate and sitting opposite me.

"You own this," I gasped, "outright?"

"Yup, paid the mortgage off years ago, my cut from Rage and my business makes good money," Apache grinned and shovelled a mouthful of omelette in his mouth. Wow, I knew Apache owned the construction company BlackRock with Rock, and I knew they'd many men working for them, but I didn't think the company was that big.

"Good money?" I asked cautiously, I didn't want Apache thinking I wanted him for his fortune.

"Yup, we got over two hundred men working for us now, we don't just build in South Dakota, we've got teams in the surrounding states too. We're looking to recruit five further teams too, what with the new plans," Apache said.

"New plans?" I asked. To be honest, I never paid much attention to what Apache had done outside of Rage, and now I was seeing a whole different side of him.

"Rock and I want to take the company in a different direction. We've been mixing housing between apartment blocks and offices, want to become more greenhouse friendly. Rock and I have bought the old warehouse district downtown, the derelict one. Got plans in place to build affordable, clean housing there and turn the district around. We've a shopping strip planned for the new estate and planning two thousand homes with front and rear yards."

"Holy shit," I gasped. The old warehouse district was huge and had been abandoned years ago when cheaper and more accessible warehouses were built. The whole locality had been an eyesore for Rapid City for years. Imagining the vastness of the region, I could see how it could hold two thousand homes.

"Yeah, it's what we're going to move into, re-claiming and re-using abandoned land. Affordable green living is expensive, so we're making housing cheap while maintaining quality. There're loads of people who can't afford to buy houses because the prices are far too high. Lots need a hand on the property ladder, and I don't believe in destroying the countryside to build more homes. We pitched the plans to the council, and they loved the idea, so Rock and I bought the land, and we've an architect drawing up the plans.

We'll build in phases, two hundred houses at a time. The land has been tested and is clean. A few patches needed treating, but that's done, and now we're going ahead with plans. Once the two hundred are built, we'll be building the next tract of houses while we sell the built ones. We're gonna see how well it does here, but we've got land in mind for North Dakota, Wyoming, Montana and Nebraska. Which is why we'll need more teams of builders, etcetera," Apache said and drew in a deep breath.

"This means a great deal to you," I said.

"Fuck yes, Silvie, my heritage is to protect the land. Everyone building in a free for all makes me ill. If I can respect the land and build on reclaimed and abandoned land left to rot, then I'll honour my heritage," Apache murmured and ducked his head. Aw, he was embarrassed.

"It's a wonderful idea, how wonderful Rock agrees with you," I said. Apache nodded.

"We've been considering this for a few years, and this year bit the bullet. Each house will have solar panels, there'll be a generator that stores excess power as well. We're also fitting small windmills to the houses; they won't be an eyesore but will fit in with the designs. Rock discovered a company that is producing small, powerful windmills that fix to chimneys and create electricity when the wind's blowing.

We're using reclaimed bricks as much as possible and recycled wood as much as possible. Each house will be insulated and made economically workable. We're offering two schemes, for those who can't get a mortgage, they can either do one of two things. The first is we lease them the house. Say the house costs, one hundred thou, then each month they'll pay rent and once they've reached the one hundred thou, they'll own the house. Second is a lifetime rental agreement. They'll pay rent each month, but a contract is drawn up, they can live there for life alongside usual caveats. Obviously, the third option is they get a mortgage from the bank," Apache said.

"Oh?" I asked, honestly interested. This was a part of Apache I'd never seen.

"Yeah, no damage to property, or they gotta pay for repairs. If they fall behind in rent and don't make arrangements, they can be evicted. No consistent wild behaviour or partying, those types of things."

"Is any of that legally binding?" I asked. What a fantastic idea and definitely something I'd have been interested in.

"Yes, a contract is drawn up between both parties. The only difference is, if they decide to live elsewhere, then they don't get to sell the house unless they own it. Of course, if they move to a bigger house on the estate, then we'll renegotiate. But yes, it's legally binding on both sides, but we'll have caveats drawn up to protect the company. But really, we're pushing for people to buy the house from a mortgage point of view. Makes it easier."

"That scheme would have been something I'd have been interested in, it sounds fantastic. I couldn't get a mortgage because I was on low pay, which is why I was saving up so hard," I mused.

"You said you suffered that shithole to buy a house?" Apache asked, and I nodded.

"Yeah, but finally working for Lindsey and the boys made life much easier. I get a great bonus, and the wages are generous. What I've saved since then is more than I ever saved beforehand. But if a scheme like that had existed, I'd have moved years ago. And I'd have even been able to pay more off the rent because I was paying rent on that shithole and trying to put money away for a home."

"That's the buyers we hope to attract, people who do an honest day's work. But can't get out of the rut they're stuck in because of something blacklisting them. We want to give them hope and a chance," Apache said.

"Honey, I admire that, fancy, I never knew this about you or Rock."

"Well, we don't talk business at the clubhouse unless we need to. The clubhouse is our break from work. Rock and I still pull shifts at the bar and shop and still patrol once a week. Got staff in the office, Rock and I spend little time there, prefer to be out on site. Both of us spend one day a week in the office for meetings unless we're needed for something else," Apache said, rubbing his hand over his chin. Yeah, I bet they both avoided the office. Neither man liked to be caged into suits or offices.

"But you both own the company?" I asked, wondering if they had a board of directors or something.

"Yeah, no board or anything like that, we run it, but we've great department managers. BlackRock is a private company, not public, and we prefer that. We've been approached about going public but decided against it. It's Rock and I who put the hours in. Why should a board of directors or shareholders reap our benefits?" I could see Apache's point. Rock and Apache worked hard, so they should be able to keep the money they earned. Damn, I didn't realise how big their company was; I was taken aback.

"Will Ace inherit?" I asked, and Apache shrugged.

"Ace ain't interested, but maybe one of our kids or one of my grandkids will want it. But I think Falcon will go the Rage route. Whatever, I'll make sure everyone's treated fairly, but I hope one of my blood will want the company," Apache said with a wistfulness in his eyes. The company meant a lot, I could tell, and I hoped one of Apache's bloodline would take the reins one day.

"Maybe share your half amongst them and make them the shareholders?" I suggested.

"Not a bad idea. Anyway, enough concerning work, what I was tellin' ya was to make this your home. Silvie, you wanna buy shit go ahead but don't make this a woman's den. Remember, a man lives here too! Jett's told me about Sin, cushions for Christmas, Easter, Fourth of July and every other fuckin' holiday going," Apache grumbled, and I laughed. That was definitely true. Several of the old ladies went crazy during holiday times. Changed décor for the holidays, I wasn't one, but then I'd never had the money to do so. But I was intrigued by the idea, and Apache groaned when he saw the expression in my eyes.

"Everything will be fine," I said, patting his arm.

"Sure," Apache muttered, and I choked back a laugh. As Apache grumpily began loading the dishwasher, I thought about what he'd admitted upstairs. The secret that had kept us apart for so many years could harm another person. There was only one person that could be, Ace. While Apache was protective of his brothers, Ace was his son, and Apache loved Ace very much. I began wondering what the secret could be and considered many scenarios. Without Apache's input, it could be any of them, so I shoved the mess to one side. There was no point worrying about the problem, I couldn't help until I knew what it was.

"Honey, have you had any flashbacks?" Apache asked as he took my hand and led me to his sofa. He sank into it and drew me into his lap. I swung my legs up and over and nestled into his embrace.

"None, still no idea what I was rambling about. Mexican surely means something to do with Santos, but I've got no idea. Shit's a total blank," I replied, and my mind went to that problem.

"Don't push," Apache insisted, and I nodded my head. Again, leaving that alone would mean the memories should return sooner rather than later.

"Who's doing my job while I've been in hospital?" I asked. Apache grimaced, and my eyes widened.

"Oh, no! Not her! She messed my mojo up real bad last time," I whined, and Apache chuckled.

"Lindsey said you wouldn't like it."

"Like it? I hate it, she moved everything around, and it took a week to straighten it out. Now she's back in my domain. Apache, I need to go to work tomorrow,"

I insisted, and Apache's face took on that stubborn expression I was so familiar with.

"Not until next Monday, Doc Paul said you can go back then and on light duties," Apache said firmly. One of his hands rose and twisted in my hair before making soothing motions.

"But she'll wreck everything!" I nearly shrieked. My desk and office were laid out the way I liked them, and last time that rotten temp had literally moved everything. Talk about a lack of respect for someone's personal space!

"Baby, no. Monday, you can sort that shit out. For the rest of this week, you can relax," Apache said.

"Fine, I'll shop and buy lots of girlie shit," I hissed, and Apache dropped a kiss on my head. He shifted and lifted his hips and yanked out his wallet. Apache withdrew a card from it and passed it to me.

"Put any shit you wanna buy on that," he murmured. Hold on, I thought we'd agreed already, I bought girlie shit, and Apache bought electrical shit.

"Apache, I can pay," I muttered.

"Yeah, you can, but I wanna spoil the fuck out of ya, and you're gonna let me this one time," Apache rumbled. Not bothering to argue, I leant my head against his chest and felt his heart steadily beating.

"Just this once," I agreed. Apache grunted, and I knew that wasn't the end of it. My eyes fluttered closed, and I fell into a restful sleep. No nightmares would dare disturb me in Apache's arms.

Abruptly, I woke up in Apache's arms in his bed. I'd been so tired I'd not even felt Apache move me during the night. When I glanced at the clock, I was shocked to see it was six in the morning, I'd slept well over twelve hours. Ever since I woke in hospital, I'd not slept so well, just catnapping, and I hadn't realised how tired I'd been. Apache lay next to me, his beautiful face relaxed as he slept.

His worry lines and stress had disappeared, and Apache looked far younger. My dream had been for so many years to wake in Apache's arms and be part of his life. But a tiny part of me kept waiting for the hammer to fall, it had with the other old ladies, why should I be any different? I scampered to the bathroom and took care of my needs, and brushed my teeth before returning to the bed where Apache still slumbered.

Apache lay flat on his back, and as I peeked beneath the sheets, I realised he only wore a pair of cut-off shorts. Greedily, I studied the physique of the god before me, and desire pooled between my legs. My eyes ran happily over Apache's body, his chest was broad, and his abs had a defined eight pack. Apache clearly took care of himself; his legs were thickly corded with muscles, his hips lean and narrow. I gently ran a hand over Apache's chest, and his nipples peeked at my touch. Happily, I ran my hand further down, tracing those lickable abs and stopped short of his shorts.

A prickle ran down my spine, and I glanced up and caught green eyes lazily watching me. Apache said nothing, I paused a moment giving him the chance to stop me, and when he didn't, I kept exploring the body of the man I loved. I slid down his body and kissed my way to the tent in his pants. If anything, Apache grew harder as I neared his cock. My hair dragged over Apache's chest as I moved back up and claimed his mouth. Apache sank deep into the kiss, a hand holding me in place as I clumsily straddled his narrow hips. Freaking cast!

Apache tasted hot, amazing and of mint. Awareness hit that he'd been awake longer than me and had brushed his teeth. Apache smelt of musk, and my nipples hardened in reaction to his scent. He always smelled amazing. I moved slowly, trailing kisses and licking his abs as I moved downwards towards his cock, pressing deep into me. Without a word, I sank my fingers into Apache's shorts and dragged them down as his cock sprang free.

Damn, my eyes widened at how huge Apache was, and I had a moment's self-doubt. How on earth could I take that into my mouth, let alone myself. Apache's hand cupped my head, and I moved boldly to his cock. I grasped Apache at the base, and he hissed. I'd fooled around with Gunner, but this was different, this was Apache, and I was unsure of myself. My eyelids fluttering shut, I bent my head and took Apache's cock in my mouth. He was too big to take fully, but I could play with what I could. Slowly, I licked him up and down his shaft and sucked on his head.

Apache's hips thrust upwards, and I revelled in the knowledge he liked this, enjoyed what I was doing. Keeping the pace slow, I repeated my actions and kept a tight grip on his base. With me controlling his cock, I continued to lick and suck, teasing Apache as he thrust several more times. I kept up a gentle pressure as I took him in my mouth and swirled my tongue around his head. Apache stretched my mouth to filling point, and I made sure to sheave my teeth, instead, I lightly grazed them over his cock, and Apache sat bolt upright.

"Fuck me!" Apache grated, and I grinned as his cock popped free from my mouth.

"That's what I'm trying to do," I replied cheekily and bent my head to retake him in my mouth. Apache let me. I upped the pace this time, and Apache collapsed back on the bed. His hands sank into my hair on either side of my head, and Apache held me in place as my head bobbed up and down. His cock hardened even further as my hand moved with my head, and his balls tightened. I licked pre-cum and encouraged Apache to spill, I discovered he liked my tonguing the slit in his head. Happily, I teased Apache to the point of no return.

"Fuck!" Apache roared as he came. Gulping, I swallowed, unsure of the taste, it was the first time anyone had spilt into my mouth, and I could understand the gag or swallow reflex. I swallowed and cupped his balls, and Apache thrust hard into my mouth and finally emptied himself entirely. Wow. Smugly, I raised my head and licked my lips and froze at the look on Apache's face. Without a word, Apache hauled me up his body and flipped me onto my back. Hands ripped my tee off, and Apache's head dipped low, claiming my mouth in a kiss as his hands released my breasts from my bra. The bra forced them upwards, and Apache growled deep in his throat as he cupped them and rubbed my nipples. My good leg wrapped around his as he fondled and teased.

With effort, Apache tore his mouth from kissing me and sank his head towards my breasts. A hot, wet mouth descended on one and my back arched in a silent plea. I whimpered as Apache sucked, and I cried out.

"Harder," I gasped, and Apache briefly broke contact.

"Sure?" Apache asked, and I nodded. With a wicked glint, Apache bent his head again and sucked harder, to the point of pain. Wetness pooled between my legs, and my hips moved in a silent plea. Apache's hand pinched and tweaked my other nipple, and he swapped his mouth and fingers and lavished attention on the other. His cock poked against my panties, and I moaned as his hand left my breast and slipped below to rub my clit.

"Apache," I cried, and he lifted himself up and tore my panties off. Apache's eyes feasted on me, bare before him.

"Baby, you shave," Apache muttered, his eyes lit with pleasure.

"I was told it made sex more pleasurable," I whispered, embarrassed.

"That baby, you're gonna find out," Apache muttered, and without warning, his tongue sank into my folds. I screamed in pleasure as Apache found my nub, and his tongue lapped at me. My hips thrust to meet him as he sucked on my nub, and pleasure exploded. I became mindless, lost to the pleasure Apache's mouth offered, and his finger slipped inside me. Again, my legs tightened around Apache as I met each thrust of his finger while his tongue aroused passion I'd never felt before.

With a cry, I exploded in Apache's mouth, and he withdrew his finger and licked my wetness away. His finger continued playing with my sensitive nub, and I screamed as my orgasm peaked and crested. Dazed, I collapsed, limbless back on the bed as Apache took care of me and then shifted between my legs. Apache's cock was rock hard again and poked at my entrance.

"Silvie, tell me no," Apache whispered, and I shook my head. No fucking way was I saying no. Apache grunted and held my hips as he slid inside me. He hit my virginity and paused.

"You're so fuckin' wet, so tight and hot. Fuck Silvie, this will hurt," Apache grunted and then thrust through my barrier. I squealed, and Apache held himself still, allowing me to get used to his size.

"You on something?" Apache grunted.

"What?" I whispered, revelling in the feeling of his cock inside me.

"Birth control."

"No, we want kids," I gasped, and Apache's eyes lit.

"Bareback?" Apache asked.

"Stop talking and fuck," I said with a lift of my hips. Apache's mouth claimed mine, and he thrust fully into me and waited. Apache was so hard and big, velvet over steel, I stretched to accommodate him, and I made a tentative move again. Slowly Apache responded, his mouth taking mine, teeth nibbling, finding the sensitive place at the hollow of my throat. I cried aloud as Apache moved slightly faster, each stroke arousing and teasing as he took his time. I wanted more, harder, faster, but couldn't articulate the words. Apache reading my face gave me what I sought and took me harder. Each push inside filled me fully, each withdrawal left me sobbing for more.

The pace fastened, and Apache held me tightly as he fucked me harder and harder. My body knew how to react to his demands, his motions, and I met each thrust with my own. Wetness drenched me as I grabbed Apache's head and kissed him, and Apache cried into my mouth, and he spilt his seed. But he wasn't finished, I needed to orgasm, and Apache kept thrusting hard against me, rubbing against my nub until I screamed into his mouth. With one last thrust, Apache collapsed on top of me and then rolled to the side. He remained inside me as he twisted my body snug against his.

"Oh my God," I whispered, my head tucked into Apache's shoulder.

"Yeah," Apache mumbled. My right leg slid over his as I pushed my pelvis closer to his. I didn't want to lose the intimacy between us, and I loved feeling his cock, softening now, inside me. With a rueful grunt, Apache pulled away and walked to the bathroom, where he came out with a damp cloth. Carefully Apache wiped me clean and dumped the cloth on the floor before climbing back in and pulling me close.

"In the heat, you agreed to bareback. If you got second thoughts, can take you to a pharmacy," Apache said softly. I shook my head against his chest.

"No, what will be, will be, fate can run free," I muttered. My hands rested on Apache's chest as he wrapped me in his arms. My leg hitched over his again, and I felt a small poke from his cock.

"Again?" I asked. Apache chuckled ruefully.

"Take a few minutes, baby, ain't as young as I was, but I get to feast," Apache said. And feast he did.

We spent the rest of the day in bed, learning each other's bodies, what made the other tick, and Apache explored the sensation of pain with me. I hated BDSM, but I didn't mind spanking, my nipples being pinched hard, light sensual slaps on my pussy.

Apache liked my teeth lightly grazing his cock, loved my tongue on his slit, his balls being squeezed.

Later that day, Apache ran a hot bath with lavender, one of my favourite scents, and told me to take it easy. We'd made love vigorously, only stopping for food, which we ate and returned to the bed. The bath relaxed my sore and unused muscles, and Apache got in with me, sliding behind as he washed my hair and body. I lay back, relaxed, happy, and content as Apache worshipped me silently. We'd not spoken more of children, but if he hadn't got me pregnant, it wasn't for the lack of trying!

James glanced up as Adam knocked on the office door. Adam walked in as James called enter and appeared perplexed.

"What's wrong?"

"Brady Whittaker is here," Adam said, and one of James's eyebrows quirked.

"Unexpected," James commented and relaxed back in his chair.

"What do you want me to do, boss?" Adam asked. James considered the situation for a few moments and decided.

"Show Whittaker in," James said. Adam disappeared and returned with a suit. James studied him for a few seconds as Brady returned the favour. And then Brady, entirely at ease, walked over to James's sideboard and poured two measures of whiskey. James watched bemused as Brady placed one in front of him and sat in a chair, and took a swallow.

"Excellent stuff," Brady said, and James nodded.

"Indeed," James replied and waited. His tactics at silent intimidation backfired as Brady continued to study him, and James dug his heels in.

"If we're both finished measuring our dicks," Brady said finally. James considered their standoff a draw. Brady's tone made it clear he hadn't backed down.

"What can I do for you?" James asked, taking a swallow of his whiskey.

"Why did you run a background check on me?" Brady said bluntly, and James nearly choked. James's admiration grew for the man opposite.

"Silvie Stanton is under my protection," James replied. Brady's eyes narrowed.

"Fucked that up, didn't you?" Brady said, and James stiffened.

"None of us had any idea there was a hit on Silvie. There's nothing, no chatter, no rumours, just empty silence," James replied.

"So again, why the check on me?"

"Because you, friend, were new in Silvie's life. And you stepped into my club with a woman I care a great deal for," James replied, and his eyes searched Brady's.

"I've only known her a couple of months, but there's no way I'd harm her. Silvie helped me through a nasty period of my life, and she's a wonderful woman," Brady said.

"You're legit; I found nothing on you except your bad spell. No man deserves shit like that," James said, alluding to Brady's relationship failure.

"Well, in the spirit of goodwill, I ran my own check on you," Brady said, and James's eyes narrowed.

"And?"

"Well, you're only just legit yourself, and I mean that as in legally. You're trying to go straight, and the fact you cared enough about Silvie to run a check on me means you're a good man. But I wanted to see that for myself."

"And now?" James asked.

"Now I'm here to offer you an investment, one that will keep you legit." James's interest peeked. Brady ran a well-known business, and James was interested in what the man could offer.

"Why?" James drawled.

"I'm looking to branch out but want a partner. And Silvie trusts you, thinks a lot of you, so yeah, if you're serious about staying straight, we can talk. If this is a blip and you're going back to your old ways, I'll thank you for the whiskey and leave," Brady said calmly. James felt an instant reaction to Brady's words. James wanted legitimacy. Desperately wanted to be a good man, someone Gunner and Autumn could be proud to call family.

"Hit me," James said. Brady swallowed the last of the whiskey and sat forward. Quietly Brady began to explain his plan to branch out.

Chapter Six.

"Wake up, honey," Apache murmured, and I moaned and rolled away from him. I was bone tired and wanted to sleep. Apache's hand trailed down my naked back, and I shivered under his light touch. "Sweetheart."

"No!" I said firmly and rolled back into his body. My leg hitched around his, and my arm snuck around his waist. Apache chuckled as I buried my head in his shoulder. Wait a minute… that was denim under my leg and cotton on my cheek. Blearily opening my eyes, I saw Apache dressed and grinning at me.

"No, come back to bed," I muttered, sure it was the early hours of the morning.

"Honey, it's eleven o'clock," Apache grinned.

"Get the fuck out!" I exclaimed and sat up in bed. The sheets pooled around my waist as I stared at the sun high in the sky and then at the clock on Apache's bedside table. "Crap," I yelled, struggling to get out of bed. Apache's hand firmly pushed me back onto the mattress, and he sat up and held a cup of coffee out. Without a word, I snatched it from his hand and took a sip. Perfect, just the way I liked it. Apache's eyes dropped to my breasts, and when he raised them again, heat turned them liquid green.

"Like what you see?" I said, sipping the coffee again.

"Silvie, you know I do, but you're gonna be sore, we were… energetic yesterday, and me being inside you again ain't what ya need right now. Instead, we are going for a ride," Apache grumbled, his eyes dropping to my breasts again. I sharply drew my head back in. That one sentence staggered me. No one rode behind a Rage brother unless it was their old lady. Only once had I in an emergency, and that had been behind Apache. That one thing showed his intentions more than a diamond ring on my finger. Apache was *claiming* me. Now he was telling me he was taking me out on his bike, where words had failed to convince me, actions fully did.

"Your bike?" I asked, and Apache grinned.

"Take you in my truck, and you'd kick my shins in spitfire, yeah my bike," Apache said. I was passing him the coffee and on my way to the bathroom before he could blink. Apache chuckled as I turned the shower on and dived into the warm water. The door opened, and Apache wandered in naked. A grin lit his face as my eyes dropped to his cock, hanging heavily between his legs.

"Not today, baby," he muttered but stepped into the shower. Strong hands caught my mass of hair, and to my surprise, Apache began shampooing and conditioning my hair. Slowly and sensually, he rinsed my hair and then washed my body, trailing kisses where the sponge touched my skin.

Frustrated, I was halfway to telling Apache to screw the soreness when his finger slid between my folds. I leant back against his chest as his finger moved lazily, his other hand came up to cup my breast, and Apache dived between my folds and found my clit. I cried out, sensitive to his touch as he began rubbing and pinching. His mouth hit the hollow of my throat, and my hands splayed on the tiles, supporting my weight. His finger touched my entrance and hesitated and pulled back to my nub. Little shivers of pleasure ran through me as he focused on my arousal. He teased me until my orgasm built up, and I orgasmed with a cry of relief.

"Wow," I muttered as he held my weight.

"Yeah," he replied, sounding pleased with himself.

"I thought you said we couldn't have sex," I whispered as I came back to reality.

"You can't Silvie, you're far too sore, and don't even deny it, woman. But I can give you pleasure," he said and turned me to face him, kissing me hard.

"You didn't…" I motioned to his hard cock.

"Nope, I can wait," he growled, and I wondered whether to give him oral relief. I didn't get the chance as he turned me again and washed me from head to toe, and then wrapped me in a fluffy towel.

"I wanted to take care of you," I muttered mulishly. Apache grinned, and I blinked, dazzled by the happiness in his smile.

"Silvie, you don't think I don't know that? You've looked after me for years, even when I ain't acknowledged it. Now it's my turn to spoil and watch over you. Let me do that," Apache said and touched the tip of his finger to my nose.

"Not saying no to that!" I grinned. Happiness swept through me as I dressed. By the time I was done, Apache was dressed and leaning against the wall. It was one of the sexiest poses I'd ever seen him take. Long legs and lean hipped, Apache rested a muscled shoulder against the wall with his arms folded across his chest. His hair was scraped back into a man bun. It was rare Apache let it loose and never when he rode.

"I want to make love to you with your hair free," I said, and Apache's eyes blazed.

"Can do that," he muttered, "come on, woman, that bike is calling us." Apache swung an arm around my shoulder and led me from the room.

I'd always loved Apache's bike, a ninety-one Dyna Glide in perfect condition. Apache had worked on the bike himself and had Texas do the paintwork. The tank was covered in an American Indian hunting scene, men on horses chasing buffalos. It was a genuine piece of art, it felt as if they were alive, so vital were the images. Gleaming chrome and black wheels capped the effect, and I loved the throaty roar the bike made. Despite not riding behind anyone before apart from Apache, that one time I knew how to mount. Although it would be difficult with one leg in a cast.

Apache threw one long leg over the bike and straddled it as I zipped up the coat he'd insisted I wear and shoved the helmet on. There was no point arguing. The brothers may not wear helmets, but the old ladies did. I put my foot on the footrest and swung up behind Apache, and wrapped my arms tightly around him as I shuffled forward to plaster myself against him.

Apache revved the throttle and shot off; I squealed in excitement as I felt the bike vibrating though my legs and moving up through my body. Wind swept my loose hair behind me as Apache hit the road and opened the throttle. Fuck me, this was the sexiest experience ever, the wind blowing through my hair, the vibration of the road, and Apache's scent hitting me despite my helmet.

We rode for two hours, taking back roads and the highways, and ended up at Magic's bar. The moment we walked in together, Magic's jaw dropped. His eyes swapped between the two of us, and Apache speared him with a stern glare.

"Fuckin' about time," Magic roared. "Fuckin' pussy finally got his act together," Magic announced to no one in particular. I gazed around and saw various brothers from other clubs. But the ones who caught my eye were Bear and Banshee from Hellfire. Shee was on his phone, tapping away and then shoved it in his pocket with a gleeful smile.

"Fuck me, Chance?" Apache groaned as Banshee grinned.

"You think he wouldn't want to know?" Bear rumbled, stomping forward and wrapping Apache up in an enormous hug. Bear turned to me and snatched me up, squeezing me tightly.

"Magic's right, time you manned up," Banshee said, slapping Apache on the back and snatching me from Bear's arms to hug me himself.

"Can't believe you texted fuckin' Chance," Apache grumbled as Magic slammed a beer in front of him.

"Brother hadn't, I'd have," Magic hollered from the bar, and I grinned at the man. He was much like Axel, except Magic was deadlier. Rumours had it, the hills behind his bar held the bodies of the men who'd pissed him off. Magic's age was hard to place, but he was younger than Axel but older than Texas.

"Ain't a big deal," Apache said, but I sensed his embarrassment and shame. He'd waited for years to claim me, and loyal idiot I was, I'd waited those years too.

"Perfect old lady for you, brother," Shee said, slapping Apache again. Banshee was often shortened to Shee.

"Yeah, she's one in a fuckin' million," Apache agreed, drawing me close and tucking me under his arm.

"Good to see you happy at last," Magic said, and I caught the undercurrent in his words. Whatever had happened to Apache, Magic was aware of it. I glanced at Apache as his jaw tightened, and he gave a sharp nod.

"Yeah," Apache replied, and Magic let the topic drop. A diet coke was placed in front of me, and as I reached out, Magic caught my hand and squeezed it. I caught his eyes and read the unspoken message there, Apache's a good man, stick with him. I offered a silent nod, and Magic relaxed.

"Apache need a word," someone called, and I saw Bat, the VP of the Fallen Warriors, approaching. By his side was Raddock, a huge guy who rarely spoke and Sniper, one of Fallen Warriors' enforcers. The Fallen Warriors were a motorbike club but clean and made entirely of ex-military men.

"Yo," Apache greeted as they clasped arms with each other.

"Got a problem. Lance needs a sit down with Drake. Got information you need," Bat said, and Apache's eyebrows rose.

"Yeah?" Apache asked. Bear nodded to a table, and the men began walking across. "Silvie," Apache called to me, and I clumped across to join him. Bat, Sniper and Raddock swapped glances with each other but sat at the table. To my surprise, Inglorious and his VP, Psych, joined us.

"You know?" Bat asked.

"Got a feeling we got similar info," Inglorious

replied. "Grats brother on your claimin', Silvie's beautiful." I smiled shyly at the Unwanted Bastards President. I knew from years back they had ties to Rage and had watched curiously from the side-lines as Drake got his club clean. Where Fallen Warriors were clean, I thought Unwanted Bastards hovered on the side-lines of barely legal.

"Arms?" Bat grunted, and Inglorious nodded.

"What arms?" Apache asked, leaning forward.

"Raddock here caught a shipment of arms being arranged in the hills. Raddock took stock and watched when he realised he was outnumbered. Happened between Black Hawk and Rapid City. Raddock says an MC was involved, but he didn't recognise the patch," Bat said. Inglorious nodded.

"We got the same, except two of my boys were jumped, bad."

"Walkin'?" Apache asked.

"One barely, the other yeah. This gang, Silvie, are the ones I think attacked you. Do you remember anything?" Inglorious asked, and I shook my head.

"What you got?" Apache growled, sitting up straight and hauling me into his side.

"Mouse heard them talking about a hit on a woman, one linked to Rage," Inglorious said, and I stiffened. That had to be me, but I didn't remember anything.

"I can't remember," I told Inglorious.

"One thing we've always agreed on, never touch family. Man to man, yeah, but you don't touch his family," Psych said, glowering.

"Silvie, they said you saw something, something that could break hell open," Inglorious said gently. I shook my head, I didn't know. Apache tightened his arm around me as I got distressed. Whatever I had seen was so important that someone tried to kill me.

"We caught the gang moving a delivery. They accepted a shipment of arms and bikes surrounded their truck, escorting it. Once they hit the open road, my people couldn't follow. They'd have been spotted and pulled back. Information was more important," Sniper said.

"Same as my two men, that's the information they got except they overheard the chat concerning Silvie. We need to call a meet," Psych said, and Apache nodded.

"Bear and Shee can get Hellfire on board. What about the others?" Apache asked.

"Gonna put feelers out to the others in our alliance. They may have info as well," Shee said. Nods abounded around the table.

"Silvie, if this is linked to something you saw, honey, you need to stay safe. No one needs Rage on the warpath," Sniper said, and I nodded.

"If I could remember what I saw, then it'd help, but I don't. I've been trying, but everyone keeps telling me to leave it alone. It will return when I least expect it. But arms shipments coming through Rapid City aren't what we need. Not with the freaking nutcase remaining free," I said. No one questioned who the freaking nutcase was. Santos. The name sent shivers down my spine, and I spun to Apache.

"My Mexican ghost, that's Santos?" I asked. Apache shrugged.

"That's what we think. You saw or heard something about Santos, but time baby, give it time," Apache agreed.

"Santos raising his head means bad times for Rapid City. That fucker got lucky with Washington," Inglorious spat. Wow, the anger coming off Inglorious shocked me, as did the hate that flowed from the man. Santos had made enemies.

"We'll call a meet," Apache said, and clasped arms with Inglorious as he rose to his feet. Apache repeated the action with the others and sat back at the table with Bear and Shee still there.

"Relax, there's fuck all we can do for now. Shee, call Chance and give him a heads up. We'll get the date and time of the meet later," Bear said, and Shee nodded at his VP. I felt scared. Many years ago, as Drake started to clean Rage, he reached out to other clubs, good clubs, and they made an alliance as soon as Drake took President. Hellfire and Rage had always been linked, brother clubs, but the other five clubs who formed part of the coalition came later.

They didn't interfere with each other but instead had oaths to support each other if called upon for help. They shared information and stayed out of each other's business. But if war came, the clubs rode at the call of aid. No club would ever involve one in a personal dispute, it had been agreed it needed to be a threat to each club in the alliance. It had never happened yet. They met up every couple of months, the inner circles of each club, rotating clubhouses each time. And while a few may cross the line or barely be legal, they held the same beliefs: honesty, brothers, family, the road, and respect.

Drake had sought similar-minded clubs and forged a path they could ride down together in peace. No club wars, no-poaching on territory, no shootings or anything, just peace and a flow of information. It was good, and this part of South Dakota had peace. We had other clubs that weren't part of our alliance, but they stayed out of our way. That was fine, but now Rage had a rogue club causing trouble.

"You okay?" Bear asked, leaning forward as Shee and Apache talked.

"Yes, no, I guess so, I'm frustrated I can't remember, and please don't tell me to give it time. I'm so sick of hearing that, Bear," I said softly, not wanting Apache to overhear.

"Silvie, you're a good lass, but you have your own answer. Hate to say it, girl, but time is what you need," Bear rumbled and sat back. Half an hour later, Apache rose and pulled me to my feet. He dropped a kiss on my mouth and tipped Magic a salute, and we left the bar.

"Hey, stop Silvie, what you know will come back eventually," Apache said, drawing me into his arms. I wondered how Apache knew I was still chewing on it. An eyebrow rose as Apache read my face, and I smiled at his expression. Apache had a duh look on his face as he answered my unspoken question. Of course, he knew what I was thinking, he understood me pretty damn well.

"Ride and then food?" Apache asked, and I nodded. I was beginning to get hungry, and my stomach was making itself known. But riding behind Apache beat my stomach hands down any day.

We arrived at the clubhouse to find the inner circle fully present and waiting on Apache. Drake was frowning at something on his phone, and I wasn't surprised when Dylan Hawthorne and Antonio Ramirez walked in with Ben behind them. The surprise was when Akemi, the man Artemis claimed as a brother, entered. The inner circle entered the sanctum, and church was called. Ramirez, Hawthorne, Ben, and Akemi joined the brothers there. I saw Hawthorne nod several times, and Ramirez ran his hand across his face. Ben asked questions, and I was watching avidly when someone stepped into my line of sight. Instantly I shrank back at the figure, and they froze.

"Silvie, it's me," Rock said, and I relaxed with a sigh.

"Sorry Rock, I didn't see you," I explained, but his eyes were watchful and alert. Slowly, he lowered his body into a seat and sat opposite me. His arms rested on his thighs, and I forced myself to relax. Rock's sharp gaze caught it, and I opened my mouth, but he beat me to the punch.

"Shit's too much, ain't it?" Rock rumbled and caught the attention of Lowrider and Lex. Both came over and stared at me.

"I'm fine," I said airily and waved a hand to emphasise that.

"Bullshit, the attack from Frenzy," I flinched as Rock said his name, "and now the hit and run. You're at breaking point."

"Rock, honestly, I'm fine. Apache and I sorted our differences, shit's great," I said, forcing a smile. Actually, I wasn't, and this perceptive man opposite knew it.

"Don't need to be strong with us," Lowrider said gently, and I swallowed tears.

"Rider…" I said, and my voice broke. There was too much going on. Frenzy's attack bothered me still. I woke screaming in the night with visions of dead women and tortured bodies. But being me, I told no one, it was a shock I'd slept soundly in Apache's bed. The hit and run remained a blank nothing, I remembered feeling fear, horror, despair, and a rampaging urge to reach Rage. Which meant what I had discovered was huge because I'd pulled away from Rage. Only something huge could have forced me to run for Rage.

I was dealing with my old pain and heartbreak, I couldn't ignore them, and even though Apache and I were together, they remained. The drama of my running away and meeting Brady, finding a rare man who only wanted friendship. Added in amongst all that, was the fact there had been a rift caused by me, between the brothers and old ladies. Even tonight, the old ladies weren't here, just skanks and whores. And there was everything else going on. Yeah,shit was too much, and I wasn't strong enough to handle much more.

"Silvie, you need a break or someone to talk to," Lowrider said. He placed a hand on my leg, and before I could understand, Apache was there at my side.

"What's wrong?" Apache demanded. His gaze narrowed as he took in my pale face and turned a glower on the brothers. "What you say to her?"

"Silvie needs someone to speak to," Lowrider said, standing and eyeing Apache.

"Silvie has me," Apache said firmly, and I snorted. I couldn't talk to Apache about all this shit in my head.

"Woman needs a professional Apache. Think what she's been through," Lex said, and my gaze snapped to him. The good time boy, who rarely sank into anything deeper than a laugh, had seen I was struggling. Lex wasn't shallow, but he couldn't be bothered to dig deeper with emotions. He blatantly avoided any emotional scene, so it proved how worried he was about me, which filled me with a warm feeling.

"Don't tell me how to look after my woman," Apache snarled, but Lex stepped forward.

"Brother, think, then tell us she doesn't need someone to speak to," Lex insisted. Apache stopped and thought, and I saw when it struck him what I'd been through.

"Fuck," he muttered, running a hand over his face. "Get me the number of the therapist Lindsey met."

"Will do," Lowrider said and walked away. Lex stepped forward, and one arm hugged Apache before slowly walking into my space and dropping a kiss on my head.

"You wanna see someone to talk?" Apache asked, crouching by my chair. I took a huge intake of breath and nodded.

"May be a good idea. I've got so much shit swirling around in my head," I whispered, and Apache lifted a hand and cupped my face.

"Then you'll get help," Apache promised.

"Has the meeting ended?" I asked, turning to look over my shoulder.

"Nah, I saw shit going down here and came out, I'll go back in if Rock will watch you."

"I don't need Rock to watch me," I muttered, and Apache grinned, and I fell silent.

"Get some food in Calamity!" Apache roared at the prospect, who sat up from where he slouched on a sofa.

"Guests?" Calamity asked.

"Yeah," Apache said and walked away after giving me a panty-melting kiss. Boy, that man could kiss. Rock gave a rare grin and sat back, playing with his phone.

"You wanna talk, I'm here," Rock said abruptly but didn't push. Calamity ducked out after a few minutes and returned an hour later with buckets of fried chicken, fries, and ribs with all the extras. He took buckets into the sanctum and shared the rest out amongst us. A squeal sounded as Lindsey bounded in, followed by the other old ladies, and Rock looked sheepish as I was surrounded by old ladies. Calamity grinned and waved at the extra buckets as the old ladies helped themselves. Skanks and whores could get their own food.

"So Apache," Lindsey whispered yelled. I rolled my eyes at her, and she grinned unabashedly.

"Yeah," I smiled as I bit into a rib.

"Silvie, you're happy?" Phoe said, and her disconcerting eyes stared into mine.

"I need help. So much has built up, I need someone to talk to," I whispered after a minute. Phoe nodded and hugged me tightly.

"That we can do," she whispered. I hated admitting to weakness, but my core of strength was whittling away. The truth was I needed the old ladies and Rage, and the further I got from them, the weaker I was. Rage had been my core of strength for so long I'd forgotten what it was to be without them. Now I knew, if I'd had them around me, I could have dealt with my issues, issues I hadn't even realised existed. The old ladies would have spotted them and confronted me before I even realised I was suffering.

"Thank you," I said. Marsha's sharp eyes caught mine, and she came over and nudged me to one side and hefted herself next to me.

"Don't be blaming yourself for the distance between brothers and old ladies," she said, getting straight to the heart of the matter. But I blamed myself. The old ladies had taken sides, even if they went against the men they loved so much.

"The estrangement is my fault," I said as she chewed a fry.

"Nope, it's their fault. Yeah, they don't treat us like whores and skanks, but they took us for granted. We understand Rage is a man's world, and we don't get a voice in what Rage do. We never have and accepted that. What we couldn't accept was that they thought we were less than them. Oh, the brothers would never say it outright, but old lady issues, were just that, old lady issues.

None of them took an active interest in our lives unless they were shacked up with us. Drake learnt a partial lesson when Phoe was gunned down on the forecourt, but as she pointed out, Drake's responsible for each of us. The brothers are Rage, but we make up Rage as well, and they forgot that. Now they've learnt, they've hurt the women they love, and they've ignored our needs as well," Marsha said, her eyes flicking to Fish.

"They spoil their old ladies rotten," I said, shaking my head.

"But do they listen? Do they sit and talk about

things that matter to us? No, they blindly go their own way and fuck what we think or feel. I thought they might wake up after what happened with Frenzy; instead only Gunner did. That man felt actual fear after your attack, but the others yet again blindly carried on. You'd survived, so life went on, but none looked for your scars, your hurts, they thought what Apache was doing was okay because you didn't show physical hurt. Apache may have got his head out of his ass now. But for so many fuckin' years, he was a total asshole to you," Marsha said with a glare over her shoulder.

"He loves me, Marsha, Apache always has, but there's something he's hiding. That's what kept us apart, no… don't ask, I don't know what it is. But Apache loves me, and I've accepted that, but I still carry the pain, embarrassment and humiliation around with me. That hasn't faded, it won't go away for a long time, Marsha. Apache made me *suffer,* and that hasn't escaped me. However, he means what he says, he loves me and will tell me what kept us apart," I said urgently, wanting Marsha to understand.

"Apache fucks up again. This will blow open in a way Drake and the brothers won't see coming. Old ladies have a place, not in deciding how the club operates, but in supporting our husbands. They need to understand that, their brothers are settled and happier when their old lady supports them. Drake understands that, he stopped the 'property of' being on our cuts and jackets. Phoe would have ripped him a new one, and can you imagine Artemis being the property of Ace?" Marsha chuckled.

"She'd have carved that in his forehead," I sniggered.

"Yeah," Marsha agreed as we both glanced at the woman in question. Artemis held baby Nashoba in her arms, smiling at Carly, who held Nokomis. I wanted that, my baby, with Apache. I wasn't greedy, the days of dreaming of a big family had long gone, but one would be nice.

"You've that look in your eye," Sin said, sitting on the arm of my chair.

"Huh?" I said stupidly, my thoughts interrupted.

"Broody," Sin giggled, and I smiled.

"One would be nice," I agreed, and Sin ran her hand down my arm.

"Silvie, we aren't close, but you've always been kind to me. Got so much respect and love for you, I truly hope your dreams come true," she said. Tears gathered in my eyes, and I blinked them back furiously.

"You lady, are a class act," I told her and hugged her. Happily, I gazed around me. Every old lady was there, even Penny. The sanctum door opened, and the men poured out. Ben nodded at us and took his leave while Ramirez joined Drake at the bar. Apache said something to Gunner, whose gaze was swapping between Autumn and me before coming over to me. He leant over the back of my chair and pulled my head back for a kiss. I felt the thaw from the women melt as he gazed into my eyes afterwards and smiled.

"Okay?" he asked.

"Yes," I replied.

"Talk your shit through with your women, let them help, they'll not do you wrong," Apache said. Approval rolled off the women towards him, but there was still a barrier, I could sense it, and while I understood, I wanted it gone.

Apache nodded at the women, caught sight of Nokomis in Carly's arms, and moved to take his granddaughter. Carly gave her up with a huff as Apache claimed Nokomis and strode away. I stifled a giggle at the pissed off look on Carly's face, which was appeased when Artemis handed her Nashoba. It didn't last long as Ace strode up and snatched him. Carly sat with a huff and glared at Ace's back as he walked away. I began laughing, and Marsha joined in, her stomach rippling alarmingly.

"Jeez, don't do that," I said wide-eyed. Marsha laughed again, and Sin joined in the merriment. I eyed their stomachs in alarm. Marsha winced as she calmed, and I watched her concerned.

"Marsha," I said.

"I'm okay, just the babies are laying wrong, and I'm sure they're bouncing on my bladder," Marsha said and struggled to get to her feet. Fish dashed over and hauled her to her feet, and Marsha gasped.

"Baby?" Fish said as Marsha bent over double.

"Oh, fuck!" Marsha exclaimed. A puddle of water formed at her feet, and I squealed.

"Marsha's water's broke!" Heads turned at my squeal, and Fish paled.

"Fish!" Drake called, striding over to us. Calamity darted out of the clubhouse as Marsha paled and rubbed her belly.

"I thought they were back pains," she gasped, and Phoe's eyes softened.

"Oh honey, we all think that," she said. Calamity returned.

"I got the truck. Let's go," he said, and Marsha began moving in his direction.

"Well, Fish, you better move," Drake chuckled, and Fish darted his head around before racing to the door without Marsha. Axel rolled his eyes.

"What the fuck is it with you assholes leaving your labouring women behind?" Axel boomed, and chuckles arose as we remembered how Ace had acted with Artemis. Ace sent him a glare as Axel wrapped a meaty arm around Marsha and began guiding her to the door. As he reached it, Fish ran back in shamefaced.

"Forgot the most important thing," he muttered, and together, Axel and Fish walked Marsha out. The old ladies swapped glances.

"Well, what are we waiting for? It's become a habit for the club to welcome in legacies," Phoe said, and we glanced at our men. The men grinned, and as a group, we darted to the doors to escort Marsha and Fish to the hospital. Even Hawthorne and Ramirez followed, laughing.

Marsha gave birth to a son called Hawk Axel Greenway and a daughter Julianna Kayleigh Greenway at eleven that night on the fourth of April. Axel, Ace, and Apache looked stunned while Artemis simply made a moue with her lips.

"Kayleigh was our first child," Fish said, handing Hawk to Artemis. Artemis gazed at the tiny face and then at Fish.

"And you and Marsha were Kayleigh's parents. She never forgot that, and neither have I," Artemis replied.

"You're not annoyed? Marsha was worried."

"No Fish, never, Kayleigh is dead, been dead years. And she'd have been honoured," Artemis said. I never got over Artemis referring to Kayleigh as gone. But the girl Artemis had been, was truly dead. Even though there was no body in Kayleigh's grave, she'd died. And out of her ashes, Artemis arose.

Marsha gazed up as Fish dropped a kiss on her head as Artemis passed him carrying Hawk and headed in Marsha's direction. Happiness radiated off Marsha, and I felt a small pang of jealously. Hopefully, that would be me soon enough. Fish took Julianna back from Axel, who glowered and reluctantly let the baby go and headed towards Marsha. Fish rolled his eyes and followed in Axel's footsteps. I glanced at Apache, who was smiling with Drake as they watched the two men walk away. Yeah, this was something I wanted, most definitely wanted.

Chapter Seven.

Of course, this was Rage. Everyone's relationships had been fraught with drama and mayhem. Why should mine be any different? The thought crossed my mind as I stared at the diminutive woman who'd just dropped a nuclear bomb on Rage. Old ladies stood at my back, eyes narrowed, and I gazed at Apache, who had paled as hurtful words left the woman's mouth.

Five hours earlier.

I rolled over in the bed as Apache's cock poked at me. With a small smile, I dashed from the bed and used the bathroom, brushing my teeth too. As I exited, I stared at Apache lying splayed out. One arm was behind his head and the other outstretched, touching where I'd been sleeping. The covers had moved down his muscled chest, and I could just see a hint of his happy trail. And over the past five days, it had been a trail I'd been most happy to explore.

Silently, I crept over to the bed and drew the covers away, my smile turning to a grin as I saw the hard cock just waiting for me. A quick glance at Apache showed he was still asleep, and I grasped his cock in my hand and bent my head. Apache twitched under my hand, and I took the head of his cock into my mouth. I loved this power. Apache never failed to let me explore his body or experiment.

Hollowing my cheeks, I took as much of his cock as possible into my mouth while my hand moved up and down the stiff shaft. A rumble reached my ears as Apache began waking, and a hand slid into my hair. I licked around the tip of his cock, and Apache shuddered under my ministrations. Hips thrust upwards as Apache sought to go deeper in my wet mouth, and I tried to take more. I sucked hard, and Apache growled as my hands slid around to cup his balls. I squeezed his tight sacs gently, and Apache moaned.

"Silvie, shit," Apache hissed as I popped him free of my mouth and used my tongue on them. I was spoilt for choice; did I suck his cock more or play with his sacs? I licked them, and Apache nearly came off the bed. Wow, he liked that. Happily, I sucked gently on them as Apache growled and his hand tightened in my hair. My hand moved up and down his hard cock as I worshipped Apache with my mouth. I spread pre-cum around the head and sucked it clean while my hands moved back to his balls.

Curiously, my finger slid towards his anus, and Apache stiffened. I stopped and wondered if I was doing something wrong, and Apache lifted his head.

"You want that?" Apache asked, his eyes lazily gazing at me. Autumn had told me Gunner loved that, so I wondered if Apache would.

"Yes," I replied boldly.

"Make sure I'm wet there, Silvie, very wet baby," Apache said and flopped back on the bed. Fuck, Apache was giving permission. I sucked his cock again, spreading the wetness down his shaft and balls and to his anus. With great gentleness, I ensured Apache was wet before gently pushing in a finger. Apache's ass clenched around the intrusion, and Apache forced himself to relax. He gave an inarticulate cry as I pushed my finger fully in and then moved it back out. Apache's cock twitched as I repeated the actions and wetness swelled between my own legs. God, this was hot. This powerful man was at my mercy and letting me fuck his ass.

"Suck me, baby, while you fuck me," Apache growled as he pulled my head toward his cock. My other hand grasped his base, and I slid his cock into my mouth. Bolder now, knowing Apache enjoyed this, I slid a second finger into his ass, and Apache's hips bucked as he came off the bed.

"Harder," Apache gasped as I began moving my fingers and mouth faster, giving him what he wanted.

With a wordless cry, Apache erupted into my mouth, and I swallowed quickly, knowing he'd come again. I pushed all the way in with my fingers, and Apache spilt a second time. I withdrew my fingers and took a wipe from the bedside table. Deftly, I cleaned Apache and my fingers before straddling his body. Apache's cock was semi-hard now, but I needed release too.

"Lick me," I ordered, and Apache's lustful eyes watched as I pulled off the tee I wore to bed. With a grunt, Apache grabbed my ass cheeks and lifted me up towards his mouth. I grabbed hold of the headboard as Apache slid down the bed and pulled me onto his face. I cried out as his tongue slid straight between my folds and found my clit. His tongue licked harshly, and his fingers prised my folds open, and I screamed as my head flew backwards as his tongue entered me.

Fuck, this was something different. Apache's tongue fucked me while one hand kept my folds open, and the other played with my clit. Sensations poured through me as I could only concentrate on what his magical tongue was doing. Apache's hand slipped away, and I felt a sharp slap on my ass.

"That's it, baby," Apache muttered before leashing an assault on my clit again. His fingers spread my wetness, and I wasn't even aware of what Apache was doing until a finger pierced my ass. Oh my god, this was amazing, even though the intrusion was slightly unwelcome. But the sensations of his mouth on my clit and finger in my ass overwhelmed me, and

I orgasmed with a scream.

"More baby, more," Apache grunted. His mouth latched back onto my clit as he fucked my ass with two fingers now, and my knuckles turned white, holding on to the headboard. Moments later, I screamed a second time and shifted to collapse next to him on the bed. My body shuddered with aftershocks as my hand crept to his chest. Apache loomed over me and his cock prodded between my legs.

"Inside, now," I whispered, blinking to clear the stars from my eyes. Without a word, Apache slid into me, and I wrapped my leg around him. Apache grunted as I rose to meet his thrust inside, and he slid through my slick wetness. Fully seated, Apache grinned and pulled out as I whimpered. No, I needed Apache to fuck me hard.

Apache rose to his knees and spread his legs, and I watched as he pulled me upwards and towards him and slid back inside. I found it harder to move and could only watch as Apache thrust again, and a strangled scream escaped me. At this angle, Apache was in control, and I was helpless. Intense lust on his face Apache pounded into me as I panted beneath him.

"You're so fuckin' tight, I love this, love you," Apache grunted with each thrust. I wailed as my orgasm built up, and Apache pulled out, denying me. He lifted me and turned me over, pulling me to my knees and pushing my shoulders to the bed. Apache pushed inside me again as I tried to thrust back, but he gripped my hips and stopped me from moving. Apache was deeper this way, and from behind, he pushed into me over and over. His hand slapped my ass again, and I cried out as my orgasm swept through me, obliterating any other thought or sensation. Apache pumped twice more and collapsed against my back.

"Holy hell," I muttered after a few minutes. Apache grunted and pulled out, and I could have wept at the feeling of loss. He dropped next to me and wrapped me up in his arms.

"Mornin' baby," Apache grunted, and I giggled.

"Morning," I replied.

"Any time you wanna wake me like that, feel free," Apache grinned. "Made my fuckin' day."

"Ditto," I said and dropped a kiss on the hollow of his throat.

"Wanna take a run to Rage?" Apache asked.

"That will be nice."

"And get breakfast?" Apache wriggled his brows, and I laughed.

"Didn't you just eat?"

"Woman!" Apache roared before laughing.

"That's me," I giggled.

"Eat you any time or place you want, but we need actual food. Got plans for this afternoon," Apache said and winked. I stared, stunned at him. Apache never winked or flirted, he just… was. Apache grinned again at the look on my face before slapping my ass slightly harder than during our lovemaking, and I scrabbled to get away from that hand.

"Shower," I growled, rubbing my ass.

"Together?"

"Duh," I snickered and yelped as Apache reached for me, and I fled into the bathroom.

Together we entered Rage, me firmly wrapped under Apache's arm, and I waved at Penny, who was sat at the bar with Marsha and Carly. Penny had Hawk and Carly held Julianna as Marsha watched over the twins proudly. I ran a critical eye over my friend; Marsha was the one I'd known the longest, and her heartbreak I'd felt as my own. Now Marsha glowed, she looked tired but shone with happiness. By Marsha's elbow stood Fish with Axel standing behind Carly, ready to catch Julianna should Carly drop her.

I let out a huff and rolled my eyes at Apache before pointing at Axel. A brief smile crossed Apache's face as he glanced at the glowering man. Yup, Axel was really taking Grandpa seriously, not that he hadn't in the past, but this time it was *Marsha's* babies. And Marsha was special to Axel, and he to her. Plus, Hawk was Axel's namesake, and I smiled. There was an emotion present in Axel I'd not seen before, satisfaction. The colossal mountain was happy, which meant the world to most of us in Rage. Axel had too much love in his heart and couldn't give it away quick enough.

"Want to hold Julianna?" Carly asked as we approached.

"Hey, it's my turn next," Slick yelled from where he sprawled on a couch. Carly shot Slick a smirk and hugged Julianna close.

"Tough," Carly said, and Slick crossed his eyes at her. Carly giggled, and it was a beautiful sound. Rock's eyes slid to Carly for a moment from the pool table and then focused back on his game. Klutz was playing against him with a huge frown. Yup, Klutz was losing again.

Drake was absent along with Phoe, and I guessed they were at the hospital. Lindsey and Lowrider had arrived simultaneously with us, with their kids, and I saw Penny's children playing swingball with Texas. I looked around for Ace and Artemis and noticed they were also missing, but Nova and Falcon were present. With a massive grin, Nova launched at Apache, and he grabbed her up as she wrapped her legs around him.

"Hey Grandpa," Nova cried and kissed his cheek.

"Hey, mini killer," Apache rumbled back, and Nova laughed. Nova may look like Ace and Apache, but she was her mother's daughter head to toe.

"I've a tournament next weekend. Are you and Silvie coming?" Nova asked as Apache placed her back on her feet.

"Yeah, got to watch Rage's mini killer in action,"

Apache said and rumpled her hair. Nova immediately batted Apache's hands away and turned to me.

"You're coming too?" Nova asked. Oh boy, Nova knew how to use those big green eyes of hers. Eyes that Nova shared with her father and grandfather.

"Yes, honey, I wouldn't miss it for the world," I said, touched Nova wanted me present. I hadn't been sure how Nova would react to my getting together with her grandfather. Nova and Falcon hadn't had Ace and Apache long in their lives, and I had worried they might be negative.

"Cool," Nova chirped and stepped closer.

"You know, Mom hates makeup and girlie shi… stuff," Nova corrected herself with a glance at Apache. "We've got a dance coming up soon at school. Could you take me dress shopping and to get girlie stuff?" Nova asked, and I was helpless in that green gaze.

"Yes," I said, and Nova whooped, and Apache interfered.

"Hold on, young lady. Don't think that because Silvie's taking you shopping, the rules don't apply. No skirts or dresses above the knee, no garish ho-bag makeup, no cleavage!" Apache rumbled, and Nova rolled her eyes.

"Grandpa!" Nova yelled, and Fish raised his head.

"What you doing to our granddaughter?" Fish shouted across the room.

"No skirts or dresses above the knee, no garish ho-bag makeup, no cleavage," Apache repeated, and Fish scowled.

"Damn right!" Fish yelled, and I felt sorry for the beleaguered Nova, who hadn't lost her sparkle.

"In that case, Falcon can't have skinny jeans as they show his package and can't have low waisted jeans because his ass shows," Nova said serenely, and Apache choked. I stifled a giggle. Falcon yelled something from across the room as Nova speared Apache and Fish with a stern look.

"Or are you sexist and elitist?" Nova asked sweetly, and Apache sent me a look, clearly demanding help. Axel waded in without hesitation.

"Ain't no fuckin' sexist, but ain't having no randy assed teenager groping my fuckin' grandbaby. Now you listen up, girlie, ho's get dicks, and classy chicks get the ring. Ain't having no grandbaby of mine ending with up with a dick, hear me, Nova?" Axel boomed, and Nova twisted her head.

"Okay, Grandpa, but you can buy my dress for the dance," Nova said cheekily, and Axel grinned.

"Take Silvie, and she'll get you classy shit, ya can have my card, ladies," Axel boomed. I expected Apache to kick up a storm and say he was buying the dress, but Apache tilted his head at Axel.

"We take turns, ain't no brother gonna deny Axel spoiling his grandkids, blood, honouree or not," Apache whispered to me. It was the same with Fish, he may not be Artemis's blood father, but he was her dad.

"Too much love in Axel," I whispered.

"Don't need tellin' that," Apache said and sat his ass in a chair and dragged me into his lap. Over the next hour, brothers arrived, and soon the clubhouse was buzzing. Kids were everywhere as old ladies arrived, escorted by their man on his bike.

"Gettin' harder to just jump on a bike and ride," Lex said, sitting opposite us.

"Yeah, kids are coming fast and furious," Apache said.

"Ain't right to ask old ladies to stay home while we ride," Lowrider said, joining the discussion. "Lindsey is often torn between riding and the kids. Obviously, the kids win out, but I'd like to ride with my woman sometimes."

"So why don't you speak to Drake and Phoe? It's an easy resolve," I said without thinking and bit my lip. Riding was the brother's business, not mine, I'd overstepped.

"Go on," Lowrider said encouragingly.

"Well, Phoe's got the Hall. Ask her if she can arrange childcare once a month and make that day a riding day with old ladies. Pretty sure, everyone with kids will chip in to cover the cost of childcare," I explained.

"Great idea," Lowrider said, craning his neck to see if Phoe was about.

"Not seen Drake or Phoe yet," Apache said. I snuggled into Apache's chest, and he wrapped his arms tightly around me. That was when Apache's body stiffened in outrage and shock. When I glanced up, Apache's face was a mask of boiling fury.

My eyes slid to where his furious gaze was staring, and I spied a Native American woman standing in the clubhouse's entrance. She was older than me and her face heavily lined. Slender and short, with greying long black hair pulled back, the stranger's eyes latched onto Apache. Despite a hard life showing on her face, she was stunningly beautiful but hard as granite.

"What the fuck are you doing here?" A roar came from behind me, and Axel barrelled past, going at full speed. Axel placed a hand on the stranger and pushed. Apache rose to his feet and set me on mine. I stared between him and the woman and blanched at the sheer anger Apache was leaking.

"Take your hands off me, Axel," the woman demanded and stood her ground. Confused, I stared as Apache strode towards her with murderous intent.

"Get the fuck out, Elu!" Apache roared, and I winced. Seconds later, one of the doors to the back rooms slammed open, and Drake flew out.

"What the fuck is that cunt doing here?" Drake roared, coming to stand behind Apache. Hate wafted from the three men facing the woman, Elu, as Apache had called her, and a sinking feeling started in my stomach.

"I want to see Ace, hear he has kids," the woman said. Apache slammed a hand into Elu's chest and shoved her back two steps.

"The fuck you're getting anywhere near my boy,"

Apache shouted, and a shiver of dread ran down my spine. Brothers had risen to their feet, and from the corner of my eye, I saw Phoe urging Marsha, the old ladies, and kids to the back rooms. Phoe motioned to me, and I shook my head.

"You'll see Ace over my dead body," Apache hissed.

"I'll see Ace now," Elu spat.

"The fuck you will," Drake roared. My head twisted between the three of them as Texas took Drake's back.

"Fuck off, Elu, now, before you regret it," Texas seethed. Whoever this woman was, all four men knew her and hated the ground she walked upon.

"Fuck you, Texas, I ain't part of this stupid club, and you don't order me around," Elu hissed and folded her arms. This woman knew Texas? What the hell was going on here?

"Elu, you were warned, next time you set foot on Rage, you'd get a bullet in your head!" Apache snarled, and I gasped lightly. Surely Apache didn't mean that?

"Fuck you, asshole, I want to see Ace now, got babies ain't he?" Elu snarled back, and Apache's fists clenched. I stepped forward and grabbed Apache's arm, more to show support than anything else. I'd the nasty feeling that this woman was part of what Apache was hiding.

"Silvie, stay back," Apache said, the venom in his voice dying when he spoke to me. Elu grabbed hold on that pretty quick.

"She your whore?" Elu hissed, eyes narrowing on me. Screw that, I glared right back.

"I'm Apache's old lady," I said calmly. Someone had to be calm. Might as well be me.

"Congratulations, I'm Tyee's fucking wife, bitch," Elu snarled. She was calling Apache by his given name, I rocked back on my heels. Shock flooded through me, and I gazed stunned and wordless at Apache. Deny it! I screamed silently in my head. Apache's face was once again furious, and his fists clenched. Apache's wife? Oh fuck no, that meant…

"Bullshit," I spat, handling the fact Elu claimed she was married to Apache and ignoring my other conclusion. Shocked or not, I knew Apache. No way would he have moved on me if married. This bitch was here to cause trouble. Well, Elu wouldn't sow it between us.

"What you say?" Elu asked, hands on hips.

"No bloody way would Apache get with me if he was married. You're a lying bitch," I said calmly despite emotions boiling inside.

"Silvie?" Apache asked, his hand touching my throat.

"What? I'm telling the truth, aren't I?" I asked, and Apache nodded. "Then fuck that bitch, Elu can spew all the lies she wants, and I ain't going to believe her. I know you, Apache, not her." Apache looked relieved, and then fury erupted on his face again.

"Fuck off, Elu," Apache snarled.

"Not happening," Elu said.

"What the fuck is going on?" Ace snarled from behind, and my grip tightened on Apache's arm. Shit was going to get nasty.

"Son, go back to your room," Axel said, stepping in the way of Ace's line of sight. Out of the corner of my eye, I saw Ace straighten.

"Ain't doing shit Axel, now as VP, I want to know what the fuck is going on. Nashoba was woken up by this shit," Ace said.

"Ace, go back to the babies," Apache said, but Elu stepped around us and stared at Ace. Elu's hand rose to her mouth and her eyes filled with tears.

"My baby boy!" Elu gasped, and my head snapped towards her. A gut reaction told me Elu's tears were false, but Apache's anger rocketed to nuclear. Calculation shone in Elu's tear-filled eyes.

"Ain't your baby boy," Apache growled, and I felt everything snap into place. My conclusion had been correct. This was Apache's dead wife. The one I thought Apache had mourned all these years, instead Elu was standing alive and kicking in front of me.

"I birthed Ace, Tyee, you can't deny me my son any longer. Not now he's got babies," Elu said. "I've let you assholes keep me away long enough."

"Dad?" Ace said, his head swivelling towards Apache, whose mouth opened and closed. Shit, Apache was lost for words.

"Ain't your mother," Apache said finally, and Elu let out a horrified cry. Jeez, could Elu be any more fake?

"I birthed Ace Apache, you chased me away all those years ago, took my son from me. I had postnatal depression, Ace, and your father used it to steal you," Elu cried, her hands reaching for Ace.

"That's the story you're going with?" Drake said in disbelief. He stepped forward, and a hand rose as if to punch Elu when Ace caught his fist in his own.

"Mom?" Ace said, disbelief in his voice.

"That cunt ain't a mother, not to you, Ace," Axel snarled. Axel's usual happy boom was full of hate, and his entire body shook with it. I'd never seen reactions like this from the brothers.

"Deny you took my boy from me," Elu cried, eyes narrowing, and I saw vindictiveness behind them. Whatever was going on, I guessed Elu had just played her trump; Apache had never lied to Ace. However, Ace's mother being alive was a big fucking lie.

"I took Ace for his safety," Apache spat, and Texas growled in agreement. Ace rocked back, and there was a flash of red, and Artemis stood behind him.

"Ace's mother was alive? All these years Apache and his mother was alive?" Artemis hissed, her hand on Ace's back.

"That cunt ain't a mother," Drake roared. My head snapped towards Drake in shock.

"Did she or did she not give birth to Ace?" Artemis snapped as Ace stared at his father in shock and horror.

"Yeah," Apache said. His eyes begged Ace to

understand, to see his side. But whatever that was, none of us knew because Apache had never discussed it. Ace's head turned slowly to Elu, and he studied her.

"So that makes her my mother," Ace said hoarsely.

"No, son," Apache said.

"Fuck you, Dad, you fuckin' lied to me. Told me Mom was dead, and she's been alive the whole fuckin' time!" Ace shouted, and I winced.

"Get the fuck out," I said, turning to Elu.

"Not without my boy," Elu said, shaking her head.

"Ace ain't yours, he's ours. He's Rage," Gunner said from behind us. He took Ace's back and placed a hand on his shoulder.

"Let Apache explain, Ace," Drake said, and Ace's eyes snapped to Apache. Apache held his son's gaze, but I felt pain radiating off him.

"Fuck that and fuck you, Drake, because you knew. And so did you two," Ace pointed to Axel and Texas. None of them looked shamefaced. All four looked ready to commit murder. Apache spun around and yanked his gun from his belt; he took aim straight at Elu's head.

"Told you, you ever set foot on Rage again; the punishment was death. Gonna carry that out right now," Apache snarled. Seconds later, the gun went flying as Artemis kicked it from his hand. Apache turned on Artemis with a snarl, but Artemis held her ground, her body loose and ready to fight. Apache would never raise a hand to Artemis, and damn if

Artemis didn't know it, but she was ready just in case.

"Get the kids," Ace said to Artemis, who glared at those standing opposite her and stormed away.

"You need to let us explain," Drake said, stepping forward and taking Ace's arm. Ace shook him off.

"Explain what? *Come on, brother*," Ace sneered, and Drake winced, "tell me what ya got to explain. Why you four lied for over thirty years? Why you chased away my mother? What ya got? Make it good."

"You gotta listen," Axel boomed. Panic rose in my throat as I saw the blank look in Ace's eyes. I'd seen that before, when Kayleigh died.

"Ain't gotta do shit!" Ace said. His eyes met Elu's. "We're leaving."

"Don't leave Elu alone with the kids, especially the babies," the words tore from Apache's throat. I wrapped my arms around Apache's waist as Artemis arrived with both sets of twins, and without a word, they left the clubhouse. Elu shot a look of triumph over her shoulder, and I moved forward to tackle the bitch, but Apache caught me in his arms. Apache held on tight, burying his head in my throat and abruptly let go and walked out. I didn't hesitate and dashed straight after him. As Apache swung on his bike, I scrambled up behind him. Apache froze, and then I wrapped my arms around him, and he throttled the bike and peeled out.

"You came with me," Apache said, staring out over a lake. We'd rode for two hours and not stopped until now.

"Yes," I said, sitting on the grass.

"Why? I just been proved a liar," Apache asked.

"Because I love you, and I know you. No fucking way would you have lied all those years unless it was life and death," I replied.

"Fuck me, hit the nail on the head there, Silvie," Apache snorted.

"When you're ready, we'll talk, but I can wait," I, but I desperately wanted answers.

"First off, that cunt ain't my wife. Got divorced when Ace was six months old. Ain't married or involved with anyone except you woman," Apache said. I nodded, I trusted Apache, and despite our history, I knew he didn't act like that.

"Apache, tell me something I don't know," I whispered, and his gaze held mine.

"I was fifteen when Elu got pregnant, fifteen Silvie. Bitch was twenty, seduced me right out of my childhood. Not that I'd a great one. See, my parents died young, my uncle raised me, the chief of the tribe, and Chief raised me as his own son. I thought Chief was my fuckin' Dad until I discovered who was my actual parents at fifteen, and Elu snagged me then. Raw and bleeding, the bitch seduced me right into her trap. Elu was the whore she aimed to be.

I did the decent thing and put a ring on her, fuckin'

biggest mistake of my life. Elu wanted me because I was gonna be chief one day. Elu wanted status. Fuckin' marrying the chief's heir was a real kick in the teeth. Even worse, Elu would sneer that her bloodline was gonna be chief one day. Bitch was scum."

"Oh, Apache, no," I said gently, and he started pacing.

"Yeah, Silvie, I was sixteen, just turned sixteen when Ace was born, and I never felt such love for anyone in my life. We'd a house, a small one provided by the reservation, and we tried to get along together. But Elu wanted money and partying, I wanted a home and my son. We'd never have lasted.

Ace was two weeks old when the first incident happened. I came home from work, got a job on a farm, and I walked in on Elu smothering Ace with a pillow as he screamed. Terrified, I grabbed Elu and smashed her against the wall and scooped my boy up safely. Ace was full of snot and gasping for breath, and his lips had turned blue. I rushed Ace to the reservation's medic, who checked Ace over for harm. In the meantime, Elu ran to my uncle and put her own side across, which wasn't the truth.

I returned home to a beating from my uncle and Elu acting innocent. Four weeks later, Elu found some scum to fuck and left early morning. I arrived home late at night to find my boy covered in shit and piss from where his diaper leaked, starving, hungry and screaming his head off. Again I called the medic, and the doctor called my uncle. Elu arrived and claimed I was meant to be at home, and I was the one that left Ace. But the medic pointed out everyone knew I'd been at work early, and my uncle believed me that time."

"Oh my god," I whispered.

"Ace was seven weeks the next time that cunt tried to kill him. Elu left Ace drowning in a bath of water, but a neighbour had popped over and asked where Ace was. She saved his life this time. Elu claimed Ace had rolled over and fallen in, bullshit, people began realising she was lying and trying to kill my son.

One night I came home and discovered the gas on in the kitchen and Ace's cradle in front of it. I got Ace out just as the house blew up. Elu arrived shrieking and crying, which stopped when she saw Ace in my arms. Too many witnesses this time, reservation police took away Elu. I left the reservation as my uncle tried to sweep it under the table. Found my way to Arrow and Rage. Arrow took me straight in, offered a room in his house; Drake was eight to my sixteen. Drake took one look at Ace, and a bond formed between them.

Arrow got me work, kept me going when I wanted to give in to adversity. Then when Ace was about a six-months, Elu arrived at the clubhouse, wanting to see Ace. Bitch got past Bulldog, and he let her take Ace, I was working, and Ace was supposed to be safe at the clubhouse. We were wrong. By the time Arrow,

Texas, Axel, and I found Elu, she'd a knife to Ace's throat and had drugged him. I shot her and snatched Ace, and we rushed him to the hospital. My six-month-old son had to have his stomach pumped, and cops were involved. A warrant went out for Elu, but the cunt fled to the reservation, and the cops couldn't snatch her.

Cunt was obsessed with killing Ace, and that was the last time I spoke to my uncle. Arrow told Chief, if he didn't keep her in check, Rage would ride on the reservation, and innocents would be killed. The threat was enough to stop my uncle dead in his tracks. Finally, I made enough money to buy a house. That cunt is not Ace's mother, she's his murderer. Twice my son was revived and brought back because of her. And now she strolls in and is giving Ace her side and poisoning my boy. *My boy*," Apache said, anguished.

"I don't know what to say, I never guessed this was what you were hiding, what kept us apart," I whispered.

"If Elu had sniffed out I'd a woman, she'd have come running back quicker than she has. Bitch hated the thought of me being with a woman. Fuckin' convenient she's come back now," Apache bit out.

"Shit," I muttered. Now everything made sense. Apache had denied us to protect Ace from his psycho bitch of a mother.

"Weren't gonna risk no woman near Ace, and then he did what I did. Discovered the girl he thought was the one early. When Kayleigh disappeared, I thought

I'd been justified in my actions. Ace changed and was hurting, and I didn't want to tell him the truth, he'd had enough pain with Kayleigh. How do you tell your son his mother tried to kill him?" Apache asked, and I shook my head. There was no answer to that.

"I'm so sorry for your pain, and that bitch will get what's coming to her," I said. Apache gazed out over the water.

"Silvie, I won't lose my boy or my grandkids," Apache finally said.

"Ace isn't stupid. Once he's over the shock, he'll have questions for you," I said reassuringly.

"My boy can hold a fuckin' grudge, Silvie. Elu's gonna twist the truth before I can get it to him," Apache mumbled.

"Let Elu spew whatever stories she wants. Apache, I know you; you must have proof, medical records and statements," I said.

"Jesus Silvie, what would I do without you?" Apache asked, spinning and pulling me up from the grass. "Yeah, I do, and I forgot." Apache's arms clenched around me, and I pressed against his body.

"Is there anything else I should know?" I asked, and Apache stiffened. For fuck's sake, hadn't we been through enough? What else was there? I held Apache tight as he bared his soul, and mine blazed in agony for him. How could anyone have treated a fifteen-year-old boy like that? When I next saw Elu, I was going to rip her hair out by its roots.

Apache was right. Ace could hold a grudge. He stayed away from the clubhouse for three weeks and refused all phone calls. Elu was working her poison through him, and not even Artemis or the twins had visited. It was clear which side they had picked; whatever fairy tales Elu was spinning; they were damn good. I was ready to commit murder when Ace blew into the clubhouse on a Thursday night and glared at his father.

"I want the fuckin' truth," Ace snarled, his eyes holding Apache's. "No bullshit."

"No bullshit, son," Apache said, rising to his feet.

"Texas, Drake, Axel, you three as well. But ya keep your mouths shut until I ask ya something," Ace growled and stormed into the inner sanctum. I reached down and pulled out the envelope I'd been carrying around for the last three weeks. Silently I handed it to Apache, who dropped a kiss on my head.

"Get your lying ass in here and stop making out with your whore," Ace spat, and I shrank back. Apache turned and punched Ace straight in the jaw. Ace took a step back as his hand rose to his split lip.

"You watch your mouth around Silvie. Whatever I did, Silvie's innocent, and I won't have you talk to her like shit," Apache snarled.

"Leave it," I whispered, tugging Apache's jeans. Ace turned, and the fury in his eyes eased a little.

"Apologies, Silvie, whatever this asshole did, you

didn't deserve that," Ace finally said. The only thing I could do was nod. My throat was that tight with tears. None of the brothers had ever spoken to me so harshly, and I was deeply hurt. Tears leaked out as they strode towards the sanctum, and seconds later, Autumn was at my side with Gunner taking the other. Together they offered comfort as my eyes stared, with burning tears, at the sanctum.

Chapter Eight.

"Start talking," Ace spat. We heard Ace's roar through the door of the sanctum, and patting Gunner and Autumn's hands, I rose to my feet. Artemis walked in and caught my gaze.

"No fuckin' bullshit Silvie," Artemis hissed. "Ace is hurting, and it's Apache's and those asshole's fault."

"You know shit Artemis, and if you left the kids with Elu, you better get home. That woman has a track record for attempting to murder kids," I spat. Artemis rocked back on her heels as I stormed past her and entered the sanctum. The men glared at me as I walked to Apache's side and slipped my hand in his.

"Baby..." Apache whispered.

"Shut up, Apache. You don't go through this alone," I hissed and glared at Ace. Artemis strode in and kicked the door shut. She took her place at Ace's side, but her eyes searched mine.

"So first things first, you're not my dad? You're my fuckin' cousin?" Ace spat, and Apache paled. A tremor ran through his body, and my eyes dropped to the floor. Elu certainly had done her work.

Three hours earlier.

"The chief wants to meet you," Elu said, sitting at the table. Ace lifted his eyes and gazed at his mother. Despite his anger at his father, he was wary around his mother. She claimed to have been terrified of Apache and Rage, but he'd turned sixteen a long time ago, and she'd plenty of opportunities to contact him. Artemis was acting hinky. She never left the kids alone with Elu but wouldn't explain why.

"Huh?" Ace asked.

"Didn't Tyee tell you anything?" Elu hissed, sounding pissed. "You're the chief's grandson, you've got family at the reservation." Ace rocked back in his chair and stared at Elu. He'd a grandfather and family? What the fuck had Apache been playing at?

"I got family?" Ace drawled.

"On both sides, Ace, mine and *his*, a big family on your Grandpa's side," Elu laid the bait and sat back and waited for Ace to bite. Ace searched her face, but all he found was concern.

"Maybe we could make a run to the reservation," Ace said slowly, and Elu offered a triumphant smile. For the last three weeks, she'd been visiting them at a cabin she thought they lived in permanently. Instead, Artemis, being her usual self, used their second home to meet Elu at, cautious as ever. Their principal residence was at the compound with the Juno Group, and Artemis wouldn't let Elu wander around that! Ace couldn't put his finger on what was bothering him, but something was.

Elu had been charming and kind, but it was false as if she was living a role. She'd asked a multitude of questions and fussed over the babies and Nova and Falcon, but again, Ace didn't detect genuine interest. Oh, Elu had been happy to slam Apache at every chance she got, and she'd certainly got her side across. That of a frightened young woman, who suffered from post-natal depression and lost her baby because Apache had contacts, she couldn't fight.

That didn't answer the question of why she'd come back now. Elu wasn't telling the whole truth, Ace had decided, but despite his misgivings, he had a mom. Ace had never suffered a lack of love from Apache, nor had he ever been ignored. Apache had made it very clear, he'd two priorities, Ace and Rage, and in that order. Not once had he felt a bother or unwanted, and while grateful to Apache for that, he missed having a mom. Something he'd not realised until he faced Elu in the clubhouse.

"Now?" Elu asked, rising to her feet. Ace dragged his attention back to her.

"I need someone to watch the kids. Give me an hour," Ace replied. Elu frowned.

"Can't Artemis?" she asked.

"Nope, she's coming with us," Ace said. Elu wriggled and looked unsure.

"Ace, darling. This is the first time meeting the chief, meeting your grandpa. Maybe Artemis should stay here," Elu suggested.

"Now, why the fuck would I let my husband walk into a situation like that alone?" Artemis drawled from the doorway. "Buzz will be here with Simone in half an hour."

"You called them," Ace stated. Artemis nodded, and her gaze held Elu's. She offered a weak smile.

"That will be fine, we'll go in my car?" Elu said.

"We'll ride Ace's hog," Artemis said, "that way we can leave when we want." Elu's eyes narrowed on Artemis. Artemis held her gaze, and Elu looked away first. An hour later, they were following Elu out to the reservation. They passed through the gate where the guard watched them with guarded eyes and radioed through to someone.

"Something's wrong," Artemis said, glancing around herself, taking everything in and checking for threats.

"Got that same feeling, Killer," Ace said.

"Why trap you? None of this is making sense," Artemis said.

"No idea, but Dad lied to me for over thirty years. Maybe we'll get answers."

"I hope so, hubby, because something is fishy, and you forced me to back off, so we're going in blind,"

Artemis said, frowning. Elu pulled up outside an extensive building that looked like a meeting hall. She exited the car and dashed up the steps to greet a tall man who stooped at the shoulders. The man's eyes rested on Ace and Artemis as they climbed off the bike and sauntered over to him.

"Ace," the man rumbled.

"Yeah," Ace said and held the man's eyes.

"I'm the chief," he said.

"Yup, so I'm told, and family," Ace said, his hand holding onto Artemis.

"More than family boy, what's that?" the chief asked, nodding at Artemis. They both stiffened and glared at the chief.

"This is my wife, the mother of my kids; her name's Artemis," Ace hissed. The chief studied Artemis, who held his gaze without fear.

"Heard you were fertile, and *that*," the chief glanced at Artemis with a sneer, "can be resolved. A divorce can be gained quickly," the chief said, and Ace's mouth dropped open. The chief spread his arms wide to encompass the surrounding landscape.

"What do you think of our reservation, son? It's beautiful and needs a strong chief to manage it. Think you're up to it?" Ace glanced around, but the chief's dismissal of Artemis stung.

"Perhaps you didn't understand, she's my wife and the mother of my two sets of twins," Ace said, and his arms folded across his chest. Artemis held the same stance.

"Boy, I'm your chief, and this marriage wasn't approved, you're my heir, and we ain't having white man's blood in our legacy. A divorce can be arranged discreetly, and then you can marry one of our women." Ace's mouth dropped open. Was this asshole for real? The chief began walking and motioned for Ace to follow him. He and Artemis swapped glances and held their stance.

"Ain't happening," Artemis said.

"Shut your mouth whore, he's my heir and the next chief, he'll do as he's told," the chief spat. The man spun to face them. "Ace is mine, you've no place here in the reservation, nor do your half breeds." Ace hissed in a sharp breath.

"Talk to my dad like that? No wonder he left," Ace drawled and watched anger cross the chief's face. Damn, the fucker hadn't even introduced himself.

"Your dad?" the chief said, looking astounded, and he laughed. "Your dad! Fuck Elu, you didn't tell him?" Ace and Artemis swapped glances.

"No, thought it best it came from you," Elu replied in a bored voice.

"Who do you think I am, boy?" the chief roared.

"My grandfather," Ace said, confused. The chief laughed again.

"I'm your father, boy. Elu was pregnant with you when she fucked Tyee to get a ring on her finger. I wasn't marrying the little whore," the chief laughed. Ace's face turned to stone, and he glanced at Elu. Artemis grasped his arm as she felt shock and pain hit

Ace.

"You're tellin' me Apache, is my what?" Ace broke off bitterly.

"Cousin, thick bastard fell for Elu's shit. Never questioned why you were so healthy at a premature seven months born. That's in the past. What's important now is that I claim you as my great-nephew, and you start learning how to run the reservation," the chief said. Ace's eyes narrowed.

"So you won't claim Ace as your son?" Artemis said, disbelief colouring her tone.

"Hell no, I'll claim him as my great-nephew, plus Tyee's name is on your birth certificate." Ace felt like he'd been punched. The asshole had dropped a massive bombshell in his lap, and all he could say was he wouldn't claim Ace.

"Did *my father* know?" Ace asked, his mind scrabbling for something to cling to. His entire life had been a lie. His dead mother was alive, his father was his cousin, his grandfather was his father.

"Tyee guessed in the end, must have," Elu said, and Ace turned hate-filled eyes on her.

"So tell me why you came back, mother because it wasn't to play happy families. Why did you want to destroy my life?" Ace said, grasping what had been in front of him all along. This was revenge on Elu's part, why he just didn't know.

"Because Apache took you and any leverage I had over the chief. I ended up doing shit jobs and crap because I couldn't get a decent living. Tyee owed me!" Elu cried, and Artemis stared at her in disgust.

"And you, you forced your nephew to marry a whore because you fathered a kid but didn't want the mother? Now you expect me to step up and be your heir? Fuck you and fuck you," Ace said, pointing at the chief and Elu. "Next time I see you, there'll be a bullet waiting with your name on," Ace threatened Elu and turned on his heel.

"Ace, don't be stupid. You got a chance now, a good one, be my heir, divorce that and marry a nice girl from the reservation. We don't want our bloodline spoiled with white man's blood. Get your wife pregnant, fuck, keep her barefoot and pregnant, I don't care. I want my heir, I'll even agree to you keeping the woman as your whore," the chief called. Artemis spun around, disgust on her face.

"You've no idea who I am, do ya? Heard of the bounty hunter Artemis? You thick ignorant bastard, I see you know my name, you think I'd let Ace go? I'd slit his throat first. Stay away from us and our kids," Artemis seethed. Ace revved the bike, and Artemis climbed up behind him. He loudly throttled the bike and flew away from the nightmare behind him.

"Fuck you, Ace, I'm your father," Apache spat. I held onto him tightly, frightened to move.

"Yeah? So you're not the chief's nephew, and I ain't his son, and you weren't tricked into marrying that cunt Elu?" Ace hissed. Pain resounded in his voice, and I winced.

"I held you the minute after you were born, I named you, fed you, bathed you, changed your diaper. I picked you up when you fell, cleaned your cuts and soothed your bruises, I watched over you all your fuckin' life. What am I, Ace?" Apache roared. Ace began pacing as Artemis and I watched. Drake, Texas, and Axel stood by the door, blocking it. Their message was simple, no one was leaving until the truth was out.

"My damn cousin!" Ace spat. Apache let go of my hand and stormed forward, and got in Ace's face.

"Your cousin?" Apache seethed. "Your fuckin' cousin. Son, I raised you. The moment I held you in my arms, you were mine. Loved you with everything I had. Knew you weren't my seed when you were born fuckin' healthy and guessed what had happened. Didn't give a shit then and don't now. Nothin' mattered except protecting you from the shit storm your life could have become. Loved you with everythin' in my soul. And you call me, cousin?" Apache roared. Hurt shone on his face, and my heart broke. Apache had bared his soul to me. I'd held his secret tightly and never said a word. Now Ace was throwing it in his face. Everything Apache had done, was being thrown in the trash.

"How dare you?" I spat, my temper igniting. "Apache loves you; he's always loved you. No one ever treated you as anything else but his son. Apache could have resented you, left you to that murderous bitch, and instead, Apache put himself on the line and raised you as his own. Fuck me, you think sperm matters? A man's actions show who the father is. You going to tell Drake he ain't those kids dad?"

"Shut up, Silvie," Artemis hissed. Hell no.

"And you, Artemis, look at what your mother did to you, look at what your stepfather did to you. You came here, and Fish and Marsha took you in and loved you. None of us treated you different. If Apache isn't Ace's father, then Master Hoshi isn't yours! Akemi's not your brother either! Family is what we make it, and you know that. Apache at least shares blood with Ace, and he raised him with every intent to be the best father ever. Go on, deny that Ace, deny Apache wasn't the best father for you!" I yelled. Apache stepped back towards me and drew me to him. I buried my face in his chest and clung to him.

"Silvie," he murmured.

"And he stayed away from me for twenty years because Apache knew Elu would come running if he had a relationship. He loved me but wouldn't let me be in your life so he could protect you. Even when you were an adult, Apache was so used to denying himself to ensure you were safe, he continued to do so!" I shrieked. Ace looked horrified as Apache's sacrifices hit him straight in the gut.

"Silvie," Apache said again. I raised a tear-filled gaze to him.

"I hate this. Elu only came here because she wanted

to wreck shit. That bitch never wanted Ace, and she tried to kill him five times. How dare they take Elu's side over yours when they don't know the truth," I cried.

"Darlin', it's okay," Axel said, rubbing my back. Drake looked at Ace with hard eyes.

"You need to wake the fuck up, brother. Fuck me, both of you bought into Elu's shit without even considering Apache's side. Without even asking questions, you bought her lies and walked out on us. Any other brother and you'd be gone Ace, it's only thanks to Apache you're still here."

"Who tried to kill me five times?" Ace said, looking shellshocked. Apache turned a dark gaze on him.

"Now, you want the truth? After fuckin' me over for three weeks, now you ask questions?" Apache said. "Screw this, Drake, I'm leavin', need time, brother."

"Take what ya need," Drake said, his arms folded and his gaze implacable.

"Dad, wait!" Ace yelled, "tell me what is going on, please." Everyone stopped dead and slowly turned to look at Ace. Please had never once left his lips the entire time I knew him. Please was a word that didn't exist in Ace's vocabulary. Today it did. I felt the word strike Apache hard, and slowly my man turned back.

"I'm your dad Ace, it's all I've ever been."

"Please explain," Ace said, sounding very much like a lost little boy. Drake and Apache swapped glances, and Apache dragged out a chair. The weight of the world hit his shoulders as he nodded for Ace to sit. Hesitantly Apache began explaining the story he'd told me. Ace and Artemis both looked horrified and gobsmacked as Drake, Axel, and Texas bolstered his story. Drake told how Arrow had found Ace that last time and Axel explained the circumstances that had arisen.

Ace sat quietly through the story, Artemis sat at his side, paler than I'd ever seen her. Neither one of them spoke or asked questions, and when Apache threw the envelope containing proof of what he was saying, Ace pushed it to one side.

"Don't need it, know the truth when I hear it," Ace muttered. He ran a hand over his eyes, and his aggression faded and disappeared.

"Well, you think I'm a fuckin' liar," Apache said.

"You lied about being my dad and my mom being alive. So no one could blame me for that. But you're right, you're my dad. That shit ain't gonna change, but this… far too much to understand."

"I never lied about being your dad. That's your take on it. The moment I held you in my arms, I was your dad and never believed any different. Am I your sperm donor? No, but am I your dad? Fuck yes," Apache said firmly.

"Why would that cunt do this now?" Ace asked.

"Because the chief wants an heir, he hasn't got one. Apache won't go back; I reckon the chief thought Apache would come crawling back, and instead, Apache made a life for himself. Which kept Ace from him, remember what he said?" Artemis said, sitting forward. "Asshole had heard you were fertile." Ace nodded.

"Yeah, he didn't want the kids or you, Artemis. Being white meant the kids were tainted. God, what a racist bastard." Ace nodded.

"Ain't changed much over the years," Apache drawled.

"Man's got hate in him," Artemis said and met Apache's eyes before dropping them. Yeah, I seethed, you won't meet Apache's eyes, ashamed of your actions. I was furious at them both, but fury wouldn't heal the wound between them. Axel stepped forward.

"Ghosted us, Ace, all of us. That's raised issues, we gonna sit down in church about that," Axel said. Texas nodded. Artemis opened her mouth and shut it again. She couldn't interfere in this; it was brother business.

"Fair enough," Ace said, but he wasn't concerned. His gaze kept drifting to Apache and then back to his hands. "Fucked up," Ace finally muttered.

"Big-time," Texas said harshly.

"Even Axel checked in when he went walkabout," Drake pointed out.

"Was shock ya know, shock of seeing her alive and standing in front of me. Didn't understand. If I'd thought, I'd have realised you kept us apart for a reason, but I kept thinking, that's my mom. But she ain't, is she? My mom died when I was born," Ace spoke softly.

"Yeah, ain't no mother that can do that to her son Ace," Apache said.

"Fuck Dad, I'm sorry," Ace said, rising to his feet and grabbing Apache in a one-armed hug. Apache didn't hesitate but wrapped Ace in his arms. Tears welled in my eyes as I watched the scene. Ace had been broken a long time ago, and we'd watched as he healed when Artemis came back into his life. But there was still that broken part of him that needed fixing and Elu, and that creep of a chief had nudged it wide open.

For twenty years until he lost Kayleigh, Ace had only known love and acceptance. Losing her had destroyed him, and only recently since Artemis, had we seen glimpses of the old Ace. The Ace who laughed, loved, and teased. A few days ago, I'd pinned Apache down and made sure there were no other skeletons in the closet, and he assured me there wasn't. Ace and Apache had to find their way through this latest disaster. I believed they could as long as Artemis let them, she'd slit Apache's throat without a second thought if she believed he'd harm Ace.

"Had to keep you safe, you're my son," Apache said. Ace nodded, and I wiped tears from my eyes.

"Yeah, always," Ace said, and I smiled tremulously at Apache, who caught my eyes. Ace slapped Apache on the back and stepped back.

"Don't want nothin' no contact with Elu, the chief, or the rest of the family if they take sides," Ace said after a few moments.

"Can't blame ya," Apache said ruefully, and Ace chuckled. Artemis popped up at his elbow, and Apache gazed at her.

"Sorry, but not?" Artemis said, twisting her mouth.

"Oh yeah?" Drake answered.

"My role is to stand at Ace's side, I did just that, and none of you can blame me!" Artemis fired back. Drake raised an eyebrow and then glanced at me.

"Artemis acted she did because of Ace. But she's got to have to face the old ladies, bitch ghosted us too," I grinned, and Artemis winced.

"Ouch," she muttered.

"Yeah, Marsha and Phoe are truly pissed. Now you're warned. There was no excuse Artemis and taking your man's back isn't one. That's expected, but what's not expected is running from your support when we weren't judging or ghosting you," I said. Her eyes narrowed on me, and she opened her mouth.

"Pot calling kettle black, Silvie," she muttered.

"Nope, Lindsey knew where I was, and I stayed in contact with Gunner. And it's not as if I didn't take calls, I just told you to leave me alone," I replied.

"Plus, Davies was on her," Drake drawled. Startled, I shot him a wary glance.

"What?"

"Silvie, Phoe would have torn the country apart if she didn't know you were safe. He checked in every so often, and we knew you were safe. Which made shit easier for Phoe, ain't apologising for that. Davies has a grudge; he says you were boring until New Orleans." I sighed; no, Drake wouldn't apologise for that. These men were such contradictions, they didn't involve themselves in a woman's business, but they tracked her down to ensure she was safe. For all my years with Rage, I'll never work them out.

"Drake, I'm not surprised," I said, and Drake relaxed at the wry look I offered.

"Is shit settled now?" Texas asked, and nods abounded.

"Thank fuck, my grandkids out there, and I'm teaching Hawk to blow bubbles," Axel boomed and stomped out, heading straight for Marsha.

"Bubbles?" Apache murmured, and I shook my head.

"Don't ask," I said. The next moment I was dragged into a solid pair of arms and Ace buried his face in my hair.

"What I said outside was fucked up, and I was wrong," Ace muttered, and I stiffened. Wow, shocks kept coming. Ace was apologising.

"Yup, but I love you, and not because of who your father is. Do it again, and I'll get Apache or Gunner to kick your ass," I teased, and Ace chuckled. Damn, that was a pleasant sound.

It'd have been nice to believe that was the end of the incident, but no, the chief wanted Ace. One of

Apache's cousins arrived with a demand for Ace to return to the reservation. Sunny, Apache called him, was a dour, stern-faced man who surprised us at home. He told Apache that the chief demanded Ace's attendance. Apache roared with laughter, slapped the idiot on the back and wished him luck.

Ace and Artemis had returned to her compound, where members of the Juno Group lived. None of us knew where that was. I thought it was crazy they had two homes, but Artemis explained, the compound was wired for an attack, couldn't risk Rage kids triggering a defence. Their kids knew where to walk and where not to and understood the compound's defences. Apache had been drawing up plans to extend their small second home now Nashoba and Nokomis were here.

Sunny demanded Ace's address, and Apache slammed the door in his face. Needless to say, Sunny never tracked down where Ace and Artemis lived, and he wasn't brave enough to reach Ace at Rage. Apache made it plain to Sunny that Apache and Ace didn't exist as far as his family were concerned, and neither wanted to be the next chief. Whether Sunny believed that, I didn't care, I just needed to move forward with life.

Weeks had passed since Apache chased me home from the hospital, and we'd had teething problems, but nothing major. My casts had also come off, and I was free at last from restrictions! For once, I'd hope about the future, and Apache spoiled me rotten.

Apache literally sidestepped me several times, such as when we girls went shopping, and I only bought a few things. Apache slipped Phoe his card behind my back. Phoe bought whatever I'd gazed at longingly and just dumped it on me when we got back to the clubhouse. I quit arguing in the end. Apache clearly needed to do this despite I believed he was trying to make up for the years he'd ignored me.

The argument concerning bills was epic. Apache came from the train of thought, that as the male, he paid the bills. I came from the point of view we were a partnership, and we shared them. There was no mortgage to pay, so it was a simple matter of splitting the bills. Finally, I ended up with groceries and Apache everything else. I felt it was one-sided, but I'd made a stand, and that was enough. Until Apache came home with bags of meat, he claimed he'd got cheap, and I gave up and just accepted his aid. So the groceries ended up being split between the two of us.

But I got my way in adding the woman's touch to his house, cushions and scatter rugs had appeared. Small ornaments, vases and candlesticks appeared, and a lovely fruit bowl I'd discovered when out with Sin. Apache said nothing, but his eyes noted everything I'd added with approval. I'd fallen in love with Apache's picture of the bike in the bedroom and bought him two more matching prints. The startled look on his face made me realise he wasn't used to receiving presents from women. He was overjoyed with my gift, which made me feel good.

It was on Sunday I woke up and realised I was four days late. I'd not had any symptoms of pregnancy, but I was definitely late. Apache was sleeping when the thought hit me like a bolt of lightning, and I sat up and gasped.

"Baby?" Apache asked, rolling over and staring at me.

"I'm late," I gasped. Apache frowned and rubbed his sleepy eyes.

"What the fuck you on about? It's Sunday, lie back down," Apache rumbled, glancing at the clock.

"I'm late, Apache," I stressed and waited for Apache to catch up with me. Slow realisation emerged on his face.

"As in late?" he asked, and I nodded. Apache leapt up and began dragging clothes on as I watched, bemused. What was he doing?

"Apache?" I asked. He turned to me and pointed.

"You're late? We need a test," Apache said and left the room as I laughed uncontrollably. I heard his hog roar, and then it faded as Apache sped away. Guessing we were up, I hopped out of bed, took a shower and walked downstairs to make breakfast. Thirty minutes later, Apache walked back in, holding a pharmacist bag with four pregnancy tests inside.

"Overkill?" I asked, passing him a plate. Apache gazed at the plate, then me, and held out the bag.

"Eat, I'll go pee!" I said, and Apache grunted and followed me to the bathroom. "Apache, you're not watching me pee. Now go eat," I said firmly, and

Apache grumbled and walked away. Sheesh.

Five minutes later, I stared at the stick ecstatic, a dark pink double line showed, and I was pregnant. Well, that was quick, was all I could think, happy and excited. I exited the bathroom and walked into the kitchen. Apache had polished off his breakfast and was leaning on the worktop. His eyes stared out the window, seeing nothing, and he turned at the sound of my footsteps.

"Positive," I said, and Apache froze. A complex mix of emotions crossed his face, fear, happiness, delight, greed, and Apache strode forward and swept me into his arms.

"A baby?" he rumbled.

"Possibly twins, knowing what Ace has been spawning," I grinned. Apache paled and then hooted.

"Twins wouldn't be so bad," Apache said.

"No? Wait till you got two of them running around, and you need to change their diapers," I teased.

"Don't give a fuck, one, two, even three, we're having a kid," Apache roared and lifted me off my feet and kissed me soundly.

"A baby Apache, a baby, a mini-you," I cried when he released me. I was so happy; everything was coming true.

"A mini you, I've got a son. A daughter would be nice," Apache said. "Ace will be a great big brother."

"Brother?" Ace's voice boomed from the doorway as he twisted his head between us. I turned to face him, and Apache pulled me back against his chest and laid a possessive hand on my stomach.

"Silvie's pregnant, you're gonna be a big brother," Apache grinned. Ace's face stilled, and I felt a dash of apprehension. Fuck, could Ace take this as rejection? Before the thought could solidify, Ace grinned.

"Holy shit Dad, about time I got a sibling, but it's a bit backwards that my kids will be older than their Aunt or Uncle," Ace grinned. Artemis shoved forward and glanced at us.

"You're pregnant?" she asked, shocked.

"Yup," I said, and Apache's hand clenched on my stomach.

"Damn, who's taking bets on twins?" Artemis grinned. "Congratulations, you two."

"Yeah, Dad grats, Nova, Falcon, get your asses here, Grandpa's gonna be a dad again," Ace hollered, and the twins appeared carrying the babies.

"Say what?" Falcon asked, his nose wrinkling.

"Silvie's pregnant," Apache said, and Nova made an 'ew' noise.

"That's gross, you're old Grandpa," Nova said, and I laughed.

"Not so old," I teased, and everyone apart from Apache made a gagging noise.

"Seriously, Dad, I'm happy for you," Ace said and gathered the two of us in his arms. He hugged us tightly, and Artemis shoved her way in, followed by Nova and Falcon holding the babies. This is what life was, happiness.

Chapter Nine.

The day after Ace came to visit and give Apache his blessings, I woke up screaming. Maybe because I'd been so distracted with what was happening to Apache that my own problems had been pushed aside. That lapse of concentration finally allowed them to surface and what I remembered wasn't pleasant. Apache came running into the room, he'd risen before me and grabbed hold of me with one arm. The other held a gun extended as Apache's alert eyes searched for an intruder.

"Apache, I remember, I remember," I gasped, wiping tears from my eyes. Apache relaxed, lowering his weapon as he held me as I shuddered.

"What do you remember?" Apache asked. He gently wiped the tears from my cheeks with his thumb pads.

"I was heading to the ladies with Lina when I

overheard Drake's name being mentioned. Lina didn't overhear it, and a guy distracted her. Five men were standing discussing Rage and how to get ears there. They wanted to send a woman in, and one said that'd be impossible. Rage didn't discuss business in front of pussy." Sharply, I drew in a breath as I remembered.

"I vaguely recognised the guy who said that, so I hid and listened carefully, gathering information. A second man, one they called Pinhead, said his gang will take care of Rage, that Rage owed them for something. Pinhead mentioned a gang called the Dark Souls of Lucifer; not one I was familiar with."

"Say that again, baby," Apache asked.

"Dark Souls of Lucifer," I repeated. Apache shook his head.

"Don't know them."

"The men were talking about drug running and arms shipments when Drake's name was mentioned. They wanted a straight run through Rapid City, and the first man said it'd never happen while Drake ran Rage. Pinhead said Drake could be taken care of, and the first man grunted, and I knew him Apache. I couldn't see his face, but I knew him."

"Okay, baby," Apache stroked my back soothingly.

"I was too scared to peek around the pillar, so I kept listening. The gang was planning to start a war between our allies and Rage, and the man said that might work, but Hellfire would never break from Rage. Pinhead laughed and asked what would happen if something happened to Phoenix, and Rage was blamed? Hellfire will ride against Rage, and the clubs would kill each other." Apache leapt to his feet and yanked his phone from his pocket. I guessed he was calling Drake.

"Put Phoe on lockdown now, Silvie's remembered, and Phoe's a target," Apache snapped as soon as Drake answered. Drake rumbled something and hung up, and Apache turned back to me. "Carry on, baby."

"I nearly jumped out when I heard they wanted to harm Phoe, but I kept calm. Obviously, I had to get as much information as possible. Then Pinhead said Santos was paying good money for Dark Souls of Lucifer to destroy Rage, and Pinhead wanted Drake's head. Pinhead said Drake fucked shit up for him before, and this time he wanted revenge.

I stayed quiet and kept listening, but after the mention of revenge on Drake, the guy I recognised chuckled. He questioned how they were so arrogant, they believed they could take down Rage when they weren't organised and didn't own a base. He said if they wanted to get serious, then they needed a base and structure. Pinhead lost his temper, and the guy shoved Pinhead back against the wall and said shit in his face, and Pinhead listened.

The man said they were running shit out of someone's home, but Rage and Hawthorne's could easily track them. Pinhead agreed the gang needed to get off-grid, and someone suggested the Black Hills. The man I knew shook his head and said it'd be an obvious area to search, and another guy spoke. Ice Dawg, Pinhead called him, said he'd the perfect place. Ice Dawg said Taxman had seen it, and a guy I assume was Taxman nodded. Taxman told Pinhead to listen to Ice Dawg and then began talking about other stuff.

Quietly, I moved away when Taxman turned and saw me. Apache, he caught sight of me at the same time as Pinhead. So, I pretended I was coming back from the bathroom and smiled and met up with the girls. Apache, I was scared, I gave it half an hour and left, I started running, and I heard bikes and a truck behind me and knew they were following. Someone had figured me to be Rage, and Pinhead caught and threw me in front of the car." I stopped the words tumbling from falling from my lips as, with dawning horror, I saw the face in the passenger seat.

"Silvie," Apache said, rubbing my icy hands as I started shaking.

"Ghost, the man I knew was Ghost," I whispered, and Apache sat up straight. Green eyes stared in disbelief.

"Ghost has been dead years, Silvie," Apache murmured. Yeah, I knew that, but I knew what I'd seen.

"Ghost is alive. He was in the truck when it hit me. Ghost looked horrified. Apache, I don't think he realised it was me they were chasing. Ghost is working for the bad guys," I said and tried to crawl into Apache's big body.

"Ghost is dead. Axel and Texas saw his body. Or what was left of it after Bulldog had finished," Apache soothed.

"Like Kayleigh was dead?" Angrily, I spat, and Apache froze. Yup, I'd made my point.

"Fuck," Apache said and held me against his body. "That make's sense how Crow's body turned up. Ghost knows where the bodies are, he was the last to fall to Bulldog. Brother was the reason… Bulldog died hard." That hadn't been what Apache was going to say; I listened and kept my mouth shut. Ace had tortured Bulldog to death alongside Apache and the others. Yeah, I knew how Bulldog had died, hearing things over the years, and I'd been glad he suffered.

Bulldog deserved the death he got; he'd tried to stab Drake in the back, had stabbed Ace instead. Manny was shot on Rage land, Bulldog had taken out Fury, the only other founder and then Ghost. Ghost had been second-gen, like Texas and Apache, he'd been a good guy. So Ghost taking up with a gun-running gang made little sense, and trying to kill me would have gone against the grain.

"Don't make sense. Ghost sided with us. If he was alive, why the fuck didn't he come home? Ghost had no problems with us, and the brother had a shitload of problems with Bulldog and his crew. Ghost helped take Bulldog's lot down, so why hide?" Apache shook his head. I didn't have the answers to that question, but I was puzzled.

"How sure are you?" Apache asked.

"One hundred and ten percent. Ghost had that white hair and those dark eyes that saw into your soul. There was a scar on Ghost's cheek that was carved with a knife. Didn't Bulldog brag he'd cut Ghost's face up?" I asked. Apache drew back startled, and gazed at me.

"How'd you hear that?" Apache asked.

"Honey, you guys never pay attention to me. Fuck Apache, I could take Rage down if I wanted. I know most of your skeletons. Even your kills Apache, I know way too much," I said and waited for Apache's reaction.

"Silvie, you've never hinted or judged?" Apache asked. I shrugged.

"The bodies in the ground are ones that escaped justice, evil men with crappy motives and bad attitudes. Bulldog would never have left Rage peacefully, and the rampaging, immoral others? One stabbed Ace, one shot Manny, four shot at Ace. Jacked, Gid, and Misty tortured Artemis. They deserve to be there, and I don't got a place in judging none of you. Rage has protected me, the old ladies and other innocents. So fuck informing on any of you, I'd die before I ever revealed your secrets," I said adamantly.

"Jesus Silvie, none of us ever guessed," Apache drawled.

"Apache, you weren't meant to!" I said with a smile.

"Silvie, how much do you know?" Apache asked curiously. Tongue in cheek and raising my eyebrows,

I bit the inside of my cheek and glanced up at him.

"As much as Marsha," I grinned, and his eyes widened. Apache guessed Marsha knew a shitload.

"Damn!" Apache chuckled at my admission. Warmth and approval flooded his eyes and spread across his face.

"Apache, we've never interfered because it was the brother's business, not ours. Ours was to support you, which we did. Small things to make your lives easier, especially at the beginning. Marsha and I made sure there was takeout, drink, smokes, cannabis for those who smoked it. We ensured the skanks that came were good skanks and not Bulldog's skanks. When one of you was in a slump, we were there to perk you back up," I explained, and Apache's eyes widened.

"Fuck, none of us guessed," he said.

"Because you weren't meant to guess. Between Marsha and I, we've both sat with every brother during a shit spell. Just making sure you knew you were loved and cherished and needed. Once we got that into your thick skulls, you came out of the doldrums. Marsha was the first one to suggest the cookouts, something Bulldog had stopped, and I suggested we spend either Friday, Saturday, or Sunday at the bar.

When you needed clothes washing, or fresh bedsheets, who do you think did it? And come on, how many times have Drake and Texas lost their tools in the clubhouse? It was us that found your missing shit and put it where you could find it.

Marsha and I reached out to Tati, Hellfire's old lady, reached out to the other old ladies from allied clubs. If the women bonded, we could smooth over egos and shit. When Rage reached out to Hawthorne, we made friends with his receptionist and females. When Ramirez arrived, we made him welcome and safe. And I suppose I could say I'm close to James Washington, probably the closest after Gunner and Autumn.

Marsha and I took the prospects under our wing as much as we did the brothers. Made sure they had clothes, smokes, booze, found out their favourite shit and got it stocked. Provided silent support for each of you, and we dealt with the old ladies that Bulldogs gang had." Ouch, I'd said too much as Apache sorted through the information.

"Dealt with?" Apache latched onto that first. Yup, said too much.

"Yes, Marsha and I have secrets too."

"Silvie, are you tellin' me your hands spilt blood?" Apache asked, stunned. Not wanting to lie, I bit my lip, a tell of mine, when I didn't want to answer, and Apache's eyes blazed. "Silvie!" Apache roared.

"Look, I don't ask about your bodies, you don't ask about the old ladies," I said and poked him in the chest. Apache's eyes grew wide as he struggled to comprehend I'd spilt blood. I'd done it twice, and Marsha three times. Not something we were proud of. But when a bitch tries to poison, shoot, stab or bash the brains in of a brother, the old ladies stepped up and dealt with that shit. Marsha had shot two in pure self-defence, they'd jumped her, and lost. I'd shot one in self-defence. The brothers weren't the only ones with bodies in unmarked graves.

"Baby, that's so fuckin' hot!" Apache burst out, and I began laughing.

"Hot because I put a body in the ground?"

"No, because you took our backs and never once claimed recognition for it. Now I understand why Lindsey and the women were so pissed."

"Next time you want to be an asshole, think twice. Marsha has mad knife skills, and so does Penny. She's a cook!" I chuckled and then turned serious. "That's why I am certain I saw Ghost. I sat with him Apache, he may be older, but I couldn't mistake the man." Apache slowly nodded. We both looked up as doors slammed and Drake and Chance, Hellfire's President and Drake's cousin, stormed into our home. Um, I guess Chance had been visiting when Apache called Drake.

"Talk!" Drake demanded, pointing a finger as he barged into our bedroom. Both men wore snarls on their faces, and I didn't bother complaining I was only covered in a sheet. I wrapped it tightly around me and began talking.

"Tell Drake, we've a Mexican ghost. Silvie meant Mexican as in Santos and a ghost as in Ghost," Drake said, staring around the sanctum. Now they had names they'd called a meeting, and the Presidents, VP's and enforcers from the other clubs were crowded into Rage's sanctum. Apache was outside explaining it to everyone else. Old ladies had gone to the Reading Nook, the children to HQ. Phoe had made sure the daycare at her HQ could cope with the influx of children. No one wanted a multitude of kids racing around the Reading Nook. Sin would have a breakdown.

"Silvie made some names, Pinhead, Taxman, Ice Dawg, they run a gang called Dark Souls of Lucifer," Ace said. Lance, the President of the Fallen Warriors, sat forward.

"Dark Souls of Lucifer is a gang that was run out of Arizona. Vague rumours, they were run out by the feds, scattered across states, guess they reformed here," Lance mused.

"Not heard of their names," Inglorious, President of Unwanted Bastards, said.

"I've heard of Ice Dawg, man's a punk, came out of nowhere with attitude and violence. Dunno where he hangs out," Scythe, President of The Devil's Scythe, said.

"And they're running with Santos. Ain't he got his own men?" Jailbait asked, President of Devil's Damned Disciples.

"From what we understand, Dark Souls of Lucifer specialise in murder, mayhem and lawlessness. Assholes took over a small town and terrorised it, and shot anyone in their way. Three DEA agents and two feds went down to them. ATF got someone inside, and they carved the man up in pieces and sent them to the agencies involved in bringing them in," Bat said, Fallen Warriors VP.

"Fuck, they're lunatics," Chance broke in, looking pissed.

"Ain't we all?" Tiger, the President of Satan's Warriors, said.

"Not on this scale, they were linked to cartels, which explains the drugs and arms coming through South Dakota. Dark Souls of Lucifer were fuckin' psychotic," Lance said.

"Took a team of… people to take them out. Guess they missed some," Bat elaborated.

"Seals?" Drake asked, knowing Lance had been a seal. Lance gazed steadily at him and refused to comment. Fuck me, Drake thought. If the feds had brought seals in to deal with Dark Souls of Lucifer, they were beyond lunatics. Never had Drake heard of the US army involving itself in home affairs, it was unheard of.

"And now they're at war with us?" Jailbait grinned.

"Think they know we're linked?" Tiger asked.

"Who the fuck cares? Dark Souls of Lucifer come for us, they come for all of us. We'll take them out in a rain of bullets!" Crunch spat, the VP of Satan's Warriors.

"Agreed," Drake nodded.

"Made a pact, ain't backing out now, no fuckin' punk is taking my town," Psych snarled, VP of

Unwanted Bastards.

"Your woman, she okay?" Lance asked, and Drake jerked his head back.

"Phoe's fine but got a target on her back, one we didn't know existed. Upped her security and the kids again, ain't our first rodeo," Drake replied.

"And your other woman?" Inglorious asked. Drake frowned. What other woman?

"The girl who overheard this shit," Bat asked.

"Silvie, yeah, she's fine, healed and with Apache. No fucker's gettin' through him, Apache's waited too long to claim her. Won't lose Silvie now," Drake grinned.

"'Bout fuckin' time," Chance murmured, and grins broke out.

"Let's get planning," Scythe said, tapping the table.

"Yeah," Drake growled. Lunatic's or not, Dark Souls of Satan were not getting a foothold in this part of South Dakota. Drake looked up as the last members of their party arrived. Hawthorne and Washington walked in together. Ramirez behind them. All the major players were here, he thought as Artemis and Akemi walked in together. Now they could start planning payback for what those cunts had done to a kind woman, a Rage woman.

Tiredly, I sat curled up in bed with a book and a lamp on, waiting for Apache to get back from the meeting. Downstairs, Klutz was guarding me inside, and Slick was outside the house. The other old ladies were being protected by the brothers and Juno group. There were two guards on each old lady, and Phoe obviously used the security team at Reading Hall. I was worried about Apache. If he followed the route of everyone else whose woman had been in danger, bloodshed would follow.

No sooner had the thought surfaced, gunshots sounded from outside, and I ducked, confused at first. Frightened, I jumped out of bed, grateful I was wearing pyjamas as Klutz belted into the bedroom. Klutz had a gun drawn and raised it in my direction. I froze half in bed, half out, and gazed wide-eyed.

"Silvie get down," Klutz shouted as he ran to the window. A flash of amber streaked across the ground outside as a gunshot echoed.

"Slick's out there!" I shrieked.

"Get the fuck down, Silvie!" Klutz roared. I did as I was told, grabbing my cell phone and dialling Apache.

"Apache, we're under attack!" I yelled as Klutz fired from my window.

"On our way," Apache replied, and my phone went dead. The front door slammed open and then closed.

"Klutz," Slick roared.

"Upstairs with Silvie," Klutz yelled back. I reached out again and pulled a gun from the bedside table. Apache always kept one there.

"Klutz, I'm hit, you gotta protect Silvie. Get her out

of here," Slick called back, and his voice sounded weak.

"Ain't leaving a brother," Klutz yelled back.

"Priority is Silvie. They want her dead because she can identify them. Do as you're told and get Silvie safe, I'll cover your backs," Slick yelled, and I crawled to the bedroom door. Gunshots hammered against the walls as Slick shot back. Leaping to my feet, I spun around and faced Klutz.

"Honey, you save Slick," I hissed and streaked out the bedroom and down the stairs. Slick made a mad grab for me as I flew past, but I was running too fast. Unerringly, I headed towards the kitchen exit and flew out into the darkness. Shots echoed again, and I choked back a frightened sob. I had to draw their fire from Slick and Klutz. Crazed with fear, I ran into the trees, and someone shouted. Loud footsteps pounded behind me, and I cursed as I realised the ground was shredding my slippers.

"Bitch ran this way," a voice shouted that I recognised as Pinhead. I fired blindly behind me, and he yelped. Terrified, I almost ran into a tree that loomed at me from the darkness as shots were fired in return. I screamed and ducked as something loomed out of the darkness, and I shot twice. There was a grunt, and a figure fell to the ground, and men crashed through the bushes towards me.

Heavily breathing, I ran again, ducking low-lying tree branches and changing direction wildly. In the dark, I'd no idea where I was, couldn't find my way back to the house if I tried. I crouched behind a tree and greedily sucked in air. Desperately, I controlled my breathing as I listened for sounds of pursuit. Minutes slowly ticked by as I held my breath, afraid of someone finding me. I could hear them in the distance searching for me, not caring how much noise they were making. It sounded like they were moving away from me, and I rose to my feet and began quietly sneaking away.

A hand slammed across my mouth and a steel band wrapped around my chest. I began struggling and shrieked in terror. I lifted my foot and kicked backwards as hard as I could, and a grunt echoed.

"Silvie, stop it's me, Tonio!" The figure holding me hissed. I slumped in his arms as he said my name. Ramirez had found me. "Hawthorne and Ben are out here, are you armed?"

"Yes," I whispered.

"Honey, don't fuckin' shoot unless you know it's not them," Ramirez hissed in my ear.

"Slick was shot," I gasped quietly.

"Davies stayed with him," Ramirez said, moving me silently backwards and away from the crashing noises.

"How did you get here so fast?" I whispered as Tonio took my hand and began leading me away.

"The fuckin' idiot rode past Ben and me. We followed," Ramirez said, and I snorted in disbelief. No way had those idiots done that! Damn fools.

"Hawthorne was behind me and gave chase too.

Drake and Apache are on their way with the others," Ramirez said and grunted. A scream left my throat as Tonio stared at me in the moonlight as blood dripped down his head, and then he collapsed. In front of me was Pinhead, who raised a gun at me, and without a second thought, I aimed and fired. Pinhead's gun spat, and I flinched, waiting for pain to overwhelm me. Pinhead blinked at me and crumpled next to Ramirez.

I didn't wait to find out where I'd shot him but took off running. Men came towards me, yelling and shouting, and I was in full view of them. A thicket appeared up ahead, and I ran towards it. I just made it when a dark figure leapt at me and took me to the ground. I began lashing out, punching and kicking and biting while the figure on top struggled to contain me. Finally, after I aimed a vicious headbutt at him, the man wrapped himself around me.

"Stay fuckin' still, woman," Ghost hissed, and my body stiffened. I'd been right.

"Traitor," I spat.

"Shut the fuck up, Silvie, if you don't want them to find you," Ghost whispered in my ear. Huh?

"What the fuck are you doing, Ghost?" I whispered. He rolled us noiselessly into the thicket.

"Shut it, woman," Ghost said as a man appeared before us. Ghost pulled a gun from his waist and shot the man straight between the eyes. He fell backwards with a thud, and Ghost pulled me to my feet and began dragging me behind him. His gun arm swept the trees, looking for people or attackers.

"Freeze, asshole!" Ramirez roared and fired a warning shot. While he was weaving slightly on his feet, his aim was steady. Ghost held me in front of him and captured Ramirez's gaze. Silently without warning, he lifted my arm, holding my gun and fired. Ramirez moved to fire back as I screamed.

"Behind you!" Ramirez glanced back at the hulking figure that had been creeping up behind him as it slumped to the ground. His surprised gaze flew back to Ghost.

"What the fuck?" he asked. Ghost bent his head to my ear.

"I didn't know they were after you. I'd never have let it happen. Shit ain't what you think, Silvie, tell Drake," Ghost muttered. Without another word, Ghost shoved me at Ramirez, whose arms shot out to catch me. When we both looked up, Ghost had disappeared, and we were alone with a body at our feet.

"He shot his own man to save me?" Ramirez asked, sounding puzzled. He wasn't the only one. What had Ghost meant?

"Silvie!" Apache roared, and behind him, Ace and Drake yelled my name.

"We're here! Antonio's injured," I yelled. Apache appeared in the distance, long legs running towards me. Ace and Drake were at his back. Behind them, to my shock, was Inglorious and Lance. Apache ran up and swept me into his arms. He held me tightly and then let go and patted me down for injuries. Finding none, Apache relaxed and snatched me back up into his arms. I began crying, everything was so confusing, and people had got hurt. Tonio was hurt, and Slick had been shot!

"Slick?" I sobbed as Drake crowded me.

"Silvie hurt?" Drake demanded, and Apache grunted no.

"Slick was shot!" I wailed, and Apache squeezed me tighter as I tried to burrow into his hard body.

"Slick's okay, ambo is on its way," Ben said, appearing behind the others. "We got fucking bodies everywhere."

"Tonio's hurt. Pinhead knocked him out," I cried.

"Lean on me, brother," Drake said, and Ramirez sent him a dirty look.

"Can walk out on my own," Ramirez said and stumbled.

"Sure you can," Ace chuckled, but there was no amusement in it. He slung Ramirez's arm over his shoulder and began marching the cop in the house's direction. Well, I hoped that was the right direction, too hard to see in the dark. I tried walking and cried out in pain as the reality of running through the woods in slippers hit me. My feet had been shredded, and it hurt to walk. Apache bent and swept me into his arms. I clutched his tee and buried my head in his throat as he began following everyone.

"I shot Pinhead," I whispered, and Apache squeezed me.

"Self-defence," Ben replied. "Don't utter a single word to law enforcement until a lawyer's present though Silvie."

"Okay," I whispered, surprised at what Ben had said. It was pretty clear he wasn't a fan of Rage.

We stumbled out of the woods and found the front of the house lit up with lights. Cop cars were parked haphazardly, and bikes were everywhere I looked. Several ambulances were present, their lights helping the cop cars light up the front of the house. Men were everywhere I looked, some coming from the trees, dragging prisoners, others milling in the yard. Rage surrounded the house, and I struggled to get down. Slick had been shot!

"Fuck the stretcher," Slick roared on my thought, and I smiled. At least he was yelling.

"You drop, I ain't picking you up," Axel boomed back. I saw the Presidents, VP's and other members of the biker clubs who'd had their meeting today. Inglorious strode forward, obviously having had enough of Slick's arguing. He swooped in and picked Slick up, to Slick's outrage, and carried him to an ambulance.

"Now get fuckin' treatment," Inglorious yelled.

"Silvie's out there somewhere," Slick yelled back.

"I'm here!" I called, realising Slick was worried. He wouldn't go to the hospital until he saw me. The thought choked me, and I began crying again.

"Stop crying!" Slick yelled.

"Let the paramedics treat you, asshole!" I sobbed.

Apache and Drake swapped amused glances, and Apache carried me over to the ambulance next to Slicks.

"Her feet are torn up from running," he said to a paramedic. The girl nodded and began checking me over. I watched bemused as Ramirez was shoved in next to me, bellowing his own outrage as he tried to direct the circus in our yard.

"Oh shut up, you got your head smashed in, I've got this," a voice said, and I turned to see Ben glowering at him. Ramirez shot his own glare back, and then Hernando Hawthorne appeared. Behind him came Marissa and Dana, Dylan's Hawthorne's sister and secretary, respectively.

"Why are you here?" I asked, bemused.

"I was eating with Nando when the call went out. You think I was leaving one of my girls in trouble?" Marissa said.

"I was at the office when Dylan called in, I came with Davies," Dana said in her quiet voice.

"Oh my God, you guys," I whispered and broke into tears again. The two women crowded me and hugged me tightly. Apache sighed, he was well and truly put upon now. Nando chatted with Ramirez. There were four dead in the woods and three severely injured. Pinhead was one I'd killed, the other man I'd shot was in critical condition, and I honestly didn't care. Klutz was okay, he'd kept the men off of Slick until help arrived.

Apache wanted to yell at him, but Klutz had been

correct. Brothers came first, and while Apache yearned to rip Klutz a new one, he couldn't. No brother would leave another. A prospect or candidate would act similarly. Brothers before everything else. Klutz looked at me guiltily several times, but I waved him off, I was fine. I wasn't even shaken from shooting two people.

"A man was here, he had hold of Silvie, seemed to know her," Ramirez said to Apache, and his gaze snapped to me. I shook my head, and Apache's eyes narrowed, trying to find the truth in me. Not now, my eyes told him, I couldn't mention Ghost in front of Ramirez.

"A big bastard, white hair, tall, heavy build," Ramirez said, glancing between the two of us, and I smoothed out the expression in my face. Apache paused for a moment and then carried on stroking my hair.

"We'll keep an eye out," Apache muttered, his hand tightening on the back of my neck. It was a sign for, we're gonna talk later, and I nodded.

"Ramirez, this ain't all of them, there's eight men here, this gang, there's more than this," Lance said, coming forward.

"Fuck, I hoped we'd taken them in one go," Ramirez said as a paramedic forced him to sit as she examined his head.

"No, there's more than this and the names Silvie offered, they ain't here," Bat said.

"Fuck me," Apache muttered, and with Ramirez's

expression, I guess he thought much the same.

"They going to keep coming after me?" I asked plaintively.

"Nah, we got too many of them here. Even if you didn't give us their names, we got them now, Silvie. You're safe," Nando said, and I smiled at him. We jumped as shots echoed in the trees, and everyone hit the floor. Cops began running to the tree line, keeping low and guns in their hands. Ramirez made to get up, and the paramedic pushed him back hard.

"Detective, you may think I do this for fun, I can assure you I don't. You have a head injury and need at least six stitches. Antonio, you are not running off into the trees to shoot someone," she said firmly, and I giggled.

"You came for me," I whispered, and Ramirez looked startled.

"Of course I did, woman, you're Apache's girl. Even if you weren't, you're Rage," Ramirez said.

"Tonio," I mustered as tears began leaking again. "What is wrong with me? I never cry like this."

"Fuck knows, but I don't like it," Apache said as men emerged, dragging a man behind them.

"That's eight of them dead or arrested," Ben said, approaching.

"They ran to forty in the gang, maybe more, not even got half of them," Bat said.

"Asshole's declared war on Rage, there won't be forty for long," Drake said, and Ben threw him a disgusted look.

"Fucking Rage," Ben said and walked away. Nando grinned and saluted me before also leaving. Drake turned a curious eye to Ramirez.

"Not leaving?"

"Fuck it, the chief made me out to be compromised. He fucked me and Ben over, claiming we were too close, and then he fuckin' brought in outsiders to investigate our case. We'd have done Crow's murder by the book, but the chief didn't trust us, so I owe him shit." Anger bled into Ramirez's voice as he gazed around.

"Tonio," Drake said gently, or gently for Drake. Ramirez turned burning eyes on Drake.

"No cunt calls my integrity into question. No one Drake. Ben and I are considering an offer from Hawthorne, and so is Nando and his partner."

"Shit," Drake rocked back on his heels. I stared in amazement at Ramirez, I'd not seen that coming.

"A cop is who you are," Ace said, stepping forward.

"No Ace, an honest guy is who I am, one who trusts in the law and justice. But also knows it fails sometimes, and bad people get off and carry on wrecking other people's lives. The entire department knows the chief didn't trust us four to investigate, we got to work there. He's been acting fuckin' odd lately. Something's wrong. Ain't a joyous atmosphere at the moment, Drake," Ramirez said. Drake reached out and clasped Ramirez's shoulder. A wordless conversation occurred between them, and Ramirez gripped Drake's hand and let go.

"She's okay, but she needs those feet to heal, so no walking on them. I've cleaned them the best I can," the paramedic addressed Apache. He scooped me into his arms and gave her a nod of thanks, and carried me into the house, which was now full of bikers. They'd left the cops outside to do their job. Apache gave everyone a head tilt and carried me to our room. He placed me gently on the bed and walked into the bathroom, and began running a bath. I was trying to get out of my clothes when he came back and helped me undress. Slowly Apache checked every inch of my body for marks and found several bruises.

"Apache, Ghost saved me," I whispered as he cupped my face. His eyes widened slightly, and he kissed me. I melted into his embrace as he ended the kiss and picked me up, and carried me into the bathroom. Once there, he placed me in the bath and, with gentleness, washed away the dirt I was covered in. Once clean, Apache carried me back to the bed, stripped and climbed in beside me, holding me until I slept.

Chapter Ten.

"Ramirez here?" Ben asked, walking into the clubhouse. I looked up, surprised and frowned.

"No, honey, I haven't seen him since the other night," I replied. Ben rubbed his hand over his face and moved to leave.

"Okay," he replied, and I felt a strange sensation from him.

"Ben, what's wrong?" I asked. He turned back to me.

"I don't get it, can't understand how Ramirez can hang with Rage. They're an MC, and we both are aware, Silvie, there're bodies in the ground that Rage put there. Recent bodies too," Ben said.

"Sit, honey," I said. Ben slumped in a chair, and I saw just how tired he was.

"Tell me why, Silvie?" Ben asked.

"Why cover for them? Why stick to them like glue, give them the benefit of the doubt?" I asked, and Ben nodded.

"Ah honey, you really don't understand who Rage are. Check your crime reports from when Bulldog was in charge. That asshole was behind every crime in Rapid City. If it was dirty, Bulldog had an inside track. But Rage wasn't like that. It started with five men who just wanted to ride bikes, have cookouts and chill. When Arrow died, Bulldog got the vote, and Drake was too young to stand for President."

"I realised that," Ben said.

"Yes, but what you don't understand was Drake had long-term plans, he'd only planned to suck shit for so long. He planned to take his father's club back, and he hated, loathed the illegal shit they were forced to do. If they didn't, Bulldog took it out on Drake's side. Women were beaten in front of them, they got shittier jobs and other punishments.

Drake, Fish, Apache, and Ace began recruiting brothers who wanted a clean club, wanted the ideals on which Rage was founded. Yeah, none of the brothers is clean, but they desperately wanted clean, wanted family and everything that came with it. When Drake organised the takeover, well, the story is legendary in Rapid City, Bulldog came unglued.

Once Drake had Rage, he resolutely weeded out the rot and kept the good. And they started working with the police instead of against them, which Bulldog had done. So, yeah, check crime rates before and after Drake. Rapid City has a shit load of arrests thanks to Rage. The streets around here are clean, no drugs, no pussy, no robberies. People who live in an area where there's a Rage presence, or a brother, understand their area's safe."

"It don't excuse them, Silvie," Ben said.

"Maybe, maybe not, ask me how many brothers have been shot defending someone Rage cares about. Ask me how many people Rage has saved and how many children sleep safely in their beds at night. How about how many criminals are off our streets thanks to Rage?

They're good men with fundamental values, they are hard, life made them that way, but Drake will take a bullet to save Ramirez without even thinking about it. Can you honestly say you'd do the same? Without hesitation, Ben,"

"Probably not, I'd hesitate and then act," Ben admitted.

"Drake wouldn't, he's got so much respect for Ramirez, and he'd even take a bullet for you. Because that's the type of men Rage are, they aren't talk and no action. They believe acts show more than words. It's always been plain where Rage stands with Ramirez, they'd never compromise Ramirez's job or values.

You can keep turning your nose up and reject the hand of friendship they offered you. Or buttercup, you can suck it up and admit they are good men, with the best interests of their home at heart. You admit that, then work alongside them. Yeah, they skirt the line sometimes and possibly cross over it. But when you got someone willing to take a bullet for you, who the fuck cares? Slick got shot the other night, protecting me, you understand how women are treated in MC's, you ever seen Rage treat us like that?"

"No," Ben said, sitting forward, enlightenment in his voice. "See, that's what I was missing, I thought you were treated like other women in MC's. Property and just pussy, but you're not, are you?" Ben sounded as if he'd been beamed in the head.

"No, take Phoe away from Drake, and you'll kill him. Remove Marsha from Fish, and hell will break loose on earth. These men adore their women and treat them as precious treasures. Not one of these women here is mistreated, ignored, or unvalued. Ben look around, Phoe runs three national charities, Sin owns her own store, Lindsey owns her own business, Autumn runs the office, and mechanics take their boots off before entering. Penny's a success in the kitchen. Artemis runs a group rescuing abused women and children. Marsha is the den mother. Do you honestly believe those women will swallow shit the brothers may dish out?

Then look at Drake, he owned the garage and other stuff, he deeded them over to the club so the brothers could share his success. Rock and Apache run a construction company employing hundreds. Gunner owns property and rents it out, Slick runs a leasing company, Ezra owns a landscaping company, these are business owners who employ hundreds of people, Ben. The thing they have in common? They want to ride bikes and be free, want family, loyalty, respect, and love. How is that different from you?" I finished, and Ben gazed at me.

"They can be grey a hell of a lot, Silvie," Ben said, and I nodded. "But you're right, I never saw past the MC bit, which makes me short-sighted."

"Yeah, honey, it did," I agreed, and Ben smiled.

"Ramirez had it out with the chief today, he's walked. I handed in my badge, and so did Nando and Justin. The chief just had his four top detectives walk out in protest. RCPD is in uproar. Chief didn't expect a walkout," Ben said. My mouth dropped open.

"Oh my God, go back! Ben, you and Ramirez can't do this because of Rage!" I exclaimed.

"I did it because of Ramirez, Nando and Justin did it because of Ramirez and me, and Ramirez did it because of Rage," Ben explained.

"We've got his back," Apache said from behind us, and we twisted and saw Apache glowering.

"You have?" Ben said with a touch of bitterness.

"Got yours too," Apache said, and Ben's eyes widened.

"Just have Ramirez's back," Ben said.

"Got all four of ya's," Drake said, appearing. "No matter what, we'll do what ya need. Ain't gonna be good without you four in the department. Four good cops gone and the chief with his head up his ass. Fuck me, I thought chief had got past our history, but shit, it keeps coming back to bite us."

"Yeah," Ben drawled. "Need to search for Ramirez, he was pissed." Ben got to his feet and studied Drake and Apache. "Misjudged you, which is on me, I heard MC and thought the worst. That's my prejudice, not yours." Drake reached out first and clasped Ben's hand, and Apache followed suit.

"Think you better see this," Axel boomed from the doorway. We shot a curious glance at the door and walked outside to the forecourt. About thirty cops milled around the forecourt, chatting with the brothers.

"Chief's out of line, we've got your back," a man said, stepping forward.

"What are you doing?" Ben asked, astounded.

"Walked out with you, the mayor is scrabbling and panicking, expect the chief's getting a call right about now," the man said.

"You got families, go back to work," Ben ordered, his voice scratchy.

"We can get jobs with Hawthorne's, Juno Group, or HQ. Phoenix has already made job offers, and so has Artemis," the guy said, and Ben turned surprised eyes on Drake.

"Told ya, we got your back," Drake shrugged, and Ben swallowed hard.

"But I expect you'll be back in your jobs before nightfall," Apache grinned.

"Screw that, wages Artemis is offering, I'm

tempted," a man called and got some ribbing from his colleagues.

"Fucking Rage," Ben muttered, but this time there was no rancour behind it. I smiled at Apache as I snuck under his arm. This was family!

Silently, I tackled Apache flat on his back, and he grunted as I landed naked on top of him. I grinned at him and held his head in my hands, and kissed him. Apache slid his hand into my hair and kissed me back.

"Silvie," he muttered, "stay off your fuckin' feet."

"Plan to, now fuck me," I ordered, and Apache gave a shout of laughter as my eyes danced merrily at him.

"Nothin' like a demanding woman," Apache grinned and rolled me onto my back.

"I want you inside me now, screw foreplay, I need your cock," I demanded, and Apache laughed again. His cock dug into my stomach, and Apache slid his hand between my legs.

"Damn, you're soaked," Apache muttered.

"Cock now!" I yelped as Apache bit my nipple and slid inside me. His thick length filled and stretched me, and I sighed in happiness as he sank into me balls deep. Oh, thank heaven, I'd needed this all day. Apache's mouth took mine as he slid out and thrust back inside. My legs wrapped around him, and my hips rose to meet him as he set a slow pace. No, no, I wanted hard, rough, fast sex. Apache held me in place as he slowly sank back inside me, and I whimpered, I wanted more, give me more.

"Apache, I love you, but if you don't fuck me hard, I'm going to scream," I threatened as he kept up that slow pace.

"You'll scream anyway," Apache said. His eyes flashed, and he rolled onto his back, taking me with him. Oh, yes, I liked this position very much indeed. I lifted my hips and slammed down hard, and groaned. His cock seemed deeper this way, and I threw my head in sheer pleasure.

"Yes," I cried out as his hands grasped my hips, and he ground against me. I rode him greedily as he met me thrust for thrust, and I felt my orgasm build. Apache's hands slipped from my hips, and one moved to my breast and one between my legs. At the same time, he pinched my nipple hard and flicked my nub, and I fell, screaming into an orgasm. Apache's hands slid back to my hips as he held me in place as he pushed furiously inside me and came himself seconds later. I collapsed happily on his chest, watching Apache strut all day had wound me into a frenzy, and I'd literally needed him right there and then.

"Damn, woman," Apache muttered.

"That was wonderful," I muttered. Apache gave me a disbelieving glance. "No, that was, I just needed you inside me, nothing else but your cock."

"Wow, now I realise how it feels to be viewed as

meat," Apache said dryly. I giggled at his tone.

"Very sexy meat," I said.

"Even better, now I'm very sexy meat," Apache said, and with a roar, rolled me over onto my back and tickled me. I shrieked with laughter as I wriggled to get away from him.

"Okay, I surrender!" I yelled, laughing.

"In that case, I claim your punishment…"

"Your cock inside me again?" I cried as Apache turned disbelieving eyes on me. "Blame my hormones, I need sex with you, and I'm horny all the time. In fact, I think you should just have a pager, and when I get horny, you should screw my brains out. I don't need fancy sex, just a quickie," I said, giggling as Apache's eyebrows disappeared into his hair in surprise.

"Are you fuckin' serious?" Apache asked, and I stretched up, making my breasts jiggle.

"Yup, you're my fuck toy until I need it," I confirmed.

"Will always need you, Silvie," Apache whispered, staring into my eyes.

"I love your cock," I muttered, reaching out a hand to claim it. Apache laughed.

"Just my cock, baby?" he teased.

"It's a fantastic part of you," I grinned, and Apache rolled me on my back.

"Kept you happy enough," Apache muttered as he began sliding his fingers between my folds.

"I love you, Apache," I said.

"Not as much as I love you," he said. My heart melted in pure joy.

We were curled up in the living room with the fire blazing when a knock pounded on the front door. Apache lifted his head and stared at the door, and got to his feet.

"Expectin' anyone?" Apache muttered, and I shook my head. I was in a post laziness glow of glory from our lovemaking, and I deeply resented whoever was interrupting us.

"Ramirez?" Apache said, surprised. Ramirez stepped in and caught sight of the fire, and wine glasses and me curled like a kitten.

"Shit, man, sorry, I'll come back," Ramirez said.

"Sit your ass down!" I told him, and he blinked in surprise.

"Okay," Ramirez put his hands up and then ran one through his hair. I saw where he'd had stitches for the head wound he'd suffered saving me.

"Are you okay?" I asked, motioning to his head.

"This? It's nothing," Ramirez said and sat. Apache walked to the fridge and pulled out two bottles of beer. He offered one to Tonio, who popped it open.

"Where you been? Everyone's been searching for you, man," Apache said, sitting behind me and drawing me tight to him.

"Out thinking, walking, getting my head straight. The chief is out of line, and I couldn't suffocate there anymore."

"What's your plans?" Apache asked, but Apache was wondering why Ramirez was here. They were friends, but it was Drake who called Tonio a brother.

"Ain't sure Apache, just wanted to check on Silvie, she was on my mind, and I bust in here, sorry for that," Ramirez said.

"We were worried, I'm glad your safe," I said, reaching out and touching his knee.

"You seen Ben?" Apache asked, and Ramirez shook his head. Apache grinned. "You don't know?"

"Know what?" Ramirez asked, taking a huge swallow of the beer.

"Ben handed in his notice straight after you, swiftly followed by Nando and Justin. Then half the force walked out in support," Apache enlightened him.

"Huh?" Ramirez said, sitting up, looking startled.

"That's loyalty, dude, real loyalty. The mayor's been up in arms as half the police force quit in an hour, and he lost four detectives. Chief's being hauled over the coals as we speak," Apache nodded.

"They quit because I walked?" Ramirez said, disbelieving.

"Yup, then they ended up on the forecourt to support Ben and you. Reckon you'll be getting a new chief soon, and everyone knows you're the one cop who can cross lines and work with an MC. The one who keeps clean when others might take a bribe. Fuck me, Ramirez, you've been in the papers more times being praised than anyone else. Mayor is shitting a brick you might bring a case against the city," Apache smirked.

"I didn't know," Ramirez said, stunned.

"Next time, try answering your phone, you must have a hundred missed calls," I teased, and Tonio smiled.

"About fifty from loads of people, I switched it off," he admitted.

"Duh!" I replied.

"Call Ben, get your head together. The only asshole who thinks you were compromised was the chief who just had half his force walk out on him. Mayor ain't gonna wanna argue shit when it hits the papers, so he'll want you back and the others," Apache said.

"Jesus, what a mess," Ramirez said.

"What the fuck made you walk out?" Apache asked, and Ramirez held his gaze.

"Two bodies turned up, surprised you don't know," Ramirez said.

"Why would I know?" Apache asked, surprised. A sinking feeling hit my gut.

"Apache, you should've had notification. One was your ex-wife, Elu, and the other is old. Been loosely identified as Martin Shaw, known as Hammer and an ex-member of Rage MC." Apache stared at Ramirez impassive.

"Elu's dead? What the chief wanted me brought in for it because she's my ex?" Apache sounded astounded, and I reached out and grabbed Apache's hand. Ramirez shrugged.

"Yup, until we found evidence, she was killed by someone else," Ramirez replied.

"Who?" Apache spat.

"Your uncle," Ramirez replied. "Elu's body was discovered the night before last, the day after events here, Apache, sorry to be the bearer of bad news. Chief pounced on you as the culprit as soon as she was identified. A witness saw a Native American driving away. Wanted you brought in, but there was a video that hadn't been watched, and I warned him about moving against Rage after the last fuck up.

Chief applied for a warrant for your arrest, I watched the footage, got a good fucking shot of the man dumping her body. Your uncle was identified by his criminal record. Went to the chief, who went ballistic. I refused to haul an innocent man in for questioning."

"Fuckin' hell. He must have killed her for Ace failing to come to heel," Apache muttered.

"Don't know Apache, but Elu was strangled. DNA has been found inside and on her, but no rape, it was consensual. Forensics' checking the DNA now against your uncle, who's being held without bail."

"Man's an asshole Ramirez," Apache muttered. I wondered if he was feeling sad for Elu, although, in my opinion, she got what she deserved. She wasn't worth more than a footnote in my story, she was that insignificant. A blip on the radar and screw her. Elu had been wicked through to her bones, and her death was no loss. Well, not as far as I was concerned away, I glanced at Apache, unsure of his reaction.

"Apache?" I asked.

"Yeah, baby?"

"You okay?" Apache looked at me, and his arms tightened around me.

"Ain't mourning her loss, baby, if that's what you're asking. Elu's been dead to me ever since Ace was a baby. Bitch got her comeuppance, but we'll have to let Ace know," Apache grunted. I reached out and clasped Apache's arm wrapped around my chest. His hand moved and took mine in it.

"The other body? Hammer's?" Ramirez asked.

"Man stuck with Bulldog, knowing how bloodthirsty that man was, it wouldn't surprise if Bulldog had whacked the man himself," Apache said. Interesting, because I knew for a fact who had whacked Hammer, and it hadn't been Bulldog. Hammer had been a drug-crazed maniac. No way had Bulldog whacked him. Especially since I knew who did. Not saying a word, I kept a wary eye on Ramirez.

"It will be done by the book. Look, Apache, I ain't going to bullshit you. If someone in Rage whacked him, and I wouldn't blame them, make sure you've a lawyer on standby. Those assholes jumped the gun with Ace, but our guys won't make the same mistake again. Forensics return with evidence, ensure you've got a lawyer on retainer. And don't tell me shit because my duty always comes first, no matter who," Ramirez emphasised the last word. Drake, I realised, Ramirez thought Drake had killed Hammer. Nope, honey, I thought silently, wrong guess.

"Rage will be fine," Apache said with a sharp nod. Ramirez studied Apache for a few seconds and, finding no answers, rose to his feet. His phone vibrated, and I guessed he'd turned it on at some point.

"Hey, look at that, a call from the mayor. Guess I better take it," Ramirez said drolly, and I giggled. Ramirez took his leave, and I relaxed back against Apache.

"You know, don't ya?" Apache murmured in my ear.

"Told ya, I'll hold Rage's secrets until the day I die," I whispered back. Apache squeezed me again and then swept me off the floor and carried me to bed. Damn, I loved this man's cock!

We told Ace later that night, and I couldn't tell how Ace was taking it. His face was impassive, but it had been since two days ago, when Drake informed Ace he was on leave for three months to sort his head out. Ace had argued, but Drake merely looked at him and told him Lowrider was stepping up for three months as VP. It was an unprecedented move, and I wondered if something had been broken between Ace and Drake. I prayed not.

Apache had taken the news stoically, and the only comment he'd made was Ace can't ghost the club because he was having a hissy fit. Ace had taken off with Artemis on vacation, I didn't know where, but Drake and the inner circle did. Possibly Ace had learned his lesson, but that wasn't for me to answer. Despite Ace having his ass slapped, the club felt more settled. The old ladies were spending more time in the clubhouse, and the brothers finally appreciated what we did behind the scenes.

Much to the envy and distaste of the old ladies who were pregnant, had recently been pregnant, or who were trying, I was sailing through my pregnancy. No morning sickness or anything like that, I was glowing and healthy, and Apache had a self-satisfied look on his face. We were rock solid. Despite the upheaval of the last few months, I realised now, nothing could tear us apart. Apache ensured I knew I was loved and doted upon. And he'd discovered a liking for covering me in white gold. Every other week he brought me a present, earrings, bracelets, or necklaces. My meagre jewellery collection was growing and looking very nice indeed.

My favourite piece was an emerald solitaire, a white gold engagement ring that he'd slid on my finger a week ago before dragging me in front of Axel and the club. Guess we got married! Rage's allied clubs had attended, as had Hawthorne's. James Washington gave me away, and members of RCPD attended. Ramirez had looked worn out and tired, not surprising when he'd arrested the chief for being on Santos's payroll. A dirty cop working for a criminal who still caused mayhem from wherever he was hiding.

Both Ramirez and Ben had taken their jobs back. The mayor refused their notice, same with Nando and Justin. The cops who'd followed them had also been reinstated, and an interim chief was temporarily installed. What no one had realised until the money trail was followed, was the chief had caved to a bribe from Santos. It had been Ramirez and Hawthorne who'd found the bribe and took it to their higher-ups. The chief coming after Rage so hard made sense. It explained why he'd brought in outsiders who knew nothing of how Rage helped the department.

Santos and the chief had intended to isolate Rage and failed. Spectacularly failed. His reputation was in tatters while Ramirez glowed in the media. Rage had been over the moon with the result, although Drake was worried about the new chief starting. We'd seen no action or retaliation from the Dark Souls of Lucifer, but everyone was alert to the now. Fallen Warriors had got into a gunfight with five members, three of whom had escaped, but they'd not got their drugs shipment, which was worth five hundred thousand. Ramirez had arrested the two wounded gang members. The haul had been highly publicised.

I lay in bed, thanking my blessings every morning as Apache insisted on bringing breakfast before we showered together. Okay, we didn't always just shower! I was sex mad and hormonal, and that was my excuse, except the truth was, I couldn't get enough of Apache. Each morning we rode to Rage on his hog, where Apache dropped me off at Made by Rage, kissed me lingeringly, and either rode to the clubhouse or his job.

Life was amazing. Brady remained a constant part of my life, having sealed a partnership with James. Brady was letting James run the operational side of the business while his factories churned out their wares. The old ladies were a vital part of my existence, and I valued that, but I also valued my other friends. The Hawthorne females remained as crazy as ever. Whatever had been happening between Ramirez and Sophia seemed to have died down for now as Ramirez hunted out more dirty cops. I guessed Ramirez was trying to keep Sophia safe and assumed that wouldn't last for long. Sophia didn't have the surname Hawthorne for no reason.

Everything was great, finally, and my life surpassed any childish or romantic dreams I might have had. Reality was far better than make-believe, and now I understood that.

Epilogue.

"Will you stay still?" Brady hissed as he caught me in his arms. I was bouncing happily around the clubhouse as he rolled his eyes. Marsha watched with a grin on her face as Brady patted my belly and froze me in place.

"Apache is going to freak!" I whispered.

"Yup, but that man loves you, honey," Brady said. Yes, he did; Apache loved me very much and had done nothing but show it the last three months. It was June, and summer was in the air and all that jazz. Brady and I had stayed close. Apache wasn't very welcoming initially, but when he realised that Brady only saw me as a friend, Apache calmed down.

"He'll be over the moon, fuck me, Axel will go crazy," Marsha said as the big man walked into the clubhouse. Axel glanced at me and saw my excitement.

"What's cookin', babe?" Axel boomed.

"Can't tell you until Apache arrives," I replied, and Axel looked affronted.

"What? Can't tell me? But I'm grandpa," Axel disagreed, but luckily we were prevented from an argument when Apache entered with Drake, Ace and Gunner on his heels. The four men stopped and eyed me suspiciously.

"Twins!" I yelled, and Apache paled.

"Seriously?" Apache asked.

"Yup, twins!" I cried excitedly. Gunner moved before everyone else and swept me into his arms.

"Congrats!" he shouted as Autumn flew through the doors behind him.

"Twins!" she squealed and joined our huddle.

"Fuckin' hell, twins, is there something in the water?" Drake asked as Phoe walked in pregnant with their one child. Apache remained frozen on the spot. Ace slapped him on the back and strode over to me.

"Proves twins run in the Blackelks then," Ace said, gathering me in a hug. Ace was much more open now, he and Artemis returned from a long vacation, and Ace spent loads of time baring his soul to Axel. If Axel couldn't put Ace straight, no one could. Drake shoved into the huddle, and Axel pushed his way through too. The only one not to greet me was Apache.

"Honey?" I asked, biting my lip.

"Twins?" Apache asked, astounded. I nodded.

"Yeah," I said happily.

"Gonna need two of everything, cots, car seats, prams, fuck me!" Apache finally said. I got worried. Was Apache mad? Then a beautiful grin erupted on his face.

"Got fuckin' twins, brothers!" Apache said, and I was in his arms, and he was kissing me. "You fuckin' clever girl, so proud of you."

"Happy?" I whispered.

"Ecstatic," Apache replied, and I settled into his arms. The last two months, Apache made sure I'd everything I wanted, including Brady time. I'd been spoilt and adored and loved. Brady was wary of Apache at first, he'd known I was running from him when we met. In Brady's eyes, Apache had much to prove, and I was pleased to say Apache met the challenge.

Brady had flown in this week because he knew I was having the first scan, and Brady was excited. He'd claimed godfather before anyone else and James seconds behind him, putting Rage's nose out of joint. Drake claimed third godfather and Gunner forth with a glower, daring anyone to dispute the fact. Apache had been mollified to find out you could have four godfathers. Phoe and Lindsey claimed godmother alongside Marsha and Carly. Luckily, having twins meant that the child wouldn't be smothered, and we'd share godparents amongst them.

The darkness looming over us in the form of Crow and Hammer's bodies being discovered was a cause of concern. I'd noticed several meetings with the inner circle and brothers who'd been around at the time of the deaths. I knew who was behind their deaths, but my lips were sealed for life. No way would I ever grass on the culprits, and considering who was dead, it wasn't a loss to polite society and the public. But as yet, no arrests had been made, and I had my fingers crossed they wouldn't be.

"Honey?" Apache asked, interrupting my thoughts.

"Yeah?" I asked with a mental shake.

"You okay?" Apache looked worried, as if I was worried about carrying twins.

"I'm fine, baby, wonderful, everything is perfect," I told him, and I grinned as Apache lit up in happiness.

"What do we do?" Lex asked Drake in the meeting later that night.

"What can we do? We move on the other bodies, then we might be caught in a trap. I want to understand how Santos knows where to dig," Ezra replied before Drake could.

"Ain't no fuckin' mystery. Ghost is spilling his guts and setting us up. Eventually, cops gonna find DNA on one of those bodies," Texas growled. Drake nodded.

"Yeah, but we got the explanation that Ace gave. That was sharp thinking. I bet if someone swabbed my cut, they'd find DNA belonging to most of you," Drake said. His mind turned to Ghost. Why had their brother turned against them? Ghost had fought alongside them, getting Rage clean. A quiet man like Texas, nothing made sense. There was no explanation for Ghost doing this shit.

"You think Silvie's message meant something?" Ace asked Drake.

"Yeah, I don't think we got the full story. I got ears to the ground; Ghost been gone years. No one just disappears. If it smells bad, then it's bad. We're missing something, something big," Drake replied.

"Ghost is bad news Drake, he's giving up bodies, wouldn't be so bad if that fucker hadn't helped put some there," Axel growled, and Drake looked up as enlightenment dawned.

"Except he didn't with Hammer." That was what was bothering Drake. Ghost hadn't been present for Hammer's death. Slick glanced up at Drake.

"No, he wasn't. Ghost was with his mom. She'd suffered that stroke. Ghost wouldn't know where Hammer was buried. How the fuck did they discover the body?" Slick asked.

"Anyone tell Ghost what happened to Hammer?" Apache asked. Everyone shook their head.

"Wanna know why Ghost turned on us, what Rage did, that was so terrible he turned against us and harmed Silvie," Lowrider said.

"Whatever his reasons, the fucker has a reckoning coming," Apache said and turned to the window where he could see Silvie. She was laughing with Calamity and Brady and glowing with sheer happiness. "No one harms my woman and walks away without the insult returned."

"Justice is coming for Ghost, and it's named Rage," Ace said, and Apache held his son's gaze for a few seconds.

"Too fuckin' right."

Characters.

Rage MC
Rage Patch. The patch is a barbed wire circular design, with flames interwoven. A Harley Davidson is in the centre with Charon in front of the bike. Charon holds a flaming scythe in one hand that curves around the back of him. On the front of the bike, in place of a light, is a blue flaming skull. On the back of the bike is a blue flaming eagle. At the top, it says, 'Rage MC'. At the bottom of the patch were words, 'Live to Ride.' Under them, it says Rapid City.

Drake Michaelson. DOB. 1975. Drake is third generation Rage, he was in the third lot of brothers recruited into Rage. His father started Rage MC and died before Drake was old enough to become President. Drake became VP and, in a hostile takeover, became President. Phoenix thinks he looks like Tim McGraw with longer hair.

Drake has a leanness to him but has well-defined muscles and broad shoulders. Drake sports dark brown eyes with laughter lines. He's six foot four. In March 2015, his son, Dante Chance Michaelson, was born. He considers Detective Antonio Ramirez and PI Dylan Hawthorne close friends.

Apache. DOB 1969. Apache is a second-gen Rage, he was in the second lot of brothers recruited into

Rage. He is one of Drake's enforcers; Ace is his only son. Apache was widowed when Ace was young. He has bright green eyes and is six foot two. He is of Native American origin. Apaches described as absolutely stunning with high cheekbones and raven black hair that hangs past his shoulders. Apache's real name is Tyee (meaning Chief) Blackelk.

Silvie Stanton has been in love with him for years, but he hasn't reciprocated her feelings. He looks like Lou Diamond Philips. Apache was married to Elu. We know he was tricked into marrying her by his uncle, who was the chief of Apache's tribe. Apache is partnered with Rock in a construction company. Ace isn't Apache's blood son but a cousin instead, but Apache doesn't care. He thinks of Ace as his son.

Ace. DOB 1983. Ace is third generation Rage, he was in the third lot of brothers recruited into Rage. Ace is Drake's VP. He's described as looking like a young Lou Diamond Philips. Like his father, he is Native American. Ace has bright green eyes and is six foot two. He is described much the same as his father, absolutely stunning with high cheekbones and raven black hair that hangs past his shoulders. Ace was in love with Kayleigh Mitchell and thought she'd left him. Ace discovers out that Kayleigh hadn't left him but instead had been tortured and left for dead. He has four children Nova and Falcon and Nashoba, and Nokomis.

We learn that Ace has a monster inside him, created when his first love, Kayleigh, disappeared. Ace is no stranger to violence and will do whatever it takes to protect his club. He was shot five times, protecting Phoe from her ex.

Fish. DOB 1978. Fish's birth name is Justin Greenway. Fish is third generation Rage, he was in the third lot of brothers recruited into Rage. Fish is Drake's sergeant at arms. He's been married to Marsha for many years, and until Rage's Terror, they thought they couldn't have children. Fish was heartbroken when he thought Kayleigh ran away; he'd taken Kayleigh on as his own when she was eleven. He is devastated when he discovers what happened to Kayleigh. Fish runs the Rage garage. He discovers in Rage's Terror, he's about to be a father of twins and is over the moon. Marsha gave birth to a boy and a girl in April 2016.

Texas. DOB 1965. Texas is a second-gen Rage, he was in the second lot of brothers recruited into Rage. Texas's full name is Blake Craven. Texas is an older man and is the MC's secretary. He works on bike design and specialised paintwork. Texas has a daughter aged twenty-one, called Rosie. Texas had information he wasn't aware of concerning Kayleigh's disappearance.

He has a robust moral code but is mindful of what the MC is capable of. He once alludes to cleaning up after their messes. Texas is tall, broad, with a goatee, dark salt and pepper hair slightly too long and piercing brown eyes. He can also play the keyboards. Texas stands at six foot four. His old lady is Penny.

Axel. DOB 1951. Axel was one of the founders of the club, which makes him first generation Rage. He is the Chaplin of the MC. The Chaplin's role is to look after Rage's needs spiritually. Axel makes sure they have their heads on straight and performs their marriages and death ceremonies. He has blue eyes, and he is heavily bearded and very loud. He's built like a mountain. Axel has wild hair which hangs to his shoulders.

He disappears in The Hunters Rage, there is mention of his messed-up kids, and Axel has gone to resolve an issue with them. He returns at the end of The Rage of Reading to marry Sin and Jett. Axel is six foot six with a salt and pepper beard.

Gunner. DOB 1976. Gunner is third generation Rage, he was in the third lot of brothers recruited into Rage. Gunner is one of Drake's Enforcers at the MC. Gunner is described as having silver-grey eyes with thick lashes. His name is Cole Washington. James Washington is Gunner's brother, and they are estranged. James is ten years older than Gunner. They had a sister, Chloe, who died at seventeen from drinking and drugs. Gunner witnessed her death. He's six foot five.

Gunner's described as having long sandy brown hair, high cheekbones and firm, soft lips. Gunner owns four houses, three of which he rents out. He also works at Made by Rage carving wood with Manny. He pays fifty percent with Manny into the pot.

Gunner starts a relationship with Silvie, (Rage's Terror), giving her his word he'll try to make it work. When he meets Autumn, he refuses to break his word, and Silvie has to set him free. Gunner claims Autumn but refuses to give up his close friendship with Silvie, and Autumn accepts it. He breaks his ankle and several ribs in the Protection of Rage because he is knocked off his bike by Santos.

Slick. DOB 1978. Slick is third generation Rage, he

was in the third lot of brothers recruited into Rage. Slick loves books and is happy reading quietly. He has soft brown eyes and is heavily muscled. Slick loves reading. He was in love with Kayleigh, but he never let on as he knew she belonged to Ace.

He has a tattoo of her on his left pec of a circle of thorns with pink and blue and purple roses and an image of Kayleigh kneeling in the circle, with two hearts on chains threaded through her hands. One heart has Ace's name, the other has his, her name is threaded through the thorns. Slick is kidnapped by Artemis in revenge, but she finds him innocent. He has a good voice and can sing.

Slick runs a leasing company, he has over twenty properties he rents, he pays fifty percent into the pot.

Manny. DOB 1983. Manny is third generation Rage, he was in the third lot of brothers recruited into Rage. Manny takes an interest in Sin and threatens to make a move on her if Jett doesn't pull his head out of his ass! He's described as tall, sexy as in the cute boy next door way, tousled blond hair, and light amber coloured eyes. Manny is firm in teaching Jett how to treat a woman like Sin.

Manny was accused of being involved in Kayleigh's death. He was beaten by Bulldog for failing to report a pregnant prostitute and then shot in the back by Bulldog's men. Manny is six foot four. He carves wood and works his own section of Made by Rage. He pays fifty percent with Gunner into the pot.

Lowrider. DOB 1984. Lowrider is third generation Rage, he was in the third lot of brothers recruited into Rage. He has ebony hair shaved short at the sides and longer on top. A roman nose and full lips, he has blue eyes. Lowrider has a tattoo of black flames that crawls up his throat. He's six foot three of lean, powerful muscle and tanned. He had a friend, Tammi, who was shot in front of him when she was 16. Lowrider has never forgotten it. (Looks like Colin Farrell.) Lowrider's actual name is Nathan Miller. Lowrider is a mechanic and makes builds from scratch.

Lowrider is hot-tempered and suspicious of anything that looks too good to be true. Because of this, he messes up his relationship with Lindsey several times before making it right.

Ezra. DOB 1979. Ezra is third generation Rage, he was in the third lot of brothers recruited into Rage. His parents died when he was sixteen in a house fire. His aunt and uncle didn't want him, and he ended up on the streets. He has a younger sister called Lindsey, who seeks him out. He has brown eyes, is tall and has shaggy dark hair.

Ezra's a broad-shouldered man with a deep, broad chest, beautiful bone structure and a neatly trimmed goatee. He is ten years older than Lindsey. (Looks like Robert Downey Junior.) Ezra owns a landscaping company which is in high demand.

Mac. DOB 1970. Mac is third generation Rage, he was in the third lot of brothers recruited into Rage. He was accused of being involved in Kayleigh's death and can play the drums. Mac also hacked into Lindsey laptop to find out what she was hiding.

He was shot protecting Lindsey from her ex-husband and becomes Lindsey's alternative guy. Mac is responsible for running the bar.

Rock. DOB 1985. Rock is third generation Rage, he was in the third lot of brothers recruited into Rage. Rock is six foot four and huge. He has a beard and drives a black 2015 Dodge Challenger RT. Rock has his eyes on Carly, we discover in the Crafting of Rage. He runs a construction company with Apache.

Lex. DOB 1984. Lex is third generation Rage, he was in the third lot of brothers recruited into Rage. Lex was accused of being involved in Kayleigh's death. He runs the Rage shop. In the Protection of Rage, Lex is kicked out by a woman he was seeing, which led to the woman and Autumn fighting and rolling over Lex.

Blaze. Blaze is a fourth-generation Rage, he was in the fourth lot of brothers recruited into Rage. Became a brother in 2016. Blaze runs the parts store.

Slate. Slate is a fourth-generation Rage, he was in the fourth lot of brothers recruited into Rage. Became a brother in 2016. He was 'put to sleep' by Master Hoshi when he denied Master Hoshi access to the clubhouse. Slate runs into Penny's burning house in Rage's Heat to save her and the children with Texas. Slate works with Ezra in a landscaping company.

Hunter. Hunter is a fourth-generation Rage, he was in the fourth lot of brothers recruited into Rage. Became a brother in 2016. Hunter is also a designer for paintwork on bikes. He plays the bass guitar.

Jett. DOB. 1990. Jett is a fourth-generation Rage, he was in the fourth lot of brothers recruited into Rage. Became a brother in 2015, his name is Alexander Cutter. Jett was drugged by Artemis in the Hunter's Rage. He's described as having black hair, dark brown eyes, high cheekbones, a square jawline and firm, soft lips. He is slightly taller than Reid and broader, and he is lean hipped, long-legged and as tightly muscled.

Jett is a mechanic, engine designer, and paintwork designer. He finds out he has a daughter Amelia, which he gains custody of with Sinclair, who he marries. Jett is estranged from his family after his brother Martin slept with Jett's fiancée, and everyone took Martin's side. Jett becomes a brother earlier than the other three because of his actions with Sinclair's situation.

Calamity. Calamity is fifth-generation Rage, he was in the fifth lot of brothers recruited into Rage. He's nineteen when he joins Rage, and his actual name is Billy Tomkins. Calamity becomes a prospect after only being on Rage for a month. He's a talented mechanic, body designer and spray painter.

He interferes and stops Frenzy from harming Silvie and gets knocked out. He earns prospect from this act. In the Protection of Rage, Calamity becomes Autumn's alternative guy and takes a bullet in the shoulder for her.

Candidates.

Savage. Savage is a fourth-generation Rage, he was in the fourth group of brothers recruited into Rage. He usually has a savage look upon his face, but he's gentle with the old ladies. Savage is thirty-two years old and is a mechanic.

Gauntlet. Gauntlet is a fourth-generation Rage, he was in the fourth group of brothers recruited into Rage. He threw down to help Manny one night in the

bar, and that was how he became a candidate. He's twenty-eight years old and works in the garage.
Klutz. Klutz is a fourth-generation Rage. He was in the fourth group of brothers recruited into Rage. The man could trip over his own feet. He's very clumsy. Klutz is a talented bartender and often pulled scenes much similar to those in the film Cocktail.

He's twenty-six years old and is African American. Klutz's roommate was dealing drugs in college, and Klutz got swept up in the sting. The cops beat him, and then his innocence was proven, and he was freed. His family were upper-middle class and turned their backs on him even though he was innocent. He saves Silvie from being shot in The Hope of Rage.

Rage Old Ladies.

Phoenix. DOB 1979. Drake's old lady. She is English and left England to escape an abusive relationship. She has six children she gave birth to and adopted eleven. Phoe is exceedingly well off and runs three National Charities. The Phoenix Trust, the Rebirth Trust and the Eternal Trust.

She has been married twice before Drake, the first husband died, and her second was a bigamist. Phoe has long, blond hair and is green-eyed and five-foot-tall. She met Hellfire MC first and is loyal to them, and is Hellfire's only sister. Ace was shot five times rescuing Phoe from her ex-husband and is Phoe's alternative guy. Phoe discovers she's pregnant again in Rage's Terror.

She has Drake's son, Dante Chance Michaelson, but during a fight with Drake, they became estranged.

Phoe was meeting Drake when she was shot on Rage's forecourt in the Hunter's Rage. She was also kidnapped by her ex-husband and killed him by stabbing him with a broken chair leg. Phoe is now married to Drake, and they are happy together.

Marsha Greenway. DOB 1978. Fish's old lady and the only old lady the club has until Phoenix meets Drake. She's known to be kind and caring. She's distraught when she discovers the truth around Kayleigh's disappearance. Her emotions were intense as she destroyed a room in the clubhouse.

Marsha discovers she's pregnant with twins in Rage's Terror. Axel is Marsha's alternative guy. Although the old ladies don't have a ranking, Marsha is Phoe's VP. Marsha has blue eyes and shoulder-length brown hair. She gives birth in the Hope of Rage to twins, a boy and a girl.

Silvie Stanton. She's looked at as an old lady even though she doesn't have an old man. Silvie's kind and generous. The MC has a lot of respect for her. She has blond, curly hair and has soft brown eyes. Gunner is her alternative guy.

Silvie knew Kayleigh Mitchell when Kayleigh was brought to the MC. Silvie is in love with Apache, but Apache ignores it. She takes a job at the Made by Rage shop, working for Lindsey, first helping cut material and then as a receptionist. Finally, she becomes the shop manager.

Silvie is attacked by the candidate Frenzy on the forecourt, and Calamity comes to her rescue. She enters into a loose relationship with Gunner but sets him free to claim Autumn in the Protection of Rage. Frenzy leaves a bite mark on her neck, which will scar. Although the old ladies don't have a ranking, Silvie is Phoe's Chaplin.

Kayleigh Mitchell. DOB 1987. Died 2003. Kayleigh was a tiny, slender blond with blue eyes. She was raped and abused by her stepfather, aged eleven, and ended up in the care of Marsha and Fish. Just before her seventeenth birthday, she discovered she was pregnant with Ace's children. She was tortured and left for dead by Thunder and Misty and several other members of Rage.

Artemis, aka Kayleigh Mitchell. She has red curly hair, green eyes, she's small, dainty and muscled. Artemis was born in 1987. She has a heart-shaped pixie face full lips. Kayleigh was taken in by Master Hoshi, and out of her alleged death, Artemis arose. She's a famous bounty hunter and runs a team that operated under the name Artemis. Artemis calls Akemi her brother and Master Hoshi her father.

She was part of a group called Revenge before she left and formed the Artemis group. The Artemis Group became the Juno group when she went legal with her efforts. She has combat skills and has killed many times. Artemis's alternative guy is Drake. Artemis thinks she has a monster inside of her that Ace can't accept but is stunned when he does. Her nickname is Killer. She is Phoe's equivalent of an enforcer. Artemis has two sets of twins.

Artemis now has a large team working for her on search and rescues for child and women trafficking. She also provides protection, and James Washington makes use of her skills. She's extremely expensive.

Sinclair Montgomery. DOB 1993. Sin takes over her father's shop, the Reading Nook when he dies, and with Reid, they turn it into something special. Sin was an only child, and Reid became her surrogate brother. She is socially awkward and inept and feels out-of-place in crowds. She's described as dainty with brown hair and big blue eyes. Sin doesn't think she's pretty, but people describe her as beautiful. She has low self-esteem created by attending college and university when she was fifteen. Manny is Sin's alternative guy.

Jett got Sin pregnant in Rage's Terror by throwing away her birth control pills. Sin adopts Jett's daughter Amelia, and they got married in the Rage of Reading.

Penny Nelson. DOB 1976. Penny is a cook and server at Reading Nook. She loves cooking and baking and makes everything from scratch. She has a warm and caring attitude. Penny has two children, a son five and a daughter three. Her ex left her for his secretary.

In Rage's Heat, her ex-husband tries to burn her and the children alive, and Texas rescues her. She's very close to her sister Carrie who lives with them. Penny has short dark hair cut into a bob and is a few pounds overweight with blue eyes and freckles. Penny is five foot six.

Lindsey Smithson. She is ten years younger than Ezra and is his baby sister. She was married to a man called Thomas Masterson, who beat her. Lindsey escaped and get to Ezra for safety. She has brown eyes and long waist-length brown hair with red highlights. She undergoes surgery to correct her face after Thomas breaks her jaw, cheekbone and eye socket.

Lindsey has her own business called Made by

Rage, Designs by Lindsey, she pays twenty percent into the pot. While Lindsey is wary around strangers, she has no worries about speaking her mind to the Rage brothers. She's kind and generous. Lindsey's books are published under the pen name of L. Smithson. Her married name is Miller. Mac is Lindsey's alternative guy.

Autumn Rydell. Autumn was in a relationship with Carter Rydell. He turned to drugs, and Autumn kicked him out of their home and broke up with him. She has a son Aiden who's just turned five, and two twin daughters, eighteen months. Rydell kept stalking Autumn and lost her a lovely home and a good job. When Rage finds Autumn, she's on her knees, unable to cope and has no money.

Autumn starts work at the Rage Garage as their office girl, and they pay her good money, and she likes the job. Autumn didn't want another relationship and fought Gunner on it. She slowly comes around to his way of thinking. Rydell breaks into her house, and she stabs him in self-defence before being kidnapped by Santos. Calamity is her alternative guy, and Autumn is also an enforcer for Phoe.

Carly Lennon. Born in 1997. She has dark long brown hair and enormous brown eyes. Carly arrived at Made by Rage, underweight, and Lindsey and Silvie decided to look after her. She had no clothes and was living in a homeless shelter. Carly moves in with Silvie. When Lindsey is attacked, she shows the ability to fire a gun and stabs Thomas in the shoulder to rescue Lindsey.

Hellfire MC.

The Hellfire patch. Circular patch with the flames starting at the bottom and going halfway up the circle. In the middle of them is a skeleton with a devil's horns on its head and holding a pitchfork. In the other hand, the skeleton holds a motorbike and above the skeleton's head is a crown of flames. Hellfire MC is written underneath in a bold freestyle script in white.

Chance Michaelson. DOB 1973. Chance is the Hellfire President. His father started Hellfire. Chance looks like Tim McGraw with long hair. He is Drake's older cousin. They were brought up together and are as close as brothers. They both fought to get their clubs clean from the filth that infected them.

There are a lot of comments that Chance and Drake could be twins. Chance is very protective of Phoenix and loves her without barriers. He has the same leanness as his cousin. Drake has brown eyes, and Chance has bright green eyes with laughter lines. He is six foot four with his hair hanging past his collar.
Bear. Bear is the Hellfire VP. Chance lets it slip to Drake that Bear has a dead sister. Phoenix calls him Bearbear. Bear loves his food.
Banshee. Shee is an enforcer for Hellfire. Shee buys houses and rents them out. He also loves shopping for women. He had a woman who's done a bunk with his kid, and they'd never found them. Shee has been searching for four years.

Rage Children.

Micah. (Phoe and Drake) DOB 1995, he wants to be a mechanic and design street racing cars. He is English. In the Hunters Rage, Micah has moved to Miami and is working for a famous garage living his dream of designing cars. In Rage's Terror, he quits his job and returns to Rapid City for Harley.

Micah had a hard time accepting Drake as his mother's husband because he wanted her to marry Chance. But Micah does come around finally. He takes his responsibility as the eldest seriously.

Carmine. (Phoe and Drake) DOB 1996, half African American and half white, he plays for the Cubs. He's from Maine and was adopted in 2010. Carmine looked after Tye, Harley and Serenity on the streets.

Tyelar. (Phoe and Drake) DOB 1996, Tye is half Mexican and half Caucasian and is from Maine. He was adopted in 2010. In the Hunter's Rage, Tye is playing for the Blackhawks. When Tye hears Harley was attacked, he went off the rails and got a three-match ban. Carmine had to fly out and sort his head out. Tye, like Carmine, looked after Harley and Serenity.

Jodie. (Phoe and Drake) DOB 1997. She likes tennis and is close to Serenity. Jodie in Crafting of Rage has a minor role in a tv drama. Drake disapproves.

We find out in The Crafting of Rage Jodie's minor role has become a more significant role. In the Protection of Rage, we find out Jodie is flying back and forth to visit Harley whenever she gets a break.

Serenity. (Phoe and Drake) DOB 1998, She is from Maine and plays tennis well but also likes ice hockey. She was adopted in 2010. At the end of Crafting of

Rage, Serenity has signed as a lingerie model. Serenity cancels her jobs to return home for Harley in Rage's Terror.

Harley. (Phoe and Drake) DOB 1999, Harley's from Maine and was adopted in 2010. In November 2015, two seventeen-year-olds attack Harley from behind, cracking his skull and putting him into a coma. Harley was protecting Christian. Harley remains in a coma.

Cody. (Phoe and Drake) DOB 2000. Carmine found Cody living on the streets in Colorado. He was adopted in 2011. After Harley's attack, Cody stepped up to protect his siblings at school.

Christian. (Phoe and Drake) DOB 2002. Christian defends Carmine against a group of seventeen-year-olds who were calling Carmine names. He runs for help from Harley and sees Harley get attacked. After Harley's attack, Christian withdrew into himself, and Marsha arranged for homeschooling for a few months. When he returned to school, Christian has taken up boxing and martial arts.

Jared. (Phoe and Drake) DOB 2004. Jared is a hothead and known to use his fists to solve problems.

Aaron. (Phoe and Drake) DOB 2005. He was born after his father died, and he never met him. Aaron, the same as Jared, is a hothead and known to use his fists to solve issues.

Eddie and Tony. (Phoe and Drake) DOB 2010. African American, adopted in 2012. Eddie is a little diva. She says what she thinks and does what she wants. She's very strong-willed and quite funny. Drake adores her. Tony is quieter and follows his twins lead.

Timmy and Scout. (Phoe and Drake) DOB 2014. Adopted 2014 Their mother was a drug addict. They have severe illnesses which Phoe hopes medical care will cure. The twins get the all-clear in the Crafting of Rage.

Garrett and Jake. (Phoe and Drake) DOB 2014. Adopted 2014 Their mother was a drug addict. They have severe illnesses which Phoe hopes medical care will cure.

Dante Michaelson. (Phoe and Drake) DOB 2015. Everyone says that Dante is the spitting image of Drake, including his father's attitude. Dante is strong-willed and possessive of Phoe. He hates to share his mother. He is the future President of Rage and claims Aria when he's twenty months old.

Nova and Falcon (Conway) Blackelk. (Artemis and Ace) The twins were born in May 2003. They look like their father, Ace. Nova countless gold medals for mixed martial arts. Falcon prefers swimming and baseball while also winning medals for mixed martial arts. They have green eyes, a straight curtain of black hair and olive skin.

Gregory Nelson. (Penny and Texas) DOB 2011. Penny's five-year-old son. He didn't remember his father and was over the moon when Texas adopts him.

Daisy Nelson. (Penny and Texas) DOB 2013. Penny's three-year-old daughter, she loves Texas and her new big sister Rosie.

Rosie Craven. (Penny and Texas) DOB 1995. Rosie is studying to be a vet at university. She is Texas's daughter.

Amelia. (Sin and Jett) DOB. She is Jett's daughter

and is adopted by Sin. Her mother had called her Ursula Letitia Jean. Sin and Jett changed her name to Amelia Abigail.

Davy Masterson. (Lindsey and Lowrider) Lowrider adopts Davy. The little girl saw her mother get beaten and snuck Ezra Junior out of the house to safety.

Ezra Junior Masterson. (Lindsey and Lowrider) Ezra holds his own against Dante even though Dante is older than him. Everyone says he's the future VP of Rage MC and Dante claims Alyssa for him. From Love's Rage, everyone calls him EJ. He has dark hair.

Aiden Rydell. (Autumn and Gunner) Born 1st of December 2011, his father was Carter Rydell, and he is the eldest of Autumn's three children. Aiden idolises Gunner and looks up to him.

Aria Rydell. (Autumn and Gunner) Born in May 2015, she is the eldest of the twins. Aria's very shy and quiet. Aria is discovered to be a natural skier, and Gunner gets her lessons.

Alyssa Rydell. (Autumn and Gunner) Born May 2015, the youngest of the twins. Alyssa is the open one and the more excitable one.

Nokomis Isis Phoenix Blackelk. (Artemis and Ace) She was the first born of the twins. Nokomis means Daughter of the Moon. Born 14th Feb 2016.

Nashoba Tyee Drake Blackelk. (Artemis and Ace) Tyee is Apache's name and means Chief. Nashoba means wolf. Born 14th Feb 2016.

Hawk Axel Greenway. (Fish and Marsha) Born 4th of April 2016.

Julianna Kayleigh Greenway. (Fish and Marsha) Born 4th of April 2016.

RCPD.

Antonio Ramirez. He is over six-foot-tall and has black wavy hair, olive tanned skin. He is Mexican and has brown soft, gentle eyes. Tonio is lean hipped and long-legged and broad-shouldered. He is a good cop, and Drake thinks a lot of him.

  In the Hope of Rage, Ramirez saves Silvie from a gang member and gets knocked out. He quits the force because he was yanked from a murder case which involved Rage. Ramirez catches his chief in a bribe from Santos.

Eric Benjamin. Known as Ben. Partner of Ramirez. He's a clean cop and thinks Ramirez sometimes turns a blind eye to Rage, but he'll always back his partner up. He leaves RCPD to support Ramirez before he gets rehired.

Hernando Hawthorne. Following in his fathers and brother's footsteps, Hernando is a cop too. He works alongside Ramirez and Ben and sometimes moonlights for Hawthorne's. He became involved in Rage's Terror when Silvie was attacked. Casually known as Nando. He leaves RCPD to support Ramirez and Ben before he gets rehired.

Justin Goldberg. Nando's partner. He leaves RCPD to support Ramirez, Ben and Nando before he gets rehired.

Officer Lucas. An officer with RCPD who attended Rage to question Ace.

Hawthorne's

Dylan Hawthorne. Owner of Hawthorne investigations. He is extremely intelligent and will bend and break the rules as he wants. He thinks of Drake as a close friend and takes Rage's back during the Artemis war. He discovers information on Artemis.
Davies. Hawthorne investigator.
Dana. The Hawthorne receptionist, she's 28 years old.
Washington's.

James Washington. James is Gunner's older brother. He appears when Gunner is shot in the Rage of Reading, with claims Santos is going to war with Rage and himself. James skirts the illegal side of life and is someone Santos is afraid of. He is ten years older than Gunner. James had a sister, Chloe, who was born when he was five. Chloe ended up dead, men tried to abuse her as her mother didn't care. She was drinking at fourteen, hooked on heroin and cocaine by fifteen and dead by seventeen. Gunner witnessed it all.

Gunner was born when James was ten. James has hair greying at the temples and the same grey eyes as Gunner. James owns five strip clubs, a hotel and casino and two jewellers shop. When Gunner is kidnapped, despite their estrangement, James goes to rescue him and pretends to have a bomb. He also runs into a fire in the Protection of Rage to rescue people when his club is blown up. In the Hope of Rage, James is clean and goes into business with Brady Whittaker.
Adam. Adam takes over Frank's position as a

bodyguard, but James holds him at arms-length.

Members of Rage MC who left or died.

Bulldog. He was the next president after Drake's father died. He took the club down a dark path which led to many illegal activities. Drake wrestled control back from him. Ace killed Bulldog. Bulldog was behind Kayleigh's torture in an effort to break Ace and weaken Drake's standing in the MC.

Ghost. Ex-member was supposed to be dead. Ghost was seen by Silvie in a club, and he was present when she was hit by the car. Ghost seems to be working with Pinhead.

Crow. Real name Kyle Reeves. He was killed by Ace for his actions against Rage after siding with Bulldog. His remains are discovered in the Hope of Rage. Crow was a known drug dealer.

Hammer. Hammer's name was Martin Shaw, and his body turns up in the Hope of Rage.

Frenzy. Drake named him Frenzy because he was so pretty, he'd cause an uproar with the skanks that hung around the club. He was a candidate for prospect until he attacks Silvie one night and Calamity stops him. Apache and Rock interrupt and beat him down. Gunner then intervenes and beats Frenzy unconscious. It turns out Frenzy is a serial rapist recently turned murderer. Frenzy is suspected of killing over one hundred and fifteen women aged from thirteen to forty-five.

Other characters.

Magic. He owns a bar out in the hills, on an open stretch of road that is a biker neutral zone. Magic doesn't allow violence in his bar, nor does he allow truces to be broken in it. He's a big man, but no one knows his age. No one wants to upset Magic, he's rumoured to have buried bodies of those who've upset him in the hills behind his bar.

Brady Whittaker. Silvie meets him in California. They become friends after Silvie discovers he was jilted at the altar and his ex is pregnant with his best friends baby. He owns a famous crockery company and is rich. He sacks his ex-best friend and then visits Silvie in Rapid City. Brady starts a business with James, helping James remain legal.

Mr Etherington. The club's lawyer.

Detective William. From New York and came to the clubhouse with eight officers to question Ace.

Detective Johnson. From New York and came to the clubhouse with eight officers to question Ace.

Other MC's.

Satans Warriors.

Tiger. President.
Crunch. VP.

The Devils Scythe.
Scythe. President.

Unwanted Bastards.

Inglorious. He's the president of the MC and was involved in Clio's rescue. He got hit by Slimy Sam driving a car at him after Inglorious rescued Clio.
Psych. He's the Unwanted Bastards VP and was involved in Clio's rescue.
Mouse. He was wounded by another biker gang but overheard them saying they were responsible for Silvie being hurt.

Devil's Damned Disciples.

Jailbait. President.

Fallen Warriors. They are an MC entirely made up of military men.

Lance. President of the Fallen Warriors.
Bat. VP of the Fallen Warriors.
Sniper. He's the enforcer for the Fallen Warriors.
Raddock. He's a member of the Fallen Warriors.

Dark Souls of Lucifer.

Pinhead. He runs the gang and ends up shot by Silvie when he attacks her.
Ice Dawg. A member of the gang that has somewhere they can hideout.
Taxman. A member of the gang.

Thank you for reading The Hope of Rage. Do check out the other titles in this series. Book One of hellfire MC is out now, Chance's Hell if you want more Hellfire MC, And please take a gander at the Love Beyond Death Series, book one of which, Oakwood Manor is out now! If you enjoyed this book, please leave a review at

Goodreads and Amazon

Remember your reviews are so important to me! Check out Axel in First Rage in the next book of Rage MC.

Thank you!

Elizabeth.

Printed in Great Britain
by Amazon